About the Author

Linda Fawke is an arts person who, for good reasons at the time, studied science but always wanted to write. Now she has retired, she can indulge this passion. She writes fiction and non-fiction, even occasional poetry, preferably late at night. She has a degree in Pharmacy and a PhD in Pharmacology. She has used her pharmaceutical background for this, her first novel, and is currently working on its sequel.

Linda Fawke is married and lives in Berkshire. She has three children and six grandchildren.

A Taste of His Own Medicine

Linda Fawke

To Lynne,
Best wishes
Linda Fawke.

First published in Great Britain in 2016
Copyright © Linda Fawke

Printed by CreateSpace

ISBN: 978-1539695097

Acknowledgements

Many thanks must go to Jonathan Veale of WriteAway Book Editing Services for his help, advice and good humour. Without him, my writing would be poorer. My long-suffering husband, Tony, has read the book more times than either of us know and his pointed but kindly criticism has been invaluable. Finally, I would like to thank Fiona Routledge for creating the book cover for me.

For Tony

She didn't think about him anymore. She hadn't thought about him for three decades. In truth, she believed she'd exhausted her thoughts where he was concerned; she protected herself from him.

There was a time when it was different. A time when she enjoyed mundane tasks because completing them got her minutes closer to their next meeting. A time when she would find herself skipping like an excited child as she walked along the street, smiling at strangers because she was inwardly smiling at him. A time when all her thoughts contained him.

It was years since she woke in the night imagining she felt the touch of his fingers brushing her spine. She stopped reacting with a start if a man wearing his fragrance happened to come near. And the phone could ring without causing a jolt to her stomach.

But joy turned to bitterness and vengeance. Desire for him became the desire to hurt him; to scar him as much as she could.

Then nothing.

He was in a locked compartment in her mind. He was her past; he was no longer her everyday.

Chapter 1

'I thought you would come.'

'Confident in your power, I see.'

'That's not what I meant. Something is sweeping us along this evening. This is a special encounter, a one-off. We're unable to stop it.'

He pulled her towards him as she expected and placed his lips softly on hers. He kissed her twice and then ran his tongue slowly over her lips. 'You used to like that.'

'I still do. But I have to say something before we go further.'

She walked across the room and stood with her hands resting on the back of a chair, feeling his eyes on her, his scrutiny. 'You need to know how much you hurt me.'

'Kate, enough. I wasn't expecting you to come to my room to lecture me.'

'It's not a lecture. But you need to understand what you did. You intended to finish our relationship but gave me no clue it was about to happen. When I needed you most, you gave me no support, no sympathy. Awful as that was, the events afterwards compounded the hurt.'

'What events?'

'Don't be naïve, Jonathan. The succession of women you paraded before me. Everywhere I went you were there with a female, usually a different one from the previous time. The wound went deeper with each encounter. I hated you for that.'

'It wasn't deliberate. We were students on campus, bound to see each other. I was lost, Kate, and confused. Don't you know

3

that? I was being honest when I told you I loved you. But then it got too much for me. I had no idea what I wanted from life. So I sought simple pleasures.'

'Sex, you mean.'

'Well, yes, I suppose so. And company. Certainly no commitment, nothing serious. Situations where I could live for the moment and start again tomorrow. I was suffering, too, I felt insecure and afraid.'

'It didn't appear that way. I hope you're not expecting sympathy! You were usually laughing, drinking and in control of life. While I had so much to cope with.'

'I don't display everything I feel. I didn't leave you for anyone else. I had no other lover, not even the glimmer of a relationship, when we split. Surely it would have been worse if I'd fallen in love with someone else?'

Kate paused and said, 'I suppose so but at the time I don't think you could have hurt me more than you did.'

Jonathan searched for words as he looked at Kate, a question on his lips he couldn't ask.

'There is no discussion, Jonathan.'

'I did try to talk to you but you ignored me. I tried to congratulate you when the results came out.'

Kate knew it was true. She remembered looking away when he came near. She hadn't trusted herself to speak. Now she turned from Jonathan, wondering if she was saying too much. The atmosphere in the room changed, as if a cloud was hiding the sun. She put her head in her hands.

Jonathan went over to the table in the corner. The silence throbbed around them like a headache.

'I ordered more drinks before you arrived. Do you want one?'

Kate took it from his hand and sipped it. He took a large gulp from his and then sat playing with the glass. Gradually they both relaxed and looked at each other, neither daring to break the gaze.

'Have you had your say?'

'Yes. No more.'

'Are you staying?'

'Do you want me to?'

'Yes.'

'Then I will.'

He moved slowly across the gap between them, the physical and the emotional gap.

'Perhaps we need to go back to where we were,' he said, putting his glass down and removing hers.

She reached out for Jonathan's hand and put it against her cheek. He drew her towards him.

'You'll taste of brandy. Luckily I like Rémy Martin.'

He kissed her again, licked her lips again, held her face in his hands, then buried his own face in her neck and breathed deeply.

'You smell the same. Do you still use the same perfume?'

'I can't remember what I used then. A cheap scent, I expect.'

'Then it's pure Kate I'm inhaling.'

She licked his neck, tracing circles with her tongue and nibbled his earlobe.

'That used to drive me wild.'

'And what does it do now?'

'It drives me wild.' He pulled her tightly against him and she could feel the warmth of his body.

'Slowly, Jonathan. You were always a teasing lover, you never rushed things. I want it to be exactly like the last time.'

'Can you remember the last time?'

'Of course I can. Making love to a person you adore – and I did adore you – isn't easily forgotten.'

Jonathan slid his hands under the straps of her dress and over her shoulders. 'Just as smooth as I remember. You always had peachy skin.'

'So you remember, too.'

'Kate, you were important to me once. I wasn't playing with you.'

Kate undid the buttons on Jonathan's shirt. She took her time over each one and carefully eased the shirt open. After each button, she kissed his chest. Then she ran her fingers through the light covering of hair, trailing her long nails so he could feel the pressure. She slid her arms round him and ran her fingers up his spine. He closed his eyes and moaned softly. It was working; her scheme was working.

'Kate, I don't think it can be like last time. Thirty years more of experience has to make it better. You are doing wonderful things to me.'

Kate had now removed Jonathan's shirt and started to remove her dress.

'Let me.'

'Soon. First, I want you to watch.' Slowly, she stepped out of her dress and he smiled at her still seductive shape.

'Stand there for a moment. I need to relish the temptation.'

Kate did as he asked, then walked towards him. She held him against her, enjoying the way they fitted together and then undid his belt, unzipped his trousers and slipped her hand inside. I'm having the required effect, she thought. No doubt of that.

'I think it's time we removed a few more clothes,' Jonathan said, stripping down to his underwear. Still the male model physique, she noted.

'Did you ever model underwear?'

'No. The guys who did that got into other things. Made plenty of money, but porn wasn't my scene.'

'You still look amazing. Sales would have rocketed if you appeared in a magazine like that.'

'You're talking too much. There are better activities for your mouth. Come here.'

6

He kissed her properly and Kate struggled to keep control of her emotions. *I mustn't get too involved, I mustn't lose focus on the job to be done.* She stepped back from him and told him to remove her bra. He undid the hook and she let it drop to the floor.

Slowly she turned to him and he held her breasts gently in his hands, then pressed his face against them. He rolled one nipple between his forefinger and thumb, feeling its erection. *I should not enjoy this,* Kate thought. *But it's hard to avoid the pleasure. Keep control, keep control.*

It was her mantra.

Jonathan slid his hands down her hips hooking his thumbs inside her knickers and rolling them down so that she was naked. He picked her up.

'This is what I always did.'

You usually said you loved me as you did it, thought Kate, and winced at the memory.

Laying her down gently, he knelt beside her, now naked himself, and started to stroke. Kate closed her eyes and let his hands wander at will. He knew where to touch and how to use his fingers. He remembered what she liked best. *This could have been my life,* Kate thought, and the pain of it made her bite her lip and gasp.

She started to caress Jonathan. At first, like feathery wisps of air, then with forceful bursts of wild passion. Or so it seemed. She went through the repertoire of what excited him; if it worked all those years ago, it would surely work now. *Such a danger of getting carried away. This could be the most wonderful sex in years; I must control my passion,* she told herself. *I must follow my plan. There is a task to be completed.* Jonathan was breathing heavily and whispering her name when she suddenly pushed him away.

'I can't do this, Jonathan. I thought I could but I can't.' She threw her legs off the bed and stood up, wrapping her arms around her body.

'Kate, come back. Don't be ridiculous. You were enjoying it.'

'I can't, I can't!' She grabbed her clothes, struggled into her dress and rushed towards the door, avoiding Jonathan's eyes.

That was the problem; she was enjoying it too much.

Chapter 2

The memory flooded back as she saw them. Two people were lying on the grass near a clump of trees, their arms round each other, their legs casually intertwined. They were blind to the life that went on around them, the bustle of chattering students, the bikes and the laughter, the cooling breeze. Theirs was a private world. Shock made her swerve and hit the kerb with her front tyre.

'Shit,' she exclaimed out loud. Bloody stupid.

She stopped the car to re-focus her mind as her heart hammered away. That was *their* spot. She lay there with Jonathan in a September exactly thirty-one years ago and as she looked across at the two strangers, she saw the past. It was the same tree, the same weather; she could almost smell the same new-mown grass. She was back there in his arms, wrapped around him in their first embrace.

***

'Kate, there's a lad called Jonathan on the phone. Can you come down and get it?'

She looked in the mirror and quickly tidied her hair. Then laughing at herself for the silliness of her action she ran down to the phone. Her father mouthed the words 'new boyfriend?' and raised his eyebrows. She shook her head and frowned, waving him away. But rushing down the stairs was not the only reason she felt breathless.

'Hello … Jonathan?'

'Hi, Kate. How were your travels?'

'They were fun but too short. I could have done with more money.' She paused. Jonathan didn't bother with pleasantries. 'I wasn't expecting you to call. Don't tell me you want to change our project?'

'To be honest, Kate, I've not given the project a single thought. But I have been thinking about you. I wondered when you were returning to uni?'

'Dad is taking me next Saturday. Why?'

'Could you come back sooner? I can't explain on the phone but I need to speak to you. I'm already here.'

'Well, I don't know. Hang on, I'll have a word with Dad.'

Her father was hovering in the kitchen in case there were any interesting snippets to pick up from her side of the conversation. She asked him if they could change their timing.

'He could take me tomorrow but I'll have to check I can have my flat early.'

'If there's a problem, you can use Eddy's room. He's not back for a few days. Will you meet me in the union coffee bar tomorrow evening at 6 o'clock?'

Kate was glad Jonathan could not see her face as she thought about the possibility of sharing his flat, even briefly.

'Can you give me a clue? I'm surprised by this.'

'Just come, Kate, will you?'

Jonathan's earnest voice gave her no choice. She had to find out what this was about.

Kate told her father she must get back to work on the project with her partner. And, no, there was no romantic involvement but yes, he was a nice guy, knowledgeable and helpful. Good looking, too. A resigned look on his face, her father wrinkled his nose and sniffed.

She decided to arrive late. She'd been the first at every one of their meetings, so this time she would not be so eager. She'd show Jonathan she could be laid-back, like him. She'd arrive at a quarter past six. They'd probably both arrive together.

Her flat, available but airless and stuffy, provided her with barely enough to do to fill the dragging time. Opening the windows, she tried to make it feel like home but her mind was elsewhere. The anticipatory pleasure that marked the beginning of term was absent.

She forced herself to delay getting ready, putting away the contents of her suitcase and tidying the bathroom. There are only so many ways of re-arranging deodorant, soap and body lotion and the task took minutes. She put sheets on her bed and a cover on her pillowcase. Books and folders were queuing up to go in their usual places, arranged by subject and then alphabetically, but there was no fun in sorting them out. It happened without her brain taking part. She made a cup of coffee she didn't want and ate a stale biscuit from a left-behind packet in the cupboard. Every few minutes she looked at her watch until she gave in, put on a fresh T-shirt, cleaned her teeth and set off. It was a ten minute walk but she slowed her usual clip-clopitty trot to a more normal walking pace to make it take longer.

Jonathan was sitting at a table near the door when she approached, a cup of coffee going cold in front of him. A student came up to him and said a few words. He replied briefly, seemingly unwilling to chat, and the visitor moved away. She saw him scanning the path, an anxious air about him. Then he saw her.

'I thought you weren't going to come. You're never late.'

'It's only five past six.'

'For you, that's late. I've been here ten minutes.'

This wasn't the relaxed Jonathan she knew. He wasn't bothered about minutes. He ran his hand through his hair, stretched his neck backwards and exhaled. His clothes looked unusually creased and mismatched as if he'd chosen them at random, not noticing their state. And he fidgeted, turning a signet ring on his finger round and round.

'Is everything alright, Jonathan? You're not ill, are you?'

'No. Not ill. Not in the conventional sense. Overwrought,

11

you might say. Worried.' His words came out in short spurts, unwillingly.

'About what?'

'Do you need a coffee, or can we go for a walk?'

'We can walk if you want.'

They went across the lawn towards a shady spot where mature trees grew and a wild, uncut area remained. Jonathan was silent, looking straight ahead, moving rapidly, so Kate said nothing. She felt sure there was some disaster in his life and she was about to become a comforter.

'Can we stop here?' Jonathan indicated a patch of grass where a few rays of sunshine penetrated the leaves, speckling the ground with flashes of light. 'I don't think I want to walk.'

Kate still said nothing. Jonathan sat down, leaned his back against a thick tree trunk and plucked a few daisies, squashing them in his fingers and throwing them to one side. Kate sat with her arms wrapped around her knees, facing him. She heard voices behind her and glanced round but their owners were moving away. They had the place to themselves apart from a few birds pecking the ground and the distant whine and clatter of a mower. It was the sort of evening which inspired indolence, told you to savour life, read an absorbing book and forget about time. But the atmosphere was different under this tree.

'Kate, do you remember when we talked about my decision never to have a girlfriend on our course? That I preferred to find my social and romantic life elsewhere?'

'Yes, I do.'

He's going out with someone in the department, she thought, and fought to keep her face expressionless. Maybe he wants my advice.

'I'm hoping to break that rule.'

'So who's the lucky lady?' She used her most flippant tone and sprang up, turning her back on him and taking a couple of paces.

'Kate, come back. Please. And don't joke.'

She sat down again, this time further away from him. So her suspicions were correct. The names of possible candidates flashed through her head. Her heart started to beat faster and she inhaled deeply in an attempt to slow it down.

'Okay, here goes. Let me tell you something. Don't say anything until I've finished.' He looked at Kate for agreement and she nodded. 'I know you think I'm a girl chaser, a couldn't-care-less user of women.'

Kate started to speak but he put up his hand.

'No interrupting. If you don't think it, then others in the department do. You've heard them talk. And I admit I've had many girlfriends. I enjoy the company of women.' He coughed and ran both hands through his hair several times. 'I enjoy your company.'

He got up and Kate could see the movement in his throat as he swallowed. He pushed his hands deep into his pockets and hunched his shoulders. After several seconds, he walked over to Kate and sat beside her. She tensed as his bare arm brushed hers.

'When I asked you out for a meal to celebrate our project at the end of term, I thought it would be just that. An enjoyable meal with an attractive girl I'd like working with. I still believed I'd never get involved with anyone in the department. But I found I couldn't get you out of my head. Your green eyes watched me; I saw your eager hands fluttering as you talked and the memory of your quizzical smile made me breathe faster. You have pursued me the entire time since term ended. You have spent the long vac with me, although you didn't know it. You have been my companion day and night. Kate, you are not just another girl. You are special.'

He hesitated and licked his lips. Then he took a deep breath. 'I think I'm falling in love with you.'

Jonathan got up and walked away as if the effort of his confession drove him from her. Then he turned, his face lined and

13

crumpled with worry. Kate's face was blank. She sat still.

'Are you going to tell me this will never work? That I'm a fool?' The question rushed out and he looked full of doubt. He walked back towards Kate, tentatively, as if he expected her to push him away. When she spoke, it was slowly and deliberately.

'I don't know if it will work. I've never let myself consider it.' Then she smiled a smile that told the true story. 'But I'm prepared to give it a go.'

Jonathan took her hand and kissed it. He had a wide grin on his face when he looked up. He stroked each finger then placed them against his cheek, trailing them across his lips, lips that wouldn't stop smiling. He put his arm around her and pulled her down onto the grass. They lay down together under the tree, gradually wrapping their limbs about each other. The sunshine had disappeared by the time they got up.

***

All those years ago. Kate wondered if the couple lying there now, under *their* tree were falling in love. Ridiculous to get romantic, she thought. She shook her head to get rid of distracting memories. Must get back to today. I need to keep my wits about me this weekend if I'm to stand a chance of punishing Jonathan. Courage, deviousness, a strong stomach; no place for sentimentality. I must not lose focus. Jonathan would feel the force of her presence.

She started the car... and moved slowly back into the present.

Chapter 3

"The year of '75 – can it really be thirty years?"

Who was asking her that? Kate saw the enigmatic email heading amongst the usual junk on her screen. Sunday at home – she shouldn't be working. But she clicked on it: a message from Gabriel Williamson. With the cursor poised over the "delete" symbol, she hesitated. She saw him: a twenty-one year old trying to be thirty-five. His round, childish face struggled to produce the beard he felt would suit him, suit the image he wanted. But the straggling, ginger wisps only served to emphasise his youth. She could hear his irritating sniff and saw the way he poked his ear with his little finger. She could see his bitten nails.

Nevertheless, he had a presence. His piercing voice could be heard in any room, usually putting forward a forceful opinion; the large sound of a small man. And although no-one wanted to admit it, he did talk sense at times, he was an intelligent guy. He walked uninvited through her memory, reminding her of distant events. There were always people around him, a man of many acquaintances. She couldn't remember who his real friends were. Had there been any? He cared mostly about himself so it wasn't easy for anyone to get close. Not that she ever wanted to. His round stomach and baggy corduroys did nothing for Kate. And as she thought back, an unmistakeable, stale smell of infrequently washed clothes made her screw up her face. Yes, she certainly could remember who he was.

And he signed himself "Gabriel", a name he hated. From the beginning of the first term he insisted no-one was to use it. Everyone knew him as "Willy". No doubt Gabriel was his current persona. She imagined him making the decision, putting his student days into a box with his inappropriate nickname and firmly closing the lid; telling himself he was now in the Gabriel phase of his life.

Well, as he said, thirty years had passed. They'd be different now; all forty of them who spent three years together studying pharmacy. And Willy – she couldn't call him anything else – was trying to get them together again for a reunion, the first time they'd met since Graduation. A thirty-year reunion on campus.

They promised to keep in touch when they parted. The elation of graduating, the over-indulgence in champagne and the hot, sultry weather intoxicated them, made them best mates for half a day; everyone said how they'd miss each other and how important it was to maintain their friendships. How university meant more than getting a degree. There was much hugging as they said goodbye and genuine, profuse tears. Kate winced when she remembered she made herself join in with all that nonsense. It wasn't her style but on that day she'd not wanted to be the odd one out. Well, maybe some of them had kept in touch. There were real friendships.

But a reunion? God, what a dreadful idea! Why in hell's name would I want to spend a weekend with that group, she asked herself. Three years were more than enough. And Willy, for a number of reasons, was far from her favourite. The prospect of supporting an idea of his made it even less appealing. The cursor hovered again over 'delete' but again she stopped.

She heard the backdoor open and close.

'Neil,' she called. 'Neil – can you come here?'

Her husband looked round the door of the study. He had just come in from his regular Sunday morning run and droplets of moisture were trickling down his face. His T-shirt stuck to him, showing his efforts to keep in shape were working. He ran sticky hands through sweat-darkened, stickier hair so that it stood up in short spikes.

16

'Hang on a minute. I must get a glass of water. It's hot out there.'

He came back drinking noisily, his suntan taking over from the beetroot glow the run had given him. He stood behind Kate as she looked at the computer screen.

'Bit of a coincidence seeing as you've just been to one. I've got an invitation to a departmental reunion.'

'Have you? Are you going to go?'

'I doubt it. They weren't the happiest years of my life.'

'There must be folk you'd like to catch up with. And it's not a coincidence – it's thirty years since my graduation, too.'

'You enjoyed the weekend, didn't you? You didn't tell me much about it.'

'Yeah. Had a great time. Only twelve of us turned up and they were people I got on well with.' He wandered round the room as he spoke, selecting bits and pieces of information to throw to Kate.

'Interesting to hear what they were doing. Mostly teachers, a couple of translators, one or two who'd left modern languages behind completely, like me. All pretty normal, mostly married, two point five kids, the usual.'

'But what did you do? How did you fill a weekend?'

'It wasn't a problem. We visited the old department, saw the new language lab, the high-tech stuff. And we drank a fair bit. Everyone relaxed and reminisced about the old days. We remembered the fun bits. Strange how your memory files away the mundane and the plain bad and you only remember how much you enjoyed yourself. And, of course, there were the amusing incidents. We searched our brains for the worst stories we could remember about each other. And about those who weren't there!'

Neil laughed, perched on the arm of the chair and grinned broadly as he went into raconteur mode. He had an eye for the details of life. He scratched his head as if determined to recall the most delicious nuances to embellish his story.

'There was the time when Phil got locked in the ...'

'Enough! I don't want to know!' Kate interrupted. 'Your "good, old times" mean nothing to me.'

Neil pulled a face, disgruntled to be cut off before he had started. He looked at Kate to see if she was willing to hear one snippet but she shook her head so he shrugged his shoulders and flopped into the chair.

'Watch out! You've got mud on your legs. Don't get it all over the furniture!'

'Whoops, sorry.'

Walking over to Kate, he put his hand on her shoulder. She reacted to his damp, clammy touch, so he removed it.

'Seriously, Kate, give it a try. I enjoyed it more than I expected. And you'll get a much better turnout. You're pharmacists so you'll be contactable through the Pharmaceutical Register.'

'Not sure that's appealing. Would mean meeting up with the whole lot of them. I can think of half a dozen I liked, some I hardly knew and a few who definitely belong to the grim past.'

'Well, mull it over. I'm off to have a shower.'

Kate re-read the email. She looked at the addressee list. Neil was right. There were thirty-six names, almost the entire group. Who were the missing four? Moved on or dead? She didn't know, couldn't remember; it didn't matter. Willy suggested a smart hotel near the university where they would stay and had a preliminary agenda, starting with a drinks reception on the Friday evening. They would visit the new department, meet various members of staff and finish with a 'formal' dinner. Willy, in his fussy, pedantic way, pointed out it wouldn't be truly formal, not black-tie formal, but the Head of Pharmacy was keen to come.

She sighed and told herself she should have deleted the message straight away. Now she started to think about it, deletion was proving difficult. She closed her eyes to get herself back into her usual, sensible frame of mind. Enough of this – what was she intending to do today? She must look at her figures before a meeting with her accountant the following week. Get on with it, she told herself, and opened up an Excel spreadsheet.

She was working on it when Neil came back into the room, a fresh smell of body spray trailing behind him, his hair clean and uncontrolled, his face still unshaven.

'It's weekend, Kate. Do you have to work on a Sunday?'

'What's this? A sudden burst of religion?'

'You know it isn't. I simply think you work too hard. You need a break. You're turning into a workaholic.'

'Wrong. I've always been a workaholic.'

'Okay. You're becoming a worse workaholic.'

'We wouldn't live in a place like this if I wasn't.'

'I know, I know, don't rub it in. We both know who earns the most.'

'I didn't mean it like that. Don't be super-sensitive. Yours is a different type of work. And I admire it.'

She sat back in her chair and stretched her slim arms above her head. Then she closed the spreadsheet with a click. 'Alright, you win. Let's go into the garden and read the papers. I'm not concentrating so the figures are better off without me. I'll make coffee.'

Neil unlocked the French doors and walked to the terrace at the end of the garden, a place that collected sunshine. He opened the parasol and settled himself in a chair. Kate smiled. It was fortunate she didn't rely on Neil to keep the place tidy. The stripes on the lawn weren't "Homes and Gardens" but they weren't bad. And the flower beds were neatly trimmed and well weeded. Her garden-savvy pensioner was worth the money.

Neil was useless at it. Even though the garden had been designed for easy maintenance, it wasn't to him. It never crept high enough up his priority list to get done; it rarely made the list. And he admitted he didn't know a weed from an expensive shrub. Well, not quite true. He could recognise a rose. But that wasn't enough for Kate.

The kettle whistled on the Aga. Kate selected Colombian from her range of coffees and a packet of shortbread. It was annoying Neil could eat as many cakes and biscuits as he liked and it never made an ounce of difference to him. I wish, she thought. As she busied herself with the cafetière – Neil accused her of always being busy and she supposed she was – she watched him. He looked at least ten years younger than his age. Still an attractive man. Especially when he stretched as he was doing now. He got up and leaned on the wall. It was old, part of the original estate boundary when the area belonged to a rich, local businessman until bankruptcy hit him. The estate was split up in the nineteen twenties and the present houses built – six of them, all solid and different, houses of character. Owned, she reflected, by solid citizens, all different, all of good character.

Neil thought the best feature of the house was this wall. She liked it, too, but not excessively, not like Neil. A neat, regular one would have been more to her taste. She asked him what was so special and he said it was its rough texture, the chipped coping along the top and the niches where brave plants grew. He liked the way sunlight hit the smooth, sharp pieces of flint buried in the bricks and ricocheted off like tiny fireworks. On bright days, the edge of the wall threw an uneven shadow across the lawn and he liked to watch its changing shape as the sun moved. Too analytical, he called her, when she shrugged her shoulders, not enough emotion, no soul. He was right. She could see him stroking the bricks, feeling their coarse, gritty warmth. He wriggled against one of them, using it as a scratching post for his shoulder, and looked back towards the kitchen.

'Coffee's made, Neil,' she called as she walked towards him with a tray. She had arranged cups, cafetière and plate of shortbread neatly and evenly on a tray.

'Doing your tactile thing with the wall?'

'You're mocking me!'

20

'Only a little!'

She sat down and looked back at the house she loved. She loved its comfort, the old oak dining table, the way the Aga warmed not only the kitchen but their chilled bodies on a winter's day. She loved the thick walls that muffled sound, making it hard to talk from one room to another. She liked their recent changes: the wooden floors, the leather sofa, the beautiful chandelier over the stairwell, the heavy silk curtains. The new cabinet with the crystal glasses lined up perfectly, like soldiers. She liked the order of it. Most of all, she loved the feeling she got whenever she arrived home. Yes, it was definitely home.

She plunged the coffee and started to read the newspaper.

'Funny, there's an article here about a guy who was in our year. Simon Featherstone. He did a law degree after pharmacy and specialises in pharmaceutical disputes. I've read about him before. He's just won a high-profile case.'

'See, you are interested in what your fellow students are doing now.'

'Only when it's in front of my nose. I don't seek them out.'

'So have you decided whether or not you're going to the big gathering?'

'No. Thought I'd give Becky a call. If she's going, I might go with her. She'll probably think it's too dull for her taste, though.'

Becky lived nearby and worked as the manager of a large pharmacy in town. She was the only real link to her student days, an easy-going, undemanding friend she saw from time to time. She was a friend – wasn't she? As students, it was Becky who made her leave her books and socialise, Becky who told her uncomfortable truths about how other students regarded her. Becky who tried to cure her obsession with studying.

***

She would regularly knock on her door in the hall of residence.

'How about watching "Coronation Street"? Today's lectures must win the prize for the world's most boring collection. I need a break. You should have one, too. You'll come back refreshed.'

Becky would wander round the room, looking at the open books on Kate's desk.

'I can't believe how thorough you are. All your results tabulated perfectly, everything neatly laid out. It must take you forever!'

'Don't mock me. It's how I work. I can't do it any other way. I'm a precise person. Pharmacists need to be accurate.'

'True. But there is life outside pharmacy, you know. It makes a change to talk to folk who aren't pharmacists! Come and mix for a bit.'

'You go and have your break, Becky. I don't need one. I've got more results to write up.'

'Can't they wait?'

'They could, but I want to sort them out now. And I can't stand "Coronation Street", you know that. Maybe I'll come down later.'

'Folk will start to think they aren't good enough for you if you never join in.' Becky gave her a warning look, then laughed when Kate looked worried.

'Only joking. But I would like your company.'

'I'll see. Maybe later as I said.'

But later saw her still at her books. She wasn't interested in wasting time in the Junior Common Room watching rubbish on television. And there was comfort and security in her room. Becky's comment bothered her. Perhaps it was a joke but something prompted it. She didn't want to be considered a snob – she knew she wasn't one – so the next time Becky knocked on her door, she surprised her and ignored work for a while.

'When you're not so intense, so wound up in your work,

you're a decent girl,' Becky told her.

'That's patronising.'

'Didn't mean it to be. I think you're great company when you relax. Unfortunately, it doesn't happen often.'

'I suppose I'm meant to take that as a compliment?'

'Don't be so complicated, Kate. Can't you simply enjoy life like I do, like the rest of us?'

Kate was about to make a sarcastic remark about not everyone having the same ideas about enjoyment when she stopped herself. She thought carefully before speaking. 'Actually, Becky, I'm trying. I would like to be more like you. There's a person inside me that wants to be happy-go-lucky. Part of me wants to be sociable, wants to have a big circle of friends. But I find it difficult. I can't do it. I don't have your self-confidence. So I have to prove myself by working, by having a routine. That's how I find my place in life.'

'Wow! I wasn't expecting a speech! It's getting too deep for me.'

'Sorry. Didn't mean to overpower you with my inner thoughts. But maybe you can understand me better now.'

Becky nodded, looking unsure. But Kate meant what she said and made a point of inviting a few girls back to her room from time to time. If one of them sat on her desk (cleared of all signs of work) and lit up, she would find a makeshift ashtray. She liked to sit on the floor with her legs crossed, a normal person for a while, one of the crowd. The buzz of conversation warmed the room and laughter rattled around it. Andrea, her neighbour, would knock on the door and ask them to be quiet. She was glad; it felt good to be slightly bad.

But she knew she was still an outsider looking in.

***

And chance moved them into the same neighbourhood.

So if Becky went along, that might make the occasion more appealing. There'd be at least one person she'd enjoy talking to. And Becky made her laugh. Her lifestyle was chaotic, a complete contrast to Kate's. It seemed she had two characters and the "home" Becky rebelled against the "work" Becky.

'How do you manage to be two such different people?' Kate asked her.

'Easy. I play a role at work. I do the job as well as I can, I provide a quality service for my customers, I'm organised, efficient and caring. You've seen, you know. But it is a role. In my social life, constraints don't exist so I can party all night and sleep until mid-day if I want. I can live in an untidy house with dirty dishes in the sink. I can wear my shabby-chic clothes and create my own style without anyone interfering.'

'You can and you do.'

'Yeah, why not? I don't have a husband on my tail. I enjoy my freedom.'

Becky would be a stuffiness-antidote. Then Neil pointed out a problem.

'It will depend if she can get a locum. But that will apply to lots of you.'

'I'll give her a call tomorrow.'

So she phoned Becky who said yes, she'd read the email and she'd go if she could, and what a fantastic idea it was, and how like Willy (or was it Gabriel?) to organise it. He was always pushing people around. She was looking forward to it; it would be fun to go together. She was verbally jumping up and down.

'I imagined you'd think a reunion would be boring.'

'It'll only be boring if we let it. I wonder if we'll still like the ones we liked all those years ago – and if the pains in the arse are still pains in the arse?'

'They'll probably all be a pain in the arse.'

'Oh, Kate, don't be such a misery! Come along. We can laugh at everyone together.'

She started to go through a list of names, asking Kate if she remembered this one or that, and how about the time when, and what if this or the other had been discovered by the staff. And what about the lecturers – would any of them turn up? Dr Cornish was probably dead. He looked half-dead when they were students! But there were younger ones. Mr Burnham was dishy – wonder what age has done to him? And Dr Passman. He was intriguing, always had a twinkle in his eye.

'Enough, Becky, enough! I can't keep pace with your enthusiasm and grasshopper mind. I'll think about it. We have a couple of weeks before Willy needs to know. I'm still not sure. But I'm not going alone so if you're keen, you'd better get your locum sorted.'

'Right. And I'll dig out my photos. I took loads. Always liked to have mementos. Haven't looked at them for ages. I could take them along.'

Kate told Neil about Becky's response. He smiled and nodded.

'Could have anticipated that. She always looks on the positive side. So will you go if she does?'

'Possibly. Probably even. But not otherwise.'

'You get on well with Becky, don't you?'

'Yes, I suppose I do. Although I no longer envy her.'

'Envy her?'

'Perhaps that's the wrong word. When we were students I wished I had her out-going nature and confidence. I was insecure.'

Neil laughed in disbelief; that wasn't the Kate he knew.

'You could come, you know. Willy says partners are invited.'

'What? I wouldn't know anyone but you and Becky. The answer is a definite "No". I don't need a reunion to talk to you two.'

'That's what I thought you'd say.'

'But I do think you should go. I bet you'd enjoy it, even if

25

it's only to show off how successful you've been. Not many will have a chain of six pharmacies. They may not realise "Kate Shaw Pharmacies, Ltd" is you.'

'True. But I don't need to boast. I won't delete the message. I'll come back to it. Becky is keen. But that's Becky. Miss Get-up-and-Go.'

The reunion then disappeared from Kate's mind as she had to focus on the meeting with her accountant. She spotted the email again a few days later but had little time to think about it as there was illness amongst the counter staff and a blocked drain in her oldest pharmacy: the usual important trivia that made up her life. But thoughts of the reunion crept back like a bad cold she couldn't shake off. She discovered she was curious to know what had happened to the people with whom she shared three years of her life. And bitter thoughts crossed her mind. Perhaps she could make use of the weekend. Maybe she could get more out of it than being pleasant to folk she never liked.

She thought about individuals who'd be there, those whose lives had marked hers, whose impacts were more than glancing blows. It was painful to dig these people out of the dark hole she'd buried them in. They were history; did she want to re-experience the pain a meeting would awaken? Part of her said "No", there was nothing to gain except bad memories; don't go back. You have a happy life now. But a hard, obsessive rancour told a different story.

Would Jonathan be there? She didn't want to ask herself but her brain had a mind of its own. It's years since I've been aware of his existence, she thought. I did a thorough job of building a wall between us. Well, if I'm going to this wretched reunion, I need to sort my head out and be prepared to face him. I'll have to treat him like the other guys there. Then the ridiculousness of this hit her like a slap in the face. It wasn't possible. He wasn't one of the "other guys". So she'd have to work out exactly how she would handle him.

26

Jonathan Carson, her beautiful man. To say he was handsome was like saying Shakespeare wrote plays. He was the epitome of good looks. Kate tried to picture him and found she was using words like "chiselled" for his features and "sparkling" for his eyes. Pathetic, she said to herself. I should be able to do better than that and he's more than a cliché. How would I describe him to a stranger? He had excellent bone structure, a clear, naturally brown skin so that he always appeared holiday-tanned. Dark, well-cut hair which he kept short. He was tall and slim, broad-shouldered and toned rather than muscular. Then there was his clothing. He had a way of wearing a sweater that made it look expensive. And he ironed his shirts. She liked him when he needed a shave which he often did. She liked his style.

Enough, she thought. This is dangerous. It was a long time ago. I have to be matter-of-fact. Jonathan is irrelevant. If he raises any emotion in me, it's contempt and scorn. She thumped the table in determination then looked down at the blood oozing from her palm. She had stabbed herself with her silver paper-knife, still in her hand. The weapon, a gift from her father, was in daily use. She opened her mail with it, liking the long, even cut of the paper and the neat envelope it produced. She never cut herself with it – until now. What violent actions the mere thought of Jonathan produces!

The beginning...

It was the welcome meeting in the department, the 1972 intake. Like most of the new students, he looked hesitant, glancing round the lecture theatre for the chance of a familiar face but seeing only the grubby, student-scuffed paintwork of a much used room and other newcomers fidgeting like himself. But unlike most of them, he stood out. Kate spotted him as he entered the room; so had everyone. The females for obvious reasons, the males with a flicker of envy and suspicion. He seemed unaware of his impact and after the meeting went to the noisy, smoke-filled coffee bar with everyone else where his loud laughter made it noisier. Kate held back and talked to a lively girl called Pauline. Jonathan was for another day when she found her feet and her confidence; or perhaps not at all.

It was the early days of mutual assessment when everyone was making choices about who to mix with, ahead of sensible judgements, and Jonathan could have joined any of the embryonic groups. But he chose to remain independent, to mix but not to belong, to sit in lectures where his whim took him, never in the same place twice. He wasn't a regular member of the front row group, nor the idlers at the back, not a creature of habit; he appeared to be neither a man's man nor a woman's man. He disappeared after lectures and labs, keeping his social life out of the department, and after a while he became pleasant wallpaper, a chanced friendly chat in the coffee bar and an occasional game of squash with one of the guys. The female section of the department gave up on him.

Four weeks into the first term, Pauline rushed up to a group of the girls before the first morning lecture, waving a page from a glossy magazine.

'Look at this!'

They crowded round to see a stick-thin girl in an elegant ball dress. The backdrop was a brooding guy wearing an expensive shirt and designer jeans. It was Jonathan.

'Is it him? Are you sure?'

'It's got to be. Doesn't give his name. They never do.'

'Where did you get it?'

'Tore it out of a mag at the dentist's. I can't afford glossies like this.'

'Well, there's one way to be sure. We can ask him.'

So they did and he nodded. 'It pays well. I was approached a couple of years ago and have been modelling ever since. I wouldn't want to make a career of it, though.' It was proper stuff, he insisted, nothing sleazy.

'You're missing a trick there!' said Colin. 'There's loads of dosh in sexy photos. Give me half a chance, I'd have my kit off!'

'Really, Colin?' asked Pauline in her mock-incredulous voice. 'What a daredevil you are!'

'Well,' he paused. 'I'd go down to my underwear.'

'And who do you think would want to see *your* Woolworth's Y-fronts?'

He went pink as everyone laughed. 'But they aren't... Oh, you're just winding me up! By now I should know you, Pauline. You're never serious for two minutes together.'

Jonathan's modelling said everything; it defined him, made him stand apart from the others. He had an alternative life. When he bothered to come to the department, his quick wit meant there was usually an audience, men and women, enjoying his humour, not only his looks. No-one could describe the peculiarities and mock the habits of the staff like he could. He wasn't only a clothes-horse. Kate was amused by him, if she thought about him at all.

Then, towards the end of the second year, mischievous fate pulled Kate and Jonathan together.

'Hey, Kate, the pharmacology project list is up!' Pauline shouted to Kate who was parking her bike in the racks near the department. She ran out of the door into the rain.

'You'll get soaked, Pauline. Go back – I'm coming in.'

'I couldn't wait. Had to tell you,' she said, shaking the water from her hair.

'Go on then.'

'Good and bad news. Which do you want first?' She didn't wait for an answer. 'The bad news is that I'm paired with Willy. Guess who you've got?'

'Probably a waste of space like Susanne.'

'Wrong. It's far better. This is the good news. You've got Mr Handsome.'

Kate frowned.

'Idiot! Don't look like that. It's Jonathan!'

Kate didn't share Pauline's excitement. She smiled but inwardly she sighed. She'd hoped for a lively individual with an interest in the mechanisms of drug action, an interest to equal her own. Jonathan didn't seem attracted to any aspect of the course. She didn't want a passenger, however amusing he might be.

'My God! You take a lot of pleasing. I thought you'd be thrilled. The rest of the females in the department would be. There'll be plenty of offers to swap!'

'A fine face doesn't mean fine marks. But if he's chosen neuromuscular blocking agents like me, then we'll make the best of working together.' She went to look at the list on the notice board and found Jonathan there.

'Worth my while turning up if I'm partnered with you, Kate.'

His comment reinforced her doubts about his usefulness even though he flashed his engaging smile at her. She was clever, a candidate for a first, and she knew he saw top marks with minimum effort coming his way. Well, I'll make sure he pulls his weight, she thought and told him they'd have to get together to do their planning. Knowing exactly what they were going to do was key to success.

'That's okay. Let me know when you need me.'

Already he was relying on Kate for a timetable and there seemed a distinct lack of enthusiasm. But Kate was determined on an early start. They decided, at her prompting, to discuss their project a few weeks before the end of the summer term.

The Students' Union coffee bar was a general meeting place, noisy and snug, with pop music in the background and people coming and going. Dirty mugs and full ashtrays littered the tables and she had to clear several away to find a place to put her note pad. The air was heavy with smoke but Kate, a non-smoker, didn't mind. She was used to it. The floor was sticky and her shoes made a sucking noise as she walked. A woman with a mop and bucket was clearing up a spill. She could see Becky and Pauline chatting to Colin who was stretched out with his sandaled feet on a table.

It was hot; everywhere was hot as summer hit the exam season. Kate pulled her hair back and retied it in an attempt to cool off. Then the elastic band snapped and her curls cascaded down in an untidy, damp mess. She cursed as she looked at her watch. She would not have chosen to come here for a work discussion. She liked it, liked its liveliness and the atmosphere but it wasn't a work place. However, Jonathan suggested it and she didn't want to take over every aspect of the project. He arrived almost on time.

'I think we should get the outline done before the long vac. Then we can start straight away in the autumn.'

'Well, we can make a start on it.'

'No. If it's only partly done, we'll lose the thread and have to start again in October. And that would be a waste of time.'

'Doesn't look like the others are doing any planning today.' Jonathan indicated their colleagues whose laughter mixed with the music.

'Well, that's their problem.'

Kate was eager to get on and if it meant organising Jonathan, she'd have to do that too. He looked bored and his

31

attention wandered, his eyes everywhere but on the diagram she was drawing. He waved and smiled at people she didn't know, almost got up to talk to another group then saw her expression and stayed where he was. He went to fetch a second coffee and took too long over it, stopping to chat on his way back. His behaviour irritated her but she kept her focus and said nothing.

Kate was full of ideas, they spilled out like a waterfall in spite of anything Jonathan did, and her constant chatter got through to him eventually. He started to respond. She stimulated him into making suggestions of his own, surprisingly original suggestions. He stopped looking around the room and the distractions diminished.

'Hey, Kate, you know what? I might start to get interested in this!'

He seemed pleased Kate liked his contributions. She started, reluctantly, to change her mind about him. He was proving useful and knew more than he made out.

She forgot about the humidity as she jotted down possibilities, flicking her hair away from her eyes, and chewing the end of her pen, engrossed in their proposals. After a while, he started to watch her and she saw him watching. He smiled at the animated way she juggled concepts, her hands darting around in front of her face as if playing a weird musical instrument.

'You love this, don't you?'

'Yes, I do. Pharmacology gives me a buzz and being able to devise our own experiments is one step better than being told what to do.'

'I like that line – drugs give me a buzz.'

'The study of how drugs work, you know what I mean – don't wind me up and start misquoting me!'

But she wasn't angry; in fact, his humour appealed to her. Working with Jonathan might be better than she expected. She became conscious of his eyes on her as she wound her long hair around her fingers, a habit that went with thinking.

'You always frown when you're working out a problem. A line creeps across your forehead. That's how you'll look when you're old.'

Kate shrugged. She wasn't expecting personal comments or Jonathan's scrutiny. She realised she hardly knew him even though two years of the course was nearly completed. Was he teasing her to cover his assumed ineptitude? Or was he expressing a different kind of interest? No matter, I'll cope, she told herself as they arranged to meet in two days' time to continue.

The plan was finished after several coffee sessions, each one in the same place with the same noise, the same messy tables and the same disturbances. Kate was afraid to suggest an alternative in case it broke their pattern of progress. They managed to concentrate and block out the rest of the world. Jonathan was still adding ideas when Kate felt it was adequate; he had changed. Kate cheered when they both decided it would do.

'Yeah! We should celebrate. Come on, it's 6 o'clock. I'm sick of this place. We've spent far too long here and given them enough custom. By the time we reach the pub, it'll be time for a beer.'

Jonathan looked surprised. 'Are you asking me out on a date?'

'A date? I wouldn't call it that. I just think we could move on from mediocre coffee to something more interesting as a celebration.'

Jonathan didn't answer straight away and Kate tipped her head sideways and studied him, wondering why drinking with her would be a problem. She thought he liked her company; they had developed a familiarity and ease with each other over the past couple of weeks. Was she misreading him?

'I've got a better idea. Instead of going to the pub, I'll take you out for a meal. I did a modelling stint last month so I've got extra cash.'

'Wow! I wasn't expecting that! But a meal out would be

33

great.' She looked down at her scruffy jeans and the shirt with frayed cuffs. 'I think I'll go and change.'

This really is a date, she thought. A date with Jonathan Carson! But then, it's not a date, not a romantic one. It's a work celebration.

***

Kate waited at the bus stop as arranged. She was early. She wore a short denim skirt and a pink, cotton top with thin straps. This was the fourth attempt at getting her outfit right and her room was unusually untidy as she tried on and rejected items of clothing, wondering why it was proving so difficult. She completed the outfit with a thin silver necklace, a birthday present from her grandmother. After more than usual care with her makeup, she decided the result was okay. Attractive but not too sexy.

Sitting on a bench, she got out a mirror from her shoulder bag to examine her face. She crossed her legs and dangled a strappy sandal from her toes, regretting she had no nail varnish on her toenails. Heat rising from the hot tarmac was sticky and she swatted at the flies buzzing around her. The air was too still; the absence of breeze seemed to make the time slow down. Half past seven arrived but Jonathan didn't. As worry started to nibble at her, she realised how much she wanted this evening out with Jonathan. Surely he hadn't changed his mind! He was happy-go-lucky and carefree, but not unthinking, not unkind. He arrived ten minutes late with a grin and no apology, unflustered. He was oblivious of time. They travelled into town and Jonathan insisted on sitting upstairs at the front of the bus.

'I always did this when I was a kid and thought I was driving. And I still like sitting here. You get the best view.'

As he settled into the seat, she could feel the warmth of his thigh as it pressed against hers, an action that made her catch her breath but which he didn't notice. He took a child's delight in spotting the unusual and kept up a continual banter, pointing this way and that, leaning across her and tapping her arm, once catching her hair with his fingers. Kate registered every contact, every casual, careless touch and tried to ignore them. His humour was cruel but funny, focussing on fat women, ugly men and others whom, he admitted, should not be the butt of jokes.

'Look at that woman! She's so flat-chested, you'd think she had her head on back to front. Her shoulder blades are more prominent than her boobs.'

'You're wicked, Jonathan. She can't help it!' Kate looked down at her own shape, glad she had curves where they should be.

'And have you ever seen a hooter like that?' Jonathan pointed to a large-nosed gentleman who was walking proudly with his head thrown back, accentuating his least favourable feature. It was blotchy and bulbous. Kate folded over with barely suppressed laughter.

She'd not known him talk so much and wondered why. Surely Jonathan wasn't the type to be nervous with a woman. Or maybe he wanted to be entertaining, to show her a different side to himself, a non-academic side. He brought his wit into the department and amused everyone. Perhaps this was his real self. She would discover.

It was a short walk to the Italian restaurant he'd chosen. Kate wondered if he'd take her hand but he didn't. She was disappointed but annoyed she felt that way. Theirs was a work partnership and anything more could complicate their project. She should be glad Jonathan felt the same, too.

The restaurant was stylish and intimate, mostly tables set for two in alcoves. The cool atmosphere washed over them, a refreshing relief from the oppressive summer outside. Italy was everywhere. The walls were covered with pictures of vineyards, Tuscan cypresses and glossy photos of tables laden with cheeses and salami. A hint of herbs and garlic hung in the air, a promise of what was to come. There was a neat array of glinting wine glasses of different sizes on a rustic dresser together with dishes of olives and bottles of red wine. Music played but it was barely audible, a hushed background to keep conversations private without intruding upon them. The lighting was subtle; the sort of place romance might start.

The Italian waiter, smart in a long white apron with the strings tied at the front, showed them to a table and lit the single candle on it. Jonathan hadn't booked but it wasn't necessary. It was only half full. They sat down facing each other.

'Have you been here before, Jonathan?'

'Yeah, a few times. But not a regular.'

'It looked as if the waiter recognised you.'

'Maybe he does. They take their jobs seriously, Italian waiters. And that includes remembering faces.'

Kate looked around. The couple to their right were holding hands across the table and leaning towards each other. She saw him trace his finger around her mouth. Quickly she turned away, their familiarity embarrassing her, and picked up a menu.

'What do you recommend?'

'I'm stuck in a rut and usually go for spaghetti carbonara but I believe the veal is excellent here.'

'Then maybe I'll have a veal dish. It would be a treat.' She noticed it was expensive and quickly looked up to see if Jonathan reacted to her choice. Price, it seemed, was not the guiding factor this evening.

Jonathan looked at the wine list and decided on a carafe of house red commenting that the house wines were worth drinking. This was his world, Kate realised; he was at home here. Previously, working on the project, he'd been in hers.

'Shall we have assorted olives and garlic bread as a simple starter?' he asked.

Garlic bread. She loved it but garlic breath was a killer. But we'll both be eating it, so that's okay. Why am I worried, she thought? I shouldn't be contemplating a kiss.

Jonathan looked round the restaurant and sighed contentedly. 'This is one reason I continue with the modelling. I enjoy fine food and wine in a pleasant atmosphere. No way could I eat here on a student's finances. It's not wildly pricey but still out of range. I'm afraid I'm developing expensive tastes.'

Kate knew nothing about posh restaurants. An occasional cheap pub meal was as far as her money went. She smoothed her hand across the starched white tablecloth and looked at the huge, long-stemmed wine glasses, each big enough to hold half a bottle of wine. The single rose in an elegant vase looked real. She touched a petal to make sure. The waiter returned to unfold the crisp napkin and place it on her lap.

The wine arrived and Jonathan tasted it. He didn't make a great show and Kate was glad. She'd been watching the couple alongside out of the corner of her eye and when their bottle of wine arrived, the guy made a show of sniffing it and swishing it round his mouth. She thought it too ostentatious by far. He was out to impress his girl but she preferred the laid-back approach. Jonathan rose in her estimation.

The waiter poured a small amount into their glasses.

'Here's to the completion of our plan and to a successful project,' Kate said, raising hers.

They clinked the glasses and toasted each other. Jonathan looked at her intently over the rim of the glass. 'Rule number one,' he said.

'Rules? You have rules for eating out?'

'I have one rule. One rule for eating out with you. No talking shop. No mention of the project. I'm beginning to know what you're like; you don't turn off.'

'Fair comment. I am obsessed. But then we've only met to discuss work so why would I have talked about anything else?'

'Most people would have wandered from the point. Would have talked about what they'd been doing apart from work. They'd have commented on a television programme or a sport they liked.

Or even what they had for dinner the night before. I would have, given half a chance!'

'You think I didn't notice? But wasn't it better to be focussed? We've got it done! We're way ahead of the others. I feel on a real high because of that.'

'This is getting dangerously close to breaking the rule. Enough.' He placed his finger on Kate's lips to seal them. His hand smelled of soap.

'Okay. So tell me about the modelling.'

'You don't have to ask about it, you know. It isn't important.'

'It makes you different. And I wouldn't be sitting here in this smart restaurant without it. So I'm bound to ask. You're the only student I know who's a model.'

'It's lucrative and at times fun. But mostly tedious and boring.'

'Boring? Don't you meet interesting people?'

'Now and then. But I'm an also-ran in the modelling world, a part-timer who happens to have a face that fits. Once I have a decent salary from a proper job, I expect I'll stop. Life as a male model is short anyway.'

He was being too blasé for Kate. She felt sure modelling must have affected him more than he was making out. She leaned forward. 'Do you wear make-up?'

'No!' Then he qualified his statement. 'Well, I have to for the photographs but not in ordinary life.'

'Just thought it might be a spin-off from the glamorous world you "now and then" live in. Thought you might have got used to it.' A touch of sarcasm; why am I doing this?

'I use moisturiser. That's all. It keeps my skin soft.'

He took Kate's hand and laid it on his cheek. She could feel slight stubble and hoped her face had not betrayed her. Moisturiser or not, she liked touching him.

The garlic bread and olives arrived so they started to eat.

Kate was glad to put food rather than wine in her stomach. She hadn't eaten anything but a sandwich for lunch hours ago and felt light-headed.

'Tell me about yourself, Kate. I know nothing that isn't work-related.'

Kate considered what to say. Not that she was a swot who spent too much time studying. Not that she'd been head-girl at her school. Not that she thought she was too boring for him. Certainly not that she found him disconcertingly attractive.

'I'm competitive. Always have been. I like tennis and am mad about skiing. I have a passing interest in fashion but insufficient money to do much about it. I've travelled a bit and intend to do more. And I love the theatre.'

Jonathan leaned back in his chair and played with his wine glass, swirling the liquid round, but keeping his eyes fixed on Kate's face. 'I like it when you talk about things that interest you. Your eyes light up and become greener. I like you when you are passionate about things. You have more passion than anyone else I know. It's infectious.'

Kate did not reply. He was confusing her. She couldn't tell where this was leading.

'Have I embarrassed you?' he said.

'Yes. A bit.'

'Well, you've learned a fact about me. I'm honest. I express my feelings. Although I try not to offend anyone by being too outspoken. In spite of my jokes on the bus, I don't go as far as telling obese women they are fat!'

Kate laughed and relaxed. The wine was helping. What the hell, she thought. I'll take the evening as it comes. The restaurant was filling up and there was a low murmur of conversation. Anyone would think we were a regular couple, she mused. Okay, let's find out a thing or two about him.

'So what do you do when not modelling, Jonathan? Do you belong to any university clubs or do any sport?'

39

'Yeah, rugby and squash. Not seen you at either of those, though!'

'No. DramSoc is more my thing. Have you been to any of the plays?'

'I saw one in the first year. "Look Back in Anger". I enjoyed it, even though I only went along because a mate had a spare ticket.'

'Well, well. You obviously didn't register who played the female lead.'

Jonathan raised his eyebrows. 'It was you, wasn't it?'

Kate nodded.

'It was a great performance.'

'You don't have to say that. But I adored it. It's a favourite play of mine and I had a marvellous leading man.'

'Whom you no doubt fell in love with?'

'Right first time. I was warned it would happen. He had great stage charisma. A perfect Jimmy Porter.'

'But it didn't last?

'Right second time. I fell in love with the actor, not the person.'

'And are you in love with anyone now, Kate?'

Kate felt herself blushing under Jonathan's questioning gaze. Without her realising, the conversation had reverted to her. 'You have a disconcerting way of looking at me, Jonathan. Stop it.'

He laughed, the easy, noisy laugh she was used to. He put a hand across his eyes. 'Will you answer the question if I don't look?'

'Yes.' She paused. 'No.'

He removed his hand and asked her what that meant.

'Yes, I will answer and no, I'm not in love with anyone at the moment.'

'So who was the guy I saw you with on Saturday night?'

'Saturday night?' She thought back. 'I went to the disco

and he was a guy I met there. Didn't realise a spy was on my tail!'

'Looked like you two were getting on pretty well!'

'Oh, come on. I bet you do much the same. Just having a good time. No-one owns me, you know.'

'Well, what about Colin and Simon?'

Kate was taken aback he asked that question and shook her head. 'I never went out with Colin – he was a pain. Kept pursuing me without any encouragement. And I finished with Simon ages ago. How do you know about them?'

'I am a pharmacy student, you know, and I'm in the department now and then. Often enough to spot what's going on. I don't miss much!'

'So it seems.'

Kate watched Jonathan enjoying the food, eating her own meal in a distracted way, and wondered how much she could ask about his relationships. Recklessness was creeping in with the alcohol so she decided to avoid subtlety and get straight to the point.

'You've quizzed me but you've not told me about your love-life.'

'No, I haven't.'

'Well?'

'Don't you remember on our first day when the staff welcomed us Dr Passman gave us a piece of advice? He suggested it was best not to become emotionally involved with each other, to find our personal involvements outside the department or life could be difficult, especially as relationships fail. After all, with lectures and labs five days a week, we would be living in each other's pockets.'

'I do remember that. Many of us ignored his advice. I got the impression he'd seen it happen. But you've never been in anyone's pocket. You're rarely there!'

Jonathan screwed up his nose in denial and then laughed. 'Well, I thought there was sense in what he said. So I've never considered a girlfriend in pharmacy.'

'Getting one would not have been difficult. You have a following!'

'Nonsense. Anyway, I've found girlfriends elsewhere. But I'm not in love if that was your next question.'

'Actually my next question was how you manage to pass the exams,' Kate lied, 'seeing as your attendance is a sporadic affair. You obviously don't need to work as hard as I do.'

'I have an excellent memory. And plenty of text books. Rarely need to read anything more than once. Lucky me. But watch out – getting close to rule-breaking!'

'Sorry!'

'Enough of work.' He leant towards her to speak quietly. 'Have you noticed the couple over there? Have a casual look in a minute. He is trying hard to impress her, laughing too much at things she says, explaining the finer points of the menu when I'm sure she doesn't need help and generally being uptight. It's amusing.'

Kate felt his breath on her face as he spoke and unconsciously put her fingers on her cheek to touch the spot. She followed his eyes and turned slightly.

'I noticed them. He made a real performance of tasting the wine. She looks fed-up and grumpy. And they look an odd couple. Why do you think they've come out together?'

'Maybe he earns a lot of money – he looks much older than her – and she fancies a night out.'

Jonathan grinned and then noticed Kate's dismayed face.

'You earn a lot of money. You don't think I've come out with you in order to scrounge, do you?'

'Oh, God, Kate. I don't want you to think that. I wasn't making a comparison!' He reached across and touched her arm. The smile had fallen off his face. 'I've asked you out as a celebration and because I like you. I hope you came because you don't totally dislike me.'

42

He couldn't maintain a serious expression, however. 'Yes, of course you're a scrounger. You've scrounged every minute of my free time for the project for weeks!'

Kate could still feel the pressure of his warm, smooth fingers on her arm and was trying to dismiss it. 'That's true, Jonathan, and I hope you're eternally grateful. And you should mind your own business and not make inappropriate remarks about fellow diners!'

'Okay. You can find the next pair to be rude about.'

He topped up Kate's glass again as they both giggled and she took a sip. The carafe was empty and she had no idea how much had ended up in her glass. She had the happy feeling whatever she said would be funny or clever. The main course was over, a delicious, well-prepared, beautifully presented, hardly noticed meal.

'Dessert?' Jonathan asked.

'Not sure if I can eat any more.'

'How about a sorbet? They're lovely and slide down with no effort. Surely you could manage that?'

Before she could protest, Jonathan nodded to the waiter who came over and took the order for two different flavours.

'These are the best ones. Wait and see. It's a great way to finish the meal. Do you want the lemon or the blackcurrant?'

Kate chose lemon and savoured its icy tartness, its delicious zing.

'You must taste the blackcurrant as well.'

Kate was about to put her spoon into Jonathan's dish when he popped his own spoon in her mouth. She coughed to cover her surprise.

'Sorry, was that too much?'

It was, but not in the way he intended. Jonathan ordered coffee and Kate realised the evening would soon be over. She got up to visit the Ladies and brushed against Jonathan on her way, enjoying his nearness. The warmth of the night, or the place, or the atmosphere, gave her cheeks a glow. Redoing her lipstick, she decided she looked good. Good enough for Jonathan to be attracted to her.

The table had been cleared when she returned and the restaurant was starting to empty. She glanced at two men in their twenties who were finishing their meal at a table in the far corner.

'There are a couple of guys eating together over there, near the window. Doesn't seem like a blokey place. Don't you think it's odd?'

'Why should it be odd?'

'Well, it's couples otherwise.'

'I expect they are a couple, Kate.'

She blushed as it hit her how naïve she was. 'Oh, God, Jonathan, you're right. I didn't think.'

'Does it offend you?'

'No, not at all. I was being innocent, I suppose. I've never been aware of a gay couple before.'

She made light of it to excuse herself but inside was worried what Jonathan would think. Although he liked to mock, he was accepting of everything. He must think her outlook narrow, must think her a silly schoolgirl. What a stupid comment to make! She cursed herself for her foolishness. Why did it matter what he thought? It did, that was all she knew. Discomfort was threatening to spoil her evening. However, Jonathan chatted on and seemed unaware of how she felt. She looked at her watch and Jonathan noticed.

'Well, Miss Shaw, I think it's time to go.'

'You're right. It was a lovely meal, a lovely evening. Thank you.'

'My pleasure.' He paused. 'I mean it.'

'Well – I'm about to break the rule. No, don't look like that, Jonathan. I just want to say I'm going to enjoy doing the project with you.'

'Ditto.'

Jonathan paid the bill and tipped the waiter, who said he hoped to see him again soon. Kate felt herself hoping it would be with her. As they headed for the bus-stop, Jonathan put his hands in his pockets. Kate was glad darkness hid her disappointment. Her problem was usually stopping the over-eager hands of guys going where she didn't want them. On the bus, upstairs at the front again, sitting unavoidably close, Jonathan asked her what she was doing during the long vac.

'Working in a café to ease myself out of poverty and then spending the money travelling with a friend in France. A girl from school – we've kept in touch. How about you?'

'Not sure yet. A few modelling stints lined up. Do you know when you'll be back here?'

'A couple of days before term starts, I expect. Why?'

'Just wondered. Give me your home phone number, I might call you to check. In case I'm back at the same time.'

Kate did as asked, confused as to what it might mean. Surely he wasn't so keen to get the project started?

Jonathan walked her back to her flat and as they said goodbye, he gave her a half-hug with one arm and a peck on her forehead.

'You're a super girl, Kate. I enjoyed tonight.'

He started to say something else, but turned it into his usual noisy laugh.

'Have a great vac, Kate.'

Chapter 4

Becky won her over in the end. Or maybe she simply persuaded herself. Once she started to reminisce, it was hard to stop, hard to close the door on the past. So she found herself driving to the university campus on a Friday in late September, a languid autumn evening with the low sun lighting up the turning leaves. People were out walking, making the most of the last of the warm weather. Younger, brave ones were still in summer dresses displaying suntans or white flesh that had missed out on earlier hot days. Others, more sensibly, had wrapped themselves up in light sweaters; there was a chill in spite of the sunshine. Children were on their bikes and in their front gardens, shouting and laughing, enjoying the last minutes of freedom before bedtime. The sounds of happy voices and the occasional squabble reached Kate although she hardly noticed.

She was debating whether or not to lower the roof on her sports car, a red Mazda MX5. She bought it the previous year when the businesses started to take off. She couldn't justify it – all she needed was a smart, reliable car to replace her old Fiesta – but now and then you need a reward, she told herself, a treat. So she ignored the question of justification and went with what she wanted. Roof up, this evening, she decided. It'll be too cold by the time I arrive. Usually she loved driving but on this occasion she went into automatic mode, gaining no enjoyment either from the car or the pleasant evening as she prepared herself for the ordeal. She switched on the radio and then turned it off again when she realised she hadn't listened to a word.

The grey, iron gates were unchanged. This was where she

entered the campus all those years ago. She was nervous then, the first member of her family to go to university, the first time she lived away from her parents.

***

Her parents drove her to this daunting place, her home for her first year, and the atmosphere in the car was tense.

'Oh, darling, will you be alright?' Her mother was transmitting her own nervousness like a radio programme.

'You know I will.' She hoped she sounded more confident than she was. 'Don't fuss.'

But the way she picked at a piece of loose skin by her thumb nail was a clue to her unease; her mother knew.

The hall of residence had the sombre walls of a prison. It looked bleak and the grey stone chilled her. The rows of even windows looked down on her, anonymous and watchful. But the garden was full of flowers and the new girls arriving buzzed around them like bees. Everyone looks much happier than I feel, Kate thought. But then maybe they were putting on a show, too. She forced a smile as another girl with her parents walked by. Life in an all-female hall would not have been her first choice of accommodation, but that was her lot.

The porter at the door welcomed her and checked her name as a stout lady swept by, wishing him "Good afternoon".

'That's the warden of the hall, Dr Minerva Jack,' he informed them. 'Not a bad old stick; her bark's worse than her bite.' It was a well-used description; he repeated those words many times.

Kate knew of her, an eminent psychologist, but was surprised at her apparent eccentricity. Her dress was grey and purple, shapeless and long with various layers that floated around her. She seemed to precede most of it across the entrance hall as it hurried to catch up with her rapid pace. A puff of smoke hung above her head like an ugly halo, the product of a cheroot, and she coughed every few breaths. She had two overweight dachshunds on leads trotting behind her. She suited her name, Kate thought, slightly exotic but short and to the point.

'Hope university doesn't turn you into a character like that!'

Kate's father spoke louder than necessary and Kate glared at him but Minerva Jack had already disappeared. I doubt it, thought Kate, who wasn't a floaty person. A year later, she realised she had been unknowingly "Minervised", as the hall residents called it, influenced by the strong, independent personality who cared for and directed those in her custody. She never, however, succumbed to grey and purple diaphanous dresses, nor cheroots and dachshunds.

Kate and her parents went up to her room on the second floor, a box containing the essentials of student life, the end one in a corridor of identical cells.

'Well, you've done well here,' her mother enthused, talking incessantly to stop herself from feeling. She sat on the bed and said how comfortable it was, how the new, patterned blanket they bought would look smart there and brighten the room. A room with plain cream walls, awaiting adornment.

'Come on, I'll help you unpack.'

They hung dresses, skirts and jeans in the wardrobe, filled the drawers with underwear, sweaters and socks and the air with useless words.

'Ah, the new mugs! Just the job. I'll make us a cup of tea. I spotted the kitchen along the corridor.'

Her mother trotted along to the communal kitchen and boiled the kettle. She put tea bags in the mugs and cursed they'd not brought any milk. Then she spotted a fridge with a couple of cartons in it. A label on the door said "For general use'. She smiled at a girl who walked in.

'I'm pleased to see whoever runs the domestic affairs here

thinks about you all.'

Kate's father said little; males of his generation and family were not effusive.

'Glad we remembered the biscuits!' Her mother clattered around, rummaging here and there and being busy. She opened the packet of chocolate digestives and handed them round, making an important job of a trivial task.

Stop the inane chatter, Kate thought. You're making it obvious that saying goodbye will be hard. Every silent moment had to be plugged, like holes in a dyke to stop the flood waters rushing through.

'Spoke to your next door neighbour in the kitchen. Andrea, that's her name. Seems a pleasant girl. I think you'll like her. She's a first year too. Studying theoretical physics.'

Must be a boring individual then, Kate thought. Then she told herself off. Don't judge people. Maybe Andrea is brilliant at physics, talks animatedly about it and would have hated pharmacy. She needed to make friends. She must try to settle in, overcome her hidden shyness, her reticence to mix. She opened the note the porter had given her when she arrived and read it.

'Mum, I have to go and meet Dr Jack in half an hour. She's seeing the new students individually. You and Dad might as well leave when you've finished your tea – no point in hanging around. Better to go early and miss the traffic.'

'If only you'd gone to a nearer university. It would have been so much easier all round. You could have lived at home.'

The plea flooded uncontrollably from her mother's mouth.

'Oh no, how many times have we had this conversation? Going away is part of the university experience. I need to learn to be independent. Anyway, you know this is one of the nearer universities where you can study pharmacy – be realistic. I'm only a couple of hours away.'

Kate was becoming stressed in an effort to hide her own feelings and spoke angrily. Leaving home wasn't easy but she hated to admit it. Then her mother started to sob. Normally well organised, she flapped around with her handbag trying to find the packet of tissues she brought along. Her Dad offered a creased white rag that was his version of a handkerchief but got a shake of the head. He blew his nose on it, folded it over, gave a final polish and a sniff, and replaced it in his pocket. He put his arm around his wife and gave her a brief hug. She shrugged him off, needing the sympathy but unable to accept it. A melange of emotions, she gathered up her belongings, put her coat on without fastening it, then walked blindly along the corridor and down the stairs to their car. They stood by the vehicle, looking at each other. Kate hugged them both. Her mother clung on to her, unwilling to let go. Getting into the car seemed too big a step; once that happened the separation would be complete.

'You will write, love, won't you? We want to know all you're doing, how you're getting on.'

'Of course I will. And I'll phone from time to time as well.'

Telling them everything was unlikely but she'd let them know about the course and how she was getting on. It was such a major change in their lives. A daughter of theirs going to university! They told their neighbours to the point of embarrassment for her. Their pride in her was a drug that kept them going. But leaving home was an event neither of them had contemplated until marriage required it. They couldn't come to terms with it.

'We'll come and visit you in a few weeks. That's something to look forward to!'

Resolutely, she refused to cry but her voice was hoarse. She was not going to let them know how much she'd miss home. But she ached, a mixture of apprehension, fear of being unable to cope and the anticipation of loneliness.

***

And now as she drove through the grey gates and saw the same forbidding walls of her first-year home frowning down, the same feeling returned. She could taste the trepidation. How little it had changed, yet how many students it had sheltered since she lived there. She wondered who was in her room, whether the walls were still cream and if the crack in the corner of the ceiling was still there. There were students wandering in and out of the main door, men and women, and with a jolt she realised it was a mixed hall. Times were different now. Where was Minerva Jack? She felt a warmth as she thought of her eccentric mentor but it was transitory. The evening clouds that were gathering didn't help. Her mood, not high when she set off, sank as the sun and the autumnal light faded.

This is stupid, she told herself. Then you were a timid eighteen-year-old with little knowledge of the world. Now you are married, a successful business woman in your fifties – she winced at the thought of her age – who has faced far bigger challenges than this. Relax! You don't know what this reunion will bring. Who knows, you might enjoy it! And if not exactly that, you could have a significant achievement by the end of this weekend.

She wished Becky had travelled with her. They'd have talked and laughed; the gloomy spirits would have been kept at bay. And Becky loved the sports car. But her regular locum wasn't available so she was obliged to work the Friday herself.

'Don't like having a stranger I don't know in the place. I'm fussy like that. I prefer to stick with Mary, my usual lady, but she can only do tomorrow. Well, I suppose I save on her fees. It's costing me enough anyway!'

She wouldn't be able to leave until after the shop closed. She'd miss the beginning of the drinks reception but would do her best to get there towards the end of it. It was only a half-hour drive.

'You should have worked for me!' Kate told her, 'Then I could have sorted it out.' Kate had offered her a job a few years

51

ago managing one of her own pharmacies.

'Becky, have you seen in the "Pharmaceutical Journal" that I'm advertising?'

'Sure. Everyone starts from the back and looks at the jobs.'

'Are you interested?'

'I thought about it. You pay well and it would be convenient.'

'You know you'd be my preferred candidate, don't you?'

'Thanks for the compliment.'

'Well, you know I rate your skills. It's not flattery. I've seen you at work and I'd like you to work for me.'

'I'll think about it.'

'I wouldn't tread on your toes, you know. You'd have the freedom to manage the pharmacy as you want.'

But she declined. In a way, Kate expected that and understood, not mixing business and social life. She tried her hardest to entice Becky; she knew the value of getting and hanging on to a quality pharmacist. That was all she could do.

'You were the one who was keen to come to this wretched reunion! Now I've got to face it alone.'

But there was no point in recriminations; it was history. She wasn't one to pull out of anything at the last minute although the thought crossed her mind. She liked Becky but felt there was a distance between them she couldn't breach. Professionalism, she told herself. I shouldn't complain about that. I go on about it enough to my staff.

Kate stopped the car and checked the instructions in Willy's message. Visitor parking was past the halls of residence, into the science area and to the right of the Civil Engineering building. Being practical put her back in her comfort zone. She drove slowly, looking at the surroundings, the lawns and flower beds, some as familiar as her own garden, others new or anyway newer than thirty years. Her memory of the campus was vivid.

After three years there, there wasn't much of it she hadn't seen. Various additional buildings had sprung up and she missed the open space. But it was the same campus. It had the air of academia, the expectation of keen student minds floated around her; it was its own world. Part of her felt like a student again.

A large sign indicated "New Theatre" on a tatty, wooden building in need of a coat of paint. Well, it's a theatre, Kate thought, even if ill-named. We didn't have one. We performed wherever anyone would have us. There were advertising posters and the current production was John Osborne's "Look Back in Anger". The word "Revival" was splashed over it. It took her back to her drama days and her spirits lifted. DramSoc had been a major highlight of her student years.

***

Her debut audition was early in the first term. She saw a note on the DramSoc notice board asking freshers to go to the auditions in the Students' Union. Kate went along and looked around nervously for instruction. One of the organisers told her to sit wherever she liked so she chose a sofa in the corner, where another girl looking equally apprehensive was perched. It required courage to turn up; auditioning at school had been much easier amongst people she knew.

She decided to wear a black sweater and tight trousers with dark makeup. It felt like a disguise and she enjoyed playing a part, hiding the real Kate behind the façade she created. The old hands, second and third year students, handed out random pieces for people to read. It was low key, no standing on a stage before an audience. It was meant to put folk at ease.

'You can have five minutes or so to prepare this, then we'll ask you to read it out loud. You can do it sitting here – no need to stand up.'

Everyone read against a low murmur of others being told

what to do. The best sounded promising but many were mediocre. Nerves produced squeaky voices and coughing. Some spoke loudly and others were barely audible. There was a touch of "Don't call us, we'll call you," in the attitude of those running the auditions. The chosen would get parts in the next play; the producer would post the cast list on the notice board and the hopefuls would read it anxiously. Then rehearsals would start.

Kate was given a speech from "Look Back in Anger": Alison, the down-trodden wife. She'd read the play, seen it and loved it. The choice was perfect for her. And it was the next production. Taking a few deep breaths of air before starting to make sure her voice came out smoothly, she read the piece with all the emotion she could. As she continued, the room went silent. Everyone was listening. There was a pause after she finished and then the babble slowly started again. She was stunned, never having held attention like that before.

'Thanks, I liked that. Think we'll be seeing you again. I'm Ian, by the way.' He took the book from her, asked her for her name, looked at her intently and smiled. He had an interesting face, crooked teeth and a scar near his lip. Not handsome but appealing. She liked his smell as he bent down to talk to her. He had obviously washed his hair recently, and it flopped forward over his eyes. He flicked it back as he stood up. A girl in the queue to read whispered to her as he walked away.

'He had the male lead in last term's production. Normally gets a big part. He has a great stage presence. All his leading ladies fall in love with him.'

She'd not been wrong. Kate's audition won her the main part in the production and she played opposite him, Alison to his Jimmy Porter. She was captivated. He coached her in acting techniques and in stage makeup, giving her time and attention. The part was developing well and the producer complimented her. As her skills improved so did her preoccupation with Ian.

'Fancy a drink after the rehearsal, Kate?'

'Love to, Ian.'

Fancying a drink led rapidly to fancying each other. But in real life, he was less exciting than on the stage and their passion soon fizzled out. They lasted as a couple barely longer than the play.

***

Kate smiled to herself and re-focused her attention; there was much to catch her eye. Students were returning to campus and groups gathered, chattering to each other, cheerful faces, shoulders weighed down with bags of books and other paraphernalia. People looked less serious than in her time; maybe the burden of doing a degree bothered them less. Bicycles were parked randomly around the campus, the most common form of transport as in her day. Everyone wore jeans, she noticed; a fashion that hadn't changed. There was a cosmopolitan feel to the place, more foreign students than thirty years ago. An interesting mix, she thought. I have to find something positive about this place. I'm here. Get on with it.

Chapter 5

They were meeting in the new pharmacy facility, the Brookman Building, a stylish glass-fronted construction built in the last five years and funded by an ex-student. An ex-student who made his money on the stock exchange – pharmacy didn't normally yield such rewards. Kate felt saddened. It didn't feel right. The reflected campus threatened her as she looked up at the imposing mirror frontage. This isn't your department, it said. The old, dilapidated buildings were Pharmacy to her. She felt surprising nostalgia. Willy said they would meet in the new premises, but it was still a blow to see her familiar surroundings gone.

She found the recommended car park and slotted the car neatly into a gap making sure she was exactly parallel with the white lines. Then she pulled down the sun visor to look in the mirror. The face that looked back was worried. Thoughts of the couple lying under the tree still lurked in her head. I must stop this. I must look my best, she told herself, and my best doesn't leave me with much to complain about. So she made herself relax and the lines faded. Not the face of her eighteen year old self, she reflected. But the frequent use she made of the local salon was to their mutual benefit, especially recently, since she passed the unforgiving fifty. The glow to her skin from a facial she had two days before remained. Her hair was still long, not the random, curly, uncut hair she had as a student, but an expensively shaped, shiny coiffure. Gym visits three times a week plus a run at the weekend completed the package.

Could pass for thirty-eight, maybe forty, I reckon, she said to herself, renewing her lipstick. And that was the boost she needed to make her entrance at the gathering.

Kate followed an arrow on a sign indicating "Pharmacy Reunion" to the Galen Lounge, passing luxurious sofas and potted plants. A hotel reception area, she thought, not a pharmacy department. The wooden floor shone and her footsteps echoed. There was too much space. There was no smell; no appropriate smell. A slight perfume from the large vase of lilies on a pedestal in the corner wafted across to her. Everything that was meant to be welcoming was alien. Not normally averse to change, her reaction surprised and bothered her. She slowed her steps and then stopped by the window, an inappropriately large window for a scientific department, she thought, to get her mind in order.

***

She cycled to the department on her first morning. Most students used bikes to get around the campus and a row of bike racks was lined up behind the main lecture theatre. They filed in and sat in the raked rows of hard, wooden benches, polished to a sheen by years of student bottoms, and rested their elbows on the scratched wooden desks, initials of predecessors gouged in the wood, testament to boring lectures.

She remembered fiddling with her bike lock for longer than necessary before feeling brave enough to go in; looking around out of the corner of her eye to make sure others were arriving and she could go in with a group. She sat three rows back, alongside two other girls and a geeky guy who kept wiping his hand around his cheeks and chin. The front row was too ostentatious but she was never a back of the classroom person.

The Head of Pharmacy, Professor Everett, spoke to them. He was a cartoon character, a lanky man wearing old-fashioned glasses he constantly took off and put back on, a tweed jacket, unpressed trousers with worn knees and a bow-tie. Such hair as he had stuck out at strange angles. Generations of students mimicked his Yorkshire accent. But the cartoon appearance belied the real man. He won the respect of all who met him.

'Welcome to the best pharmacy course in the UK. You are the privileged few. Ten times as many students applied to this course as places available. We are glad to have you here. The next three years will be hard work. They will stretch and challenge you. But you will come out of it with a superb qualification that will set you up for life. You will be proud to call yourselves pharmacists. Work hard and most of all, enjoy it!'

She could still hear the Professor's words which inspired and motivated her. Then they collected their timetables and went on a tour of the department.

It was the smell she remembered most. Years of experiments imbued the walls with an odour. There was a strong whiff of hydrogen sulphide – bad eggs – but it was mixed with so many other chemicals it was hard to describe the final cocktail. It was particularly strong in the store rooms but nowhere escaped. No amount of cleaning by Ivy, a robust lady with a duster, mop and much determination could diminish it. After a while, it became homely, a welcoming familiarity that reassured and cheered the hard-pressed student. On one occasion, she took her parents to see the department.

'Ugh! What a disgusting smell! However do you manage to work in here? It would drive me out.' Her father was loud in his dislike.

'You know, it's so much part of the place I hardly notice it now.'

'I'd have thought a department with the reputation this one has would have better facilities. It's run down. Appearances matter.'

He straightened his already immaculate tie.

Kate shrugged and said there were more important factors; he made a few comments to himself about the sloppiness of youth.

Reputation was more than buildings, but the buildings

were key. On their first morning, they'd been taken round the labs: chemistry, with shelves and shelves of bottles. She could never reach the top ones and always had to ask for help. Pharmacology with its recorders and water baths and strange pieces of kit she would eventually learn to use; pharmacognosy, a dry world of botanical samples, bits of twigs, roots and resins, the natural sources of many drugs; and pharmaceutics, real pharmacy where she would learn to compound and dispense medicines. The age of the premises didn't matter as she learned her trade.

***

And it was gone, destroyed if not fallen down. Nothing but a memory. Not even its footprint was visible. Everything was smarter now but she could not believe it was better.

Right, ready to go, you can handle this, she told herself.

She automatically smoothed her skirt and elongated her neck to give a centimetre more height as she reached the allocated room. A short, plump guy was waiting by the door, an array of printed name badges on a table beside him. She would have known him by the now ample ginger whiskers without looking at his badge. She could hear his sniff as she approached.

'Willy! Well, well! You don't look much different.'

He did, of course. Many kilos heavier with the rotund waistline and blotchy nose of the spirit-drinker.

'Gabriel now, my dear. Nice to see you, Kate. You've not weathered badly.'

He was always slightly askew with his compliments, when he bothered with them. This was a brave effort. They did the compulsory minimal kiss on both cheeks, like a pair of necking birds about to dance. A handshake would have been too business-like, a hug too familiar; it fitted the occasion.

'So how many of us are you expecting?'

'Well, of the forty who graduated I sent emails to thirty-

59

six and thirty-five responded. Didn't hear from Jack Parr, don't know why. Poor old Carol Mead and Dave Longley died last year, car crash for her, heart attack for him. Couldn't find Stephen Black or Brian Foster. They've left the register. Presumably changed their careers. Not that I could ever see either of them making it as successful pharmacists even though they got a degree!' He laughed loudly at his own tasteless joke.

'So we are thirty-five?'

'No, thirty-four, plus a few hangers-on. Partners, I mean. Unfortunately, a few won't arrive until tomorrow. The usual problems with getting a locum. Jennifer Watson said she didn't want to come. The only person of our entire year who said she wasn't interested. Miserable old cow. Never liked her anyway.'

'Looks like we need to be here to avoid being talked about,' Kate said without a hint of a smile. Willy didn't know how to take it.

'Oh, I'll talk about anyone, you know me. Whether they're here or not!'

'Well, I'd better watch my step.' She paused and then added, 'Willy.'

It was true. Willy was never one to think before speaking but at least he was open and you knew what he thought. If you could follow him, that is, and not get lost in all the details that littered every conversation.

Fresh arrivals came through the door: a couple of well-worn women wearing little makeup and unremarkable clothes. Kate was shocked not to recognise them. There were students she'd not known well – she struggled to place the names Willy had thrown at her – but she expected faces to be familiar. Then it became clear as two guys she did know appeared. Jeremy and Miles had brought their wives, the "hangers-on" Willy mentioned. So there'll be at least two bored individuals, Kate thought, glad to have Neil out of the way. They can talk to each other.

'See you later, Kate, my dear. Go and get a drink.' Willy

moved on to his latest arrivals.

Kate looked around the room. No Jonathan as far as she could see. But he'd be there, Willy had verified that without realising it. She wondered how she would react at the first sight of him for thirty years. Would there be any reaction? She thought so as her heart rate increased with anticipation. But perhaps he was now fat and bald; others around the room had gone that way. Was it possible?

She took a glass of white wine from a tray and moved across to a nearby group. Their eyes quickly scanned each other's name badges to make sure they didn't make fools of themselves. They could then go ahead with the pretence of recognising each other whether they did or not.

There was much helloing and cheek kissing and 'What are you up to now?' and 'Are you married?' and 'Is your "significant other" with you?' and 'Don't you look well!'

What a useful phrase it was! "Looking well" covered "Seems like you have a large appetite and don't care what shape you are." Or, "Your high colour implies you have a blood pressure problem." Or, "I can't think of anything nice to say to you so this will have to do." Or even, "You look dreadful but I can't tell you that!" Occasionally, it meant what it said.

Kate gathered a large share of the compliments and while she knew she was not herself always telling the truth, chose to believe others were. She could tell. The way the women looked her up and down with envy in their eyes, eyes that wondered how she maintained her shape and looks. Pauline, her old friend and flatmate in her final year, one of the few she liked, came up and threw her arms around Kate's neck. She was looking lively and forty-ish herself. She held Kate at arm's length and admired her.

'My Goodness, you look great! It's so lovely to see you.' Then she whispered, 'Just wondered if you're a hundred percent real. Any artificial help there? Tell me later. Have to admit to a bit myself.' She squeezed Kate's hand and then bounced off to talk to another group, determined to speak to everyone as soon as they got through the door.

And there were looks from the men. She saw their shaded glances at her legs, the unheard but noticed comment made between friends as she passed, the raised eyebrow hastily rubbed as if a fly had flicked by when she caught them watching her. It pleased her. They were a sexist bunch and she would normally have been annoyed but if they admired her then maybe Jonathan would, too.

She spotted Amanda who was sitting in a wheelchair.

'Amanda, so glad you're here! But I didn't expect to see this. What's the problem?'

'A riding accident ten years ago. You know I was always a keen rider. Paralysed from the waist down.'

She raised her hand as Kate was about to make the appropriate comments of sympathy.

'No. Don't say what I'm sure you were going to. The horse fell and landed on me. Nothing I could do about it but I've moved on. I spent months in hospital, wallowed in despair for two years, especially as my relationship with a long-term partner fell apart with the stress, contemplated suicide and thought there was nothing left in life for me. Then one day I decided I was being a fool. I took up archery and I'm bloody brilliant. Got into the British Paralympic Team. Married another archer and now suffer from loads of stupid jokes about long-standing radio series and country folk.'

'Wow. You've silenced me. I don't know what to say. What a well-balanced person you are! You have my admiration.'

'I know lots of people who've had to cope with more than I have. You would too, if you had to. Not that I'm wishing an accident on you. We all have strengths we don't know about. I work in the pharmaceutical industry. The building is adapted for the disabled and everyone accepts me. I get on with my job and I do it well. My husband is marvellous, totally supportive and I love him to bits. If I'd not had the accident, I might never have met him. Funny how fate works. Life couldn't be happier.'

I couldn't cope with anything like that, Kate thought. I've pretended but I haven't yet come to terms with what happened in my own life. Why would I be thinking about revenge if I had? And it's been nothing like Amanda's lot. She chatted for a few more minutes with Amanda, promised they'd talk more later, then moved on, circulating, speaking to this one and that, her mind preoccupied and her eye on the door.

She was half listening to a group of bland people, folks she had no particular feelings for in any direction, learning about their hospital positions, their dreadful hours, the demands placed upon them and the lack of decent pay, when Jonathan came in. She spotted him immediately and the instant impact shocked her. She hoped her face had not revealed the turmoil she felt as obsession and hatred fought for control of her emotions. As he fiddled with his name badge and chatted to Willy, she had time to calm herself and inspect him before he joined the crowd.

He had changed little, she could be truthful there. A touch of grey in his hair. Why does that do so much more for a man than it does for a woman? He was still slim and the few lines on his face only enhanced his bone structure. He wore a pale blue shirt with the cuffs turned back revealing a darker blue lining. It could have looked cheap but not on him. As he spoke to Willy, the old, engaging smile flashed across his face and she heard his distinctive laugh. Kate made a couple of sympathetic comments to her nearest companion to show she'd been listening then made her excuses to the group around her. She moved across the room so he would see her; she did not want to approach him first. There was a table with bowls of nibbles in an ideal spot and she stood by it as if to select what she wanted.

They had not spoken since the day he dropped her. There were no threads to pick up. There was nothing to say. What would he do? He might walk past her and nod, a cool movement of air to dismiss her, and that would be it. No, it wouldn't. That was not what she had in mind. But it needed his cooperation.

'Kate.' He stopped beside her and smiled tentatively. 'Are we talking?'

She waited before answering as if weighing his words.

'It's a long time to remain resentful,' she replied, carefully controlling her breathing.

'I was worried this could be a difficult meeting.'

'So was I. So apparently is everyone else.'

Kate realised they were the focus of covert attention; the room had gone quieter. Their break-up had hardly been a secret.

'Come and sit over here and tell me about yourself. Everyone is too busy talking about themselves to take notice of us for long.'

Jonathan picked up a glass of wine and a handful of nuts and they sat on one of the sofas in a corner of the room. Most people had now arrived, the noise and laughter level was high like the first day back at school, waitresses were replenishing the drinks and folk were involved in their own conversations. After a few minutes when it was clear there was nothing to watch, Jonathan and Kate ceased to be objects of interest. Jonathan was right. The warmth of the room reflected people's emotions; everyone had come to enjoy themselves and have their say about the last three decades.

Jonathan was rapidly on to his second glass of wine but Kate was sipping slowly. He lent back against the arm of the sofa and openly looked Kate up and down.

'Mighty fine, Miss Shaw, if I might say so!'

'Thank you, Mr Carson. You've scrubbed up pretty well yourself.'

They slipped easily into the banter they used as students, the banter that covered confused emotions before they openly admitted how they felt about each other. The banter they continued to use even after they passed the "I love you" barrier.

'But are you still Miss Shaw? Has some lucky guy snapped you up?'

'I'm married but I've retained 'Shaw' for professional purposes.'

'Married long?'

'Around twenty years.'

'Happily?'

Kate hesitated. She needed to think how to answer this. 'Yes, but that's my business. What about you?'

'Yep, married. Got married last year.'

'You took your time.'

'Third marriage.'

'Always liked a succession of women, didn't you?'

Jonathan didn't reply.

'Sorry. Shouldn't have said that.'

'It's okay. And you're right. I do like women. But I didn't intend to be a serial husband. It's the way things turned out. And if you want to know, my second wife left me, I didn't leave her. So I'm not always the bastard you take me for.'

'Depends on why she left you.'

'Don't be bitter, Kate. It doesn't suit you.'

Kate fiddled with her necklace and sighed. She wasn't sure the conversation was going how she wanted. Although did she know what she wanted? The physical presence of Jonathan was unsettling her. She was acutely aware of the smallest detail about him: the way he tied his shoelaces, the make of his watch, a cut on his left hand, the neatness of his hairline. And she hated herself for being so aware; hated him for making her this way.

'Let's change the subject,' she said.

'Okay. Tell me about yourself.'

'You don't want to know I own a chain of pharmacies, a chain of successful pharmacies, in fact. That I thoroughly enjoy my work, that I'm always looking for challenges, trying to improve and expand the business. That I work too hard and too long although I play hard too.'

'Ah, now I might be interested in the playing side. The rest I could have forecast. You were always ambitious and clever, always put in two hours to my one.'

'Wrong. Three hours at least to your one.'

'I stand corrected.'

'Seriously, I don't want to detail my business plan and bore you to death. What do you want to know?'

Kate chose only to tell him what she wanted him to know. She selected her words carefully, creating the impression she wanted, hoping she appeared relaxed and laid-back. But it was more difficult than she envisaged in her clinical way at home. She draped her arm along the back of the sofa and crossed her legs. I wasn't in DramSoc for nothing, she thought.

'I want to know about you as a person, not a list of your achievements. What makes you happy? What makes you sad? Are you still the same Kate or have you changed?'

'Being needed and loved makes me happy. Being able to rely on my partner without fear of being let down.'

Jonathan blew out a puff of air. 'That hurt. I suppose I deserved it. So does your husband fulfil these requirements?'

'You want to know, don't you? I married my husband because I loved him. I still do love him. He's dependable, faithful and loves me. But he's welcomed middle-age like an amiable friend shut out for too long. He likes having enough money and not needing to push himself. He loves his work but isn't very interested in mine. He likes staying in with an Indian take-away and a film. He even likes going to bed early. He calls it "The Good Life". He likes security.'

'And you don't?'

'Oh, it's not bad. I do like it. I like not having to worry if there'll be anything in the bank at the end of the month. I love our home. But it's not enough. I need excitement.' Especially now I've passed the dreaded half-century, she thought. 'I need a purpose to my life. I need the added sparkle that makes me breathe faster. I need a reason to look my best apart from satisfying myself. I'm the skier who comes down the black slope; Neil chooses an easy red.'

'So where do you get your kicks?'

'From my business. From sport.' She hesitated. 'From networking, from contacts.' 'But that's enough. Let's talk about you now.'

'I think you're more interesting, but okay, my turn. Fire away with the questions.'

'What did you do after graduation?'

'Couldn't settle. Had no idea what I wanted from life. Couldn't bear the thought of doing a boring pre-registration year with an old fart of a pharmacist who would disapprove of my style, my attitude – my life, full-stop. I wasn't even sure I wanted to be a pharmacist any more. So I did more modelling to refill the coffers then travelled for a couple of years. Did the Machu Picchu trail, a few months' volunteer work in a school in Peru, spent time in Thailand, paid my way with casual work and ended up in New Zealand. Stayed there and got married to a Kiwi.'

'But you're a pharmacist now? You're on the Register?'

'No. Why do you think that?'

'I assumed Willy got our names from the Pharmaceutical Society, from the Register.'

'I kept in touch with Eddy Lawton, my old flat-mate. Over there.' He pointed to a guy standing nearby, chatting animatedly to an amused group.

'He passed my details on to Willy.'

'So what do you do?'

'I'm a photographer. Mostly travel work. Got into it in New Zealand.'

Kate opened her eyes wide. Different field from Neil, fortunately. The prospect of her husband knowing Jonathan professionally wasn't one she anticipated.

'When did you marry – for the first time, that is.'

'About eighteen years ago. She died of cancer five years later.'

'I'm sorry.'

'Felt it was fate having a go at me. I loved her. I couldn't imagine what I'd do without her. But I survived.' He shrugged his shoulders. 'Couldn't stay in New Zealand so came back here.' He changed his position, drained his glass and stood up.

'This is getting too serious. We need refills.' He took their glasses and wandered off in search of more wine. Kate got up and headed for the Ladies. She stood in front of the mirror and questioned herself. How was it going so far? On track, she thought. There was still a thread between them, a stretched elastic band that could pull them closer or snap. The intensity of their old relationship had left its mark, its scar. She shouldn't be surprised by that. It was what she needed if her scheme was to work.

Chapter 6

By the spring term, they became accepted as a fixture. The initial reaction to Jonathan dating a girl in the department wore off, as did the envious, partly joking remarks towards Kate. No-one was surprised to see them holding hands after lectures, or sneaking a kiss by the bikes before they headed off in different directions. In the work environment, however, Kate maintained a serious professionalism and would not allow their relationship to distract her, in spite of Jonathan's frequent efforts to the contrary.

'Do you have to work this weekend, Kate?'

'I need to, but we can go out Saturday night and I can see you Sunday afternoon and evening, as usual. Why?'

'Well, something has come up. My parents have tickets to a musical in London on Saturday and a hotel for the night. But they can't go because of a funeral. It's a colleague of Dad's and he feels he should show his respects. So they've offered the tickets and hotel room to me.'

'Are you inviting me?'

'I don't see any other contenders here!'

Kate threw her arms around Jonathan's neck then stopped abruptly. 'I'll have to reorganise my work schedule.'

'Kate, you are too practical. Can't you forget about work for a couple of days and enjoy a weekend in London with me? You'll come back refreshed.'

Kate's hesitation was brief.

'I can! I can!' She was jumping up and down like a child. 'Don't worry. I won't bring any work with me.'

Jonathan looked at her in amazement, shaking his head.

Only Kate would consider the possibility of taking work with her.

'How will we get there?' She stopped jumping and the start of a frown spoiled the delight on her face.

'I can borrow Mum's car. Don't worry, there's no train fare to pay.'

Kate put her hand over Jonathan's and squeezed his fingers. He thought of everything down to her frequent money worries. And he must have told his parents about her or why would they have offered him a pair of tickets and the hotel? She wanted to ask him what they knew but apprehension stopped her. If they assumed he had a girlfriend in tow, a girlfriend he'd happily spend the night with – or worse, that he could find one at short notice – then perhaps she didn't want to know.

Jonathan worked out the best way to get there. A drive to a cheap car park and then the underground, overnight bags in tow.

'How do you know your way round so well, Jonathan?'

'I've always visited London. It's less than an hour on the train from home. And much of the modelling I do is there.'

His world, yet again, she thought.

They ate in an inconspicuous restaurant after the theatre. Kate couldn't stop singing songs from the show. Jonathan had deliberately not told her what it was and "The Rocky Horror Show" was no disappointment. She smiled to think that Jonathan's parents had bought tickets for it; it would have been the last choice for hers. She was making a bad job of "The Time Warp" and didn't notice where they ended up.

'Hope this isn't too expensive, Jonathan. I was thinking I'd pay as a way of saying thank you.'

'You can eat very reasonably in London. Expensively, too. But there are loads of cheap places serving tasty food. This is one of them.'

Kate paid, knowing even "cheap" would knock a hole in her next week's finances. But for once, she didn't care.

The hotel was better than anywhere she'd stayed although

she noticed Jonathan accepted it without comment. She explored the room, examining the toiletries and wondering if she could take those she didn't use. Seconds after she spotted the elegantly wrapped chocolate on her pillow, it was in her mouth.

'I'll have to wear this gorgeous dressing gown, even if I don't need it,' she said, wrapping the fluffy white towelling around herself.

'You're like a kid let loose in a toy shop! Come here, my excited little girl. We've got better things to do than examine the room in minute detail.'

Kate ran to Jonathan, the intoxication of the experience being stronger than wine. She let him remove her clothes, then gently pick her up and lay her on the bed, whispering to her. He caressed her with warm, smooth hands, his long fingers delicate in their touch. There was a risqué thrill about a night at a hotel, as if they shouldn't be there, and Kate savoured it. She'd been in bed with Jonathan many times but never overnight.

In the early hours of the morning, they decided they should go to bed properly and sleep. Kate went to the bathroom and closed the door. She'd not thought about this. The mundane aspects of getting ready for bed, cleaning teeth, using the toilet, were activities whose noises he would hear. And she would hear him. There was no magic in this. She spat out her toothpaste as quietly as she could with the tap running and was glad she only needed a wee, flushing the pan before she finished. But in the morning, things might be different. She emerged in the dressing gown to find Jonathan had put the television on quietly and was watching a rugby match, unaware of her anxious bedtime preparations. She envied his laid back attitude.

Jonathan went to the bathroom and used it as he would have done at home. Kate smiled to herself. This is the next phase of our relationship, she thought, and it pleased her.

***

Her mother phoned several weeks into the term to say she and her father would be coming to visit the following weekend. Kate enjoyed their termly visits. It was a pleasant respite from routine, a chance to catch up and a better than usual meal. But this time she felt irritated. A day given to her parents was a day without Jonathan.

'You know we were intending to spend Sunday afternoon together? Well, Mum and Dad are coming and they'll take me out to lunch. So you'll have to spend the time studying.'

'Huh! Second best, eh? Don't suppose I'm invited, am I?'

Kate wasn't sure whether this was a joke. 'You wouldn't come, would you?'

'I haven't been invited. Seems I'm not up to the parental standard.'

'Of course you can come. They'd love to meet you. Didn't think it would be your scene.'

'Well, I'm sure they're not ogres and if I can be with you, I'll put up with making small talk. And a Sunday lunch out would make a change.'

Kate had casually mentioned Jonathan in a letter home, saying her pharmacology partner was now her boyfriend. She knew there would be unwarranted enthusiasm from both her mother and father if she introduced him; he was their sort of person, well-spoken, well-dressed, amiable and amusing. But she was reluctant. They had been known to frighten off boyfriends before with too much keenness.

The lunch was a success. Jonathan was his most charming, talking to her Dad about car maintenance and then discussing gardening with her Mum, neither of which he knew much about but managed to fool them. When Jonathan went to buy them a drink, her mother was all nudges and whispers and her Dad appeared to have an eye problem, he winked so many times.

'Calm down, you two. He's a great guy but we've only been going out a few months. No need to buy a new hat, Mum!'

When it was time for her parents to leave, her Mum threw her arms around Jonathan saying how much she hoped they'd see him again. Her Dad pumped his hand up and down half a dozen times more than normal.

'You were Mr Charm himself,' Kate said once they were alone. 'I think Mum has fallen for you.'

'They're okay. I enjoyed the lunch. But I'm glad they only come once a term.'

Right, thought Kate. I think I'll keep the parents and Jonathan apart. But two weeks later, her intentions were ruined when her mother was rushed into hospital. Her father phoned her at her flat.

'Kate, don't want to worry you but Mum's in hospital. The doc thinks it's gall stones. She was in great pain last night and I took her to A & E this morning when it was no better. They kept her in and I think they're going to operate this evening. Thought you'd want to know.'

'Of course, I want to know. I'll come home.'

'You don't need to do that. I'll keep you informed.'

'I'm coming. I'll look into the trains and buses and see which works best.'

'I'd come and get you but I think I should stay here.'

'Don't even think about it. I'll be with you as soon as I can.'

She put the phone down as Jonathan rang the doorbell.

'Whatever's wrong?'

Kate's face was eloquent. She explained the situation, wondering if he'd think she was making too much fuss over what was a simple operation.

'I'll drive you there. I've got Mum's car this week because of getting to that modelling job I mentioned. We can go now if you want.'

Kate burst into tears and put her arms around Jonathan's neck. 'You are so kind to me. I wouldn't have asked but if you

73

don't mind…' Her words disappeared into his sweater.

So Jonathan again spent time with Kate's father, stayed the night chastely in the guest room, went with Kate to visit her mother after the successful operation and then drove Kate back to university. He was, necessarily, covered in praises, thanks, hugs, petrol money and kind words.

'You've got a smashing guy there, Kate. Hang on to him,' were her father's parting words. She hoped Jonathan hadn't heard. The nature of their relationship was not lost on others, either.

'Can I be a bridesmaid?' Becky asked one evening when she saw them together, arms wrapped around each other. She was being flippant but it made Kate realise she wasn't the only one who noticed how serious they were becoming. Marriage, a convention that happened to her parents' generation, vaguely crossed her mind. Only in passing; she dismissed it. It was too early for that. They were far too young. Theirs was an easy relationship but special, a friendship and a passion. She wanted it to last. Jonathan heard Becky's question and laughed.

'No-one's claiming me yet!'

Kate glanced at him apprehensively but he did not add any more. Jonathan, of all people, could appreciate a joke.

Two weeks later they completed their project. Jonathan was relieved and Kate was elated. She hugged Jonathan, there and then, in the pharmacology lab. They sat on the stools and looked at each other, hardly able to believe it was finished.

'That's gone well. We should both get excellent marks. And we finished a whole week ahead of schedule!'

Jonathan had said long ago they should celebrate the end of the project at the Italian restaurant where their relationship started. But then he seemed to forget about it. And completion didn't act as the expected prompt. Kate thought maybe money was tighter than usual in spite of his recent modelling and as she never had anything to spare, she didn't like to mention it. There are other ways to celebrate, she thought.

But then Jonathan disappeared. They no longer needed to meet in the laboratory, so he didn't turn up in the department. He ignored lectures and made no other contact with her. She heard nothing from him, or saw him, for five days.

'Odd to see you on your own, Kate,' Pauline commented as they came out of a lecture. 'I thought you were glued to Jonathan. Both in and out of the lab.'

'Well, we finished our project early.'

'Lucky you! Willy can't stop tweaking ours. He's driving me mad. Not that he lets me have much input. I leave him to it. Still, he knows what he's doing. I'll get a top mark as compensation for putting up with him.' She sighed and linked arms with Kate.

'Come and have a coffee. Haven't seen much of you since the great amour started. You'd hardly know we shared a flat. You're never there.'

Kate said nothing but Pauline prattled on and didn't notice her friend's unusual silence. Kate's mind was on Jonathan so as soon as they finished their coffees and Pauline went in search of Willy, she went to a phone box and called him at his flat. There was no answer and she was starting to worry. Wandering aimlessly about was alien to her. She went to the library, thinking the time would pass more quickly if she was occupied. But she couldn't settle to work, her usual recourse to sort out her mind. On her second attempt at phoning, he answered.

'Is everything alright, Jonathan?'

'Er, yes, why?'

'I haven't seen you lately.'

'I've been busy.'

'You sound strange.'

'I'm tired. Tired of studying. That project took it out of me. I'm not used to your pace of working. I need a break before the last push for finals. The atmosphere is too intense around the department so I've kept clear. And I've got modelling work so won't be around for a few days.'

'Oh, that's a shame. I mean, a shame we won't see each other. You should have told me. Then I wouldn't have been so worried. When do you think you'll be back?'

'Not sure. Probably Thursday.'

'We still need to celebrate the completed project. It's worth celebrating!' Then she added, 'And I miss you.'

She expected him to say he was missing her, too, or to suggest going to the restaurant but he said nothing. Their conversation felt odd and she wasn't sure why. She thought she could read Jonathan but he could still puzzle her. She went out to the supermarket and bought a bottle of Asti Spumante. We can celebrate when he comes back, she thought. We don't need a smart meal. But on Thursday, Eddy came up to her in the department.

'Message from your man. He wasn't feeling too well and has gone home. Says he won't be back before the end of term – not worth it with only a few days to go. He'll call you.'

Kate felt deflated. This wasn't like Jonathan. He never sent messages with Eddy. And now she had no idea when she'd see him next.

He called her that evening.

'Kate. Sorry I disappeared. I had a dreadful headache and felt completely antisocial.'

'What's up, Jonathan? This isn't like you.'

'Oh, I don't know, Kate. I don't feel myself. I even turned down one of the modelling jobs they offered me. Didn't feel like it.'

'So when will I see you again?'

'After Easter. At the beginning of next term. I know you want to work over the vac and I feel guilty about dragging you away.'

Kate had agreed to give up a couple of days of studying to see him. She was glad Jonathan couldn't see the unwitting tear that ran down her face. She would not enjoy the extra study time.

'What about celebrating the project?'

'Next term. Come round to the flat on the first evening, just before term starts.'

'Okay. Love you, Jonathan.'

'You too, Kate.' The words sounded odd; she couldn't hear the warmth, the smile that always went with them.

It was hard to accept but maybe Jonathan needed to take time out. He approached work differently from her and she had to get used to their differences. And he still loved her. Hadn't he said so? She'd stick to her first plan and work. But she had mentioned to her parents she might visit Jonathan in London. They quizzed her about it.

'So when are you seeing him? He could come here, you know. We'd make him welcome. But going to London would make a change for you. Such a nice boy! Charming manners. Quite the best boyfriend we've ever met.' Her mother chattered on, not waiting for a reply or even expecting one. She entertained herself with her soliloquy, accompanied by the nodding of her father's head.

'Shut up about him, will you?' Kate fired at her after several days' comments. 'I'm going to get on with my work.' She left the room so they wouldn't see how hard she was struggling to hold back her tears but heard their comments as she went upstairs.

'Not like her. Stressed with the exams coming, I expect. Make allowances,' her mother said, her father agreeing in his usual, mechanical way.

***

On the agreed evening at the beginning of term, she arrived wearing a new perfume, with her bottle of Asti, a packet of crisps and a rapidly beating heart. This wasn't the celebration she looked forward to. Her world had changed. She couldn't wait to be with Jonathan again; she thought of nothing else all day. But a shadow clouded her mind. What would he say?

She rang the doorbell and opened the unlocked door, calling out she was there, walking into the familiar sitting room.

'It's not champagne, I couldn't afford that, but I thought we needed something a bit special to celebrate.'

She threw her arms around Jonathan's neck and hugged him tightly. Let's have the bubbles first, she thought. It might help. She went into the kitchen. It was neat but tatty and old-fashioned. The chipped cupboard doors hid an array of mismatched cups, plates and glasses. There was a saucepan soaking, the evidence of burnt scrambled egg in the bottom. A pair of muddy running shoes sat by the back door. Several pieces of paper were tacked to a cork board: an advert for a jazz concert in the previous term, a couple of phone numbers and a postcard from Greece. A cardboard box on the floor held half a dozen beer bottles. She took it in without noticing; nothing unusual.

'Hope it doesn't explode everywhere. It's got shaken up on the way here. Should go in the fridge for a while but it won't. Can you open the crisps? I put them on the coffee table. I'm so happy to see you again. It's been so long! I've missed you so much. I've missed your touch.' The words tumbled out, each chasing its predecessor without any notion of sense, her thoughts in disarray.

She found two non-matching wine glasses with no chips in the rims. 'These will have to do. I'll open it over the sink.'

There was a loud pop as the cork hit the ceiling and bounced off the wall.

'Oh, God! What a mess!' The glasses were dripping and a fair amount went down the sink. 'Glad I didn't spend a fortune on this.' Kate laughed, a forced, unnecessary noise.

She wiped the glasses with a well-worn tea towel and took them into the sitting room. Jonathan was sitting stiffly on the sofa, his face strained.

'What's up? I thought… we were celebrating. You look

78

like someone's died.'

She went over to him and kissed him on the cheek. He said nothing but got up and stretched, walked across to the window and stood with his back to Kate, rubbing the back of his neck.

She took his glass to him.

'We should toast our success – and the number one team who did it!' There was little enthusiasm in her voice despite her words. She breathed in deeply. 'But first, I need to tell you something.' Her mouth felt dry and she licked her lips.

Jonathan appeared not to have heard. He turned slowly.

'Kate, we need to talk.' He took her hand and led her back to the sofa, sitting down with a gap between them.

'Oh, no, there's something wrong. I had a feeling, you know. I said you sounded strange on the phone. You're not ill, are you? Or is it your family?'

She waited for a reply, her heart thumping and assorted illnesses they learned about flashing through her mind.

'It's none of those things.'

He remained silent for a while. A long pause hung ominously in the space between them. Kate reached out for his hand but he pulled it away. She sat with her arm outstretched and watched him, fear creeping up on her like a stalker.

'Well, I have to tell you something and it won't wait. Something you're not expecting.'

He turned towards her, still distracted.

'I found out this morning I'm pregnant.'

There was a silence as Jonathan realised what she had said. He stood up. 'I don't believe you. You're on the pill. Is this a stupid joke?'

He changed from preoccupied to angry.

'You, the careful one. You, the career planner. You don't do "unexpected". You can't expect me to believe such rubbish. What is this? A trick to try to trap me? Did you expect me to turn

79

sentimental? To say our lives were bound together and this is what I wanted?'

'Stop it, Jonathan, stop it now!' The force of her words silenced him. 'This is as big a shock to me as you. I'm telling the truth.' She spoke quietly and slowly. 'Do you remember the bug I had a couple of months ago? I vomited a lot. I think I must have vomited up my pills. I assume they didn't work that month.'

Jonathan was now pacing around the room, waving his arms around, knocking over a sad glass of bubbles. 'Well, this convinces me I'm right.' He sat down heavily in an armchair. 'I said I needed to talk to you. Now I will.'

Kate curled herself up in the corner of the sofa, happiness wiped from her face like yesterday's makeup. 'What is it, Jonathan? You're acting like a stranger.'

'It's us, Kate. It's too much for me. I can't cope. Our relationship has become too intense and I'm not ready. I can't handle it.'

Kate looked at him in horror.

'You're getting too serious. This silly story proves it.'

'What? I'm getting too serious? I'm the one who's serious, you're saying? Did I hear that? I thought we were in love. That means we're both in a serious relationship. Didn't you tell me you loved me? What about the wonderful times we've had together? Don't they mean anything? Don't I mean anything to you? Have you lied to me? Have you simply been leading me on?'

Her voice became a whisper as energy drained from her. She ran out of questions. She wanted to shout but it was impossible.

'No, that's not true. I've never deceived you, never lied. I have loved you, but I can't make a commitment. I'm frightened. I'm not ready for it.'

'When did you decide this?'

'It wasn't a matter of making a decision. It's been a creeping feeling. And when I heard folk mentioning marriage, I

80

thought maybe you discussed it, had been planting the seeds. I think that was the tipping point. I felt pressured. And I certainly feel pressured now!'

'Well, you're wrong there. I said nothing to anyone, not even Becky or Pauline. I don't bandy our relationship about. It's too important to me. It's not a story to be aired for public consumption. You're not a fashionable accessory!' She found the strength to emphasise her words. She had to make him understand.

'But I can't deny I thought there was a future for us, that the end of the degree would not be the end of our love.'

'Is that what you told your parents?'

'No! No! I didn't discuss you with them. I said we'd been going out a few months. It's the way they are – over-enthusiastic when I go out with a guy they like. And, incidentally, quite the opposite if it's someone they dislike. I wish you'd never met them.'

Jonathan shrugged his shoulders and screwed up his face.

'The last few months have been so special. I thought they were special for you, too.'

'They were special. I don't deny it. So I don't understand why you are trying to trick me now.'

'I don't understand why you think it's a trick. I didn't miss pills deliberately and I don't want to be pregnant. But I am. I'm not pretending . Why would I even think of deceiving you? This has happened and we have to handle it.'

He stood rigidly and watched as Kate collapsed before him.

'Kate – if you are pregnant, and I'm not convinced that is the case, then you have to handle it, not me.'

He wiped the back of his hand against his chin and blew out a long breath. 'I think we should finish.'

'No, no, Jonathan. Please, no. The comments about marriage were nothing, simply idle chatter. And forget about Mum and Dad. They are irrelevant. Can't we just enjoy each other?

Can't we carry on as we were? Can't we give ourselves a chance, a bit more time? See how things go? Can't you help me? I'm not asking for any more than that.'

He shook his head.

'I can still finish the degree before the baby comes. Then we can decide what's best.'

'I've thought hard about our relationship, Kate. It's the main reason I've not been around. The reason why I didn't see you during the vac. I had to have space to think. Space without you in it. I've made up my mind. What you've said today has confirmed my decision.'

The beauty disappeared from his face and she saw ugly determination.

'If you've any sense and you are pregnant, you'll get rid of the baby.'

She flopped down on the sofa and gazed vacantly ahead. Her face was wet with unsobbed tears that simply poured down her cheeks. Jonathan looked at her in stubborn silence, then turned away and sat on a stool by the window. She gnawed on a nail, a habit long since dropped, until there was nothing left to chew. She was empty; there were no words to say. She barely noticed Jonathan getting up, putting on his coat and leaving. Sometime later, maybe an hour or more, she walked into the kitchen, tipped the remainder of the Asti down the sink, put the bottle and the glasses into the rubbish bin and left, slamming the door.

***

And now, thirty years later, it could be time to rebalance the scales. The memory of their last conversation was as vivid as the denouement of a novel read yesterday. I'd no idea the extent to which you can still affect me, Jonathan, she said to herself. Well, maybe I can affect you, too.

She walked slowly back, chatting to a couple of people on

the way to shake herself out of her visit to the past and found Jonathan waiting for her.

'Thought you abandoned me.'

'Switching roles, you mean?'

'Don't, Kate, don't.'

As he handed her a glass, his fingers brushed her hand. She jumped.

'Is it so bad if I touch you?'

She looked intently at him, her face serious, for several seconds. Then she spoke slowly. 'Actually, no. No, it isn't bad.'

Neither of them spoke. Then she broke the atmosphere by turning towards a group nearby.

'We should circulate. We've hardly spoken to anyone else. And it's becoming obvious.'

'Not sure I want to talk to anyone else right now.'

'Then talk to yourself. See you later.'

She walked away from him. Well, she thought, he's interested; the fireworks they experienced in their days together were waiting to be lit again. Passing a large fern in the corner of the room, she watered it with the contents of her glass. She needed a clear head ... and not only for driving.

Chapter 7

Kate was exhausted. Her body felt fragile and her hand was shaking as she put the key in the car door. The reception was breaking up and people were leaving for the hotel. She could hear the noise from the coach as the wine was shouting its presence. Her single glass followed by plenty of water meant she had no qualms about driving her car. She saw Jonathan get into the bus with Eddy, laughing and talking, and was glad he hadn't asked for a lift.

I could close my eyes and sleep right here, she thought. But that wouldn't do. She had to carry through her strategy. The act with Jonathan had drained her and she was horrified when she looked in the driving mirror. God, I've aged ten years! The ghost that looked back at her was enough to get her moving. She headed as fast as she dared to the hotel, thinking of nothing, focussing on the reviving shower waiting for her.

She could still feel the touch of his hand. She'd not meant to react. She was furious with herself. I should be able to control my emotions better, she thought. But then, his touch had been so special. She remembered his first caresses.

***

They moved on from the tree to his room. She felt unexpectedly shy as he lay on the bed and pulled her towards him. He kissed her gently and caressed her hair and neck. The world was moving in slow motion. She was used to being kissed passionately, used to the frantic removal of clothes and the ardent desire of young men whose own needs drove them towards sexual satisfaction. Love-making, if you could call it that, was not normally a drawn-out affair. But Jonathan was different. He touched her as if her skin were silk, as if each caress was a fresh discovery, and the warm, smooth feel of his fingers as they explored her were a marvel to Kate. He was as interested in her pleasure as in his own. She wondered who taught him but was afraid to ask, afraid to learn.

Late in the evening as he idly ran his hand over her stomach, propped on one elbow on the bed beside her, she tried to put her thoughts into words.

'It was like a three-act play.'

'What was?'

'Having sex with you. A three-act play rather than a short story. I loved how long it took and how you touched me.'

He laughed and she could see he liked her description. 'How about a photo-collage rather than a snapshot?'

'No, I prefer my description. Yours is too static!'

She thought for a while trying to find another analogy. 'A chain reaction rather than a . . . what?'

'This sounds too much like chemistry, far too technical.'

'It is chemistry. Our chemistry. I just can't think of an opposite to a chain reaction. An acid-base neutralisation?'

Jonathan roared with laughter. 'I can't believe you've said that. I've never come across anyone like you, Kate. No-one else would find such analogies. Let's stick with the three-act play. And if you're not careful, there might be an epilogue.'

And so their relationship continued. He taught her how to touch. And now, so many years later, a brush of his fingers could evoke the memory. Kate rubbed her hand to remove the feel of him. Barely an hour and a half before they met for dinner but time for thinking as she went through her automatic beauty routine. She must get Jonathan into perspective. She needed to; he was draining her energy like a black hole.

She shook her head vigorously and forced her thoughts

elsewhere. There were opportunities here, additional amusement. Or perhaps potential satisfaction was a better description. In the few moments when she wasn't preoccupied with Jonathan, she glanced around the room and ideas were forming in her head. There were others who marred her time at university, other scores she wouldn't mind settling.

There was Colin for a start; the plague of her first year. She remembered how he looked then. His blond, curly hair was long, longer than was fashionable, but it worked for him. He knew women liked it, liked the way he cared for it and washed it daily. It was "run through your fingers" hair. He didn't have Jonathan's way with clothes but he had an athletic shape and an appealing swing of his hips. It was a calculated look. Everything he did was calculated, his narcissistic strategy. Rarely had she met anyone who thought so highly of himself. And his voice carried across the room today as he talked about himself. She'd not spoken to him but she heard him. He hadn't changed. Shorter hair, not so slim, but the same Colin.

***

His main belief was if he wanted something, he could get it. The "something" was usually a woman, and he was usually right. A charismatic guy, there was no shortage of pretty girls lining up. Unlike Jonathan, he had no qualms about dating his colleagues.

'Hey, Kate. Doing anything on Friday night?'

This was his first request, term one, year one. It was a friendly enough question; most girls would have been pleased. She didn't know why but she turned him down.

'I'm busy, Colin. Thanks for asking.'

That was it, she thought, move on. He'd ask another girl. The next week, however, it was, 'Do you want to go to the disco on Saturday? There's a few of us going.'

'No thanks, Colin. I'm going to town with a girlfriend.'

She wasn't but a niggling unease stopped her from saying "yes".

Colin wasn't one to accept defeat. He waited at the end of Friday chemistry lab for her every week and pestered her to go out with him. He was a shadow glued to her as she walked back to her hall of residence. She found him physically attractive but being number seventy-two in his line of conquests wasn't for her. Initially, she was happy to chat to him but the predictability of his presence started to gall.

'Colin, you're being a pain. Go away.'

Then he added in waiting at Tuesday lunch time after pharmaceutics with the constant request. When she sat with her friends in the refectory, he would sit at the same table and fix his eyes on her every move. It was amusing at first and became a joke among her group.

'Where do you think he'll turn up next? Wish I had an admirer pursuing me like that!'

'I bet you don't!'

'Oh, I don't know. It'd be wonderful to think a guy wanted me that much.'

And it was something of a compliment. Kate laughed at first, flattered, but then he started phoning her hall of residence at odd times, often late in the evening. The hall porter would come knocking on her door, telling her there was a phone call in reception. The first time, she thought there must be a problem at home, so to hear Colin's voice was a relief. Then it became a nuisance, a predictable nuisance. If she had more sense – if she'd not been an immature eighteen-year-old – she'd have reported him for stalking but she regarded that as an admission of failure. And at the time she didn't think of it as stalking. She could cope with him. He didn't frighten her, he was just Colin. An annoying splinter: not particularly painful but an irritant you want to remove.

It became a macabre game. He wouldn't give in on principle and nor would she. Whether or not he appealed to her became irrelevant. Her pride wouldn't let her give in. And she had got to the point of finding him unattractive anyway and was going out with Ian from DramSoc, her leading man who enthralled her for a while. So she had an excuse, if she needed it.

'Colin, I don't go out with two guys at the same time. You know I have a boyfriend. Leave me alone.'

Then, in the second term, the requests changed. He continued his pursuit in a new way.

'Kate, you're being unfair. Can't we talk? If you don't want me as a boyfriend, can we be friends? You reject me as if I'm sub-human, unworthy of your superior glance, a piece of shit to be kicked aside.'

'That's a bit much, Colin. Don't over-dramatise. I've never said you were inferior in any way. You're simply not my type. But we can talk if you want to.'

'Gracious lady, I'm honoured.'

He bowed with a glint in his eye. Kate sighed.

'With such a performance, you should join DramSoc. You'd get a leading role.'

'I might do that.'

I hope not, she thought; the spectre of an ever-present Colin was not one she relished.

'Well, come and have a coffee with me.'

Kate was trapped. She couldn't say "no" and still be reasonable, so she mentally put aside the report she was going to write and went with him to the coffee bar in the union building. She headed towards the far corner.

'Hey, Kate! Come back. It's too hot and smoky back there. Much better by the door.'

'But you smoke, Colin. I didn't think the atmosphere would bother you.'

'I still prefer fresh air. And I don't smoke much.'

He took out a pack of cigarettes and extracted one, nevertheless. He liked the smoking aura; it was part of his image.

As he lit it, he looked around him, waved to a couple by the counter and pointed out two pharmacists chatting at the other side of the room. He knew everyone. Kate had the awkward feeling she was on show; fresh air wasn't the main reason for sitting in a conspicuous place. She wedged herself between the table and the wall, as far from him as a small table in a crowded room would allow.

'Okay then, Colin. What do you want to talk about?'

'Kate, don't be so precise. You sound like my tutor, allowing me a fixed number of minutes to state my problem. I don't want to talk about anything in particular. I want to chat, to get to know you better. Then maybe I'll understand why you keep rejecting me.'

'To be honest, Colin, I don't know why I don't want to go out with you. I just don't. You're not for me. It wouldn't work. And your persistence is irritating. Why do you keep on pursuing me when I've made my position clear?'

She played with a shabby drinks mat on the coffee-stained table and wondered how soon she could leave.

'It's always the same.'

'What is?'

'I fail to get anything I want.'

'I can't believe that. How many girls have you been out with since you started university?'

'That's irrelevant.'

Kate raised her eyebrows and blew out a puff of air.

'Don't look like that. It is irrelevant. I always fail to get what I *really* want. None of those girls count.'

'Then you've not been fair to them. What have you wanted and not been able to get?'

Colin hesitated for a long time, debating what to say. 'You don't want to hear about my problems.'

'But I expect you'll tell me, anyway. For Goodness' sake, if there's a tale I've got to hear, get on with it.'

'Okay, I'll tell you.'

He paused again and looked seriously at Kate. There was a look about him she'd not seen before, a vulnerability. He seemed ill at ease, his usual swagger absent. Kate thought maybe she should listen, listen properly if he needed help, not be so dismissive.

'Please don't laugh at this.' He dropped his voice and moved his chair nearer the table. 'The one thing I wanted most, and didn't get, was for my mother to be proud of me.'

'Proud of you? Why wasn't she?'

'Both of my sisters got into medical school. I didn't even apply.'

'Did you want to be a medic?'

'No. I wanted to be a pharmacist. But Mum couldn't get her head around that. She thought I was second best. Third best, in fact. I never did as well at school as the girls and it was always pointed out. She would have preferred a third girl. I was a disappointment from the start.'

'Colin, is this true? This sounds like a story you've cooked up to get round me. It doesn't sound like you. Are you spinning me a line?'

'Don't be so distrustful, Kate. I wish I were. It's not something I tell everyone. But you asked. Disappointment has shaped how I am. You are the woman I want but it seems I'm fated to be let down.'

Colin dropped his dramatic display and looked disconsolate. Kate placed her hand over his. This was an unexpected revelation. There was a silence while they looked at each other.

'Colin. Let's be friends. There is no point in pretending we can be anything else, but I'm sad you feel this way. If your mother treated you like that then I'm truly sorry.'

He smiled, looked hard at Kate and put his other hand over hers. 'Think about it. Don't turn me down totally.'

Kate removed her hand, picked up her cup and swallowed a mouthful of coffee in an attempt to break the sombre mood that swathed them.

'Come on, don't be mournful. Let's talk about something else.'

To her relief, one of the pharmacists from the other side of the room came to join them and the conversation turned to organising a party. She was glad not to be the sole focus of Colin's attention and didn't want to be his confidante for any more miserable stories. Ten minutes later, she made her excuses and left.

The following day, Becky gave her a strange look at breakfast.

'You're a sly one!'

'What do you mean?' Kate said.

'The grapevine was buzzing last night. Seen holding hands with Colin in the coffee bar. I thought you were trying to shake him off!'

'Holding hands? Oh, my God! I wasn't holding hands with him. I simply placed my hand on his as a way of showing sympathy for him.'

'Not what I heard. All soft looks and sloppy faces.'

'Rubbish. Who's spreading rumours?'

'General knowledge. And Colin heard us talking and didn't deny anything.'

'I felt sorry for him.'

'You didn't fall for the story about him being second best to his sisters in his mother's eyes, did you?'

Kate looked aghast and clattered her cutlery onto her plate.

'Oh, Kate, you did! He's tried that with loads of girls. It's a way into your bed.'

Kate was furious. Furious with Colin and even more furious with herself for her gullibility. Her immediate reaction was to tell him what she thought of him but then she realised she would be making a fool of herself. It was a set-up and she'd fallen into the trap. More fool her. He'd smirk if she even mentioned it. So she would ignore him. She'd have to endure a few more comments from the rest of the department until they forgot about the incident in the wake of better gossip. She'd ignore that, too.

But Colin wouldn't ignore her. His approach was now crude and direct.

'Kate, Kate. Just sleep with me. I'm not bothered about your company, your clever head or your sense of humour. I don't want to show you off. I just need to fuck you.'

'Colin – you are repulsive. I don't want you socially or physically. I can't think of anything I want to do less than sleep with you.'

'Once, Kate, just once. I want to experience your lovely body.'

She waved two fingers at him, not a gesture she often used. He drove her to unaccustomed rudeness.

'You're not short of girls, plenty of them leap into bed with you at first asking. Go and find one.'

But it seemed he had no desire for the easily obtainable. And Kate, by sticking her ground, became the most desirable object of all.

'Can't you understand me, Colin? When I say "No" I mean "No", not ask me again tomorrow. You really struggle to accept there is one person in the world who isn't susceptible to your charms, don't you?'

Colin shrugged and she knew by his face she was right. Eventually he gave up but it took most of the first year to admit defeat.

***

And the forceful charmer was here. His voice caught her ear when she was talking to Jonathan. He sounded exactly the same, an easy talker, outgoing, friendly, mixing with the crowd.

'Hello Gill! I'd have known you anywhere. No need for you to wear a name tag, you've hardly changed! Anyway, I think I saw you a few months ago. You work for Boots, don't you?'

'Yes, I rotate through several pharmacies in Shropshire.'

'I was driving through – where was it? Can't remember the name of the place – and I popped in for a packet of throat sweets. Thought it was you slaving away over a box of tablets. Didn't have time to stop and you looked busy. Usual queue of people expecting instant service because their prescription was "only pills". Thought I'd be a nuisance.'

'What a shame you didn't come and say "hello". I'd have found a few minutes for a chat.'

'You're right, I should have,' he said, patting her hand; he was a hands-on person.

How typical, Kate thought, a Colin characteristic. He always touched as he spoke, resting on an arm here, a shoulder there. She remembered his fingers on her; she remembered the number of times she removed them. Invading personal space was the appropriate description. But with him, it appeared to come naturally, endearingly. A cynic might have said it was calculated; there was much of the cynic in Kate.

I've come reluctantly to this artificial party so I might as well get a reward out of it, she thought. She could create some mischief here; light relief from Jonathan. She was developing a few ideas. Taking Colin down a peg or two shouldn't be difficult. She'd work on it. She couldn't focus solely on Jonathan; it was too intense, too wearing. And dealing with Jonathan was serious; dealing with Colin was on a different level.

But what other opportunities were there?

Chapter 8

Opportunities – well, there was Willy. She couldn't make herself call him Gabriel. Gabriel was an angel in the nativity story, a piece of her childhood. It now had a discarded feel to it, a rejected name along with a redundant religion. And she could not believe an adult man would choose to use the name, even if his parents had given it to him. Willy was a name with character, maybe unfortunate connotations but a grown man could handle it. Whatever he said, she would refuse to call him Gabriel.

She had no reason to want to please him anyway. As she thought about him, resentment flooded through her. She was a student again. He was a bastard, a real bastard. What had he said to her? "Nice to see you, Kate." And he called her "My dear", an expression he liked. Had he forgotten?

***

He was a clever guy, a top student from the start. And he made sure it was apparent to everyone. Their course was littered with progress tests and there he was on the results list proudly sitting at the top of the column.

'How have you done, Kate?'

He could read as well as she could but it pleased him to ask as they looked at the latest results. He sniffed and exhaled a waft of stale breath, the lunch-time onion soup persistent.

'Almost as well as you, Willy.'

Kate should have been happy with her results, usually second to Willy, but it spurred her on to beat him. She'd have reacted like that if he'd been her closest friend; she wanted to be the best. But as he was pompous, always enjoying an audience, always ready to expound his views, he irritated her. She admired his brain but not his manner.

She got to know him, his habits and peculiarities, better than she wanted. Working together in the lab simply fuelled their competitiveness. It was an achievement the first time she beat him in a test.

'How did you do, Willy?'

'Ha! You know exactly how I did. Must have been an off day.'

'Not very gracious of you!'

'All's fair in love and pharmaceutics tests!'

A joker opened a book on who would get the most wins during the term. They were the recognised top students, out of the reach of anyone else.

So she was surprised when he didn't turn up to the usual chemistry lab one Friday, several weeks before Finals. Normally he missed nothing. Then after lunch he arrived, too late to do anything useful but needing to let everyone know what had happened.

'Bloody burglars! Broke in during the night. Took a load of stuff.'

'What have you lost?'

'Max's radio, Jim's TV, four bottles of wine, a load of LPs, my rucksack and worst of all, my watch.'

People abandoned their experiments and gathered round.

'Did you hear them?'

'No, didn't hear a thing. They forced the lock on the back door and only took stuff from downstairs. Neither Jim nor Max heard anything, either. The flat next door was broken into, too.'

'You'd think they'd target folk richer than students!'

'I bet they reckoned on these old flats not having much security. And they were right. The landlord's going to install extra locks now.'

'Sounds a bit like horses and stable doors to me!' a joker added.

'Yes, but it could happen again. I'm so annoyed I left my watch downstairs. I usually have it by my bed. It was my twenty-first birthday present from my grandfather. It cost him more than he could afford but he was so proud of me he'd have given me everything he had. It was the last present he bought me before he died.'

The group were silenced by this, touched for the first time by Willy. He was a victim and they forgot the way he annoyed them. Everyone moved closer as if this helped to share his loss. Pauline laid her hand on his shoulder and spoke quietly.

'So what have you been doing today?'

'The police have been round. Interviewed us, taken statements, made lists of what we've lost. Difficult to know exactly what's gone. They turned everything upside down. The sitting room was a mess before they broke in; you should see it now.'

'What do you think the prospect is of getting anything back?'

'Huh! The police aren't hopeful. They know of a number of gangs working locally but they move stolen goods on so quickly they always arrive too late. They only steal easy to sell items.'

Willy sat down on a lab stool, put his elbows on the bench and his head in his hands. His self-importance and arrogance were gone and he was broken, bereaved by his loss.

'Do you want any help in tidying up?' Pauline, the mother-figure of the group, was always generous with her time.

'Thanks, but no. Jim, Max and I need to do it. We need to be sure we've identified everything that's missing.'

Kate, along with the others, felt for him. Pretentious prig he might be but he didn't deserve this.

On the following Monday morning, Willy arrived looking haggard. Things were worse than expected.

'The police found my rucksack by the motorway. The thieves had obviously taken it because it was heavy and they thought there'd be saleable items inside. I'd forgotten I put a load of chemistry notes in there. I was aiming to go home next weekend to revise. A few pages were left in the rucksack, the rest were blowing around the fields or stuck in the hedge. They're gone. The police said they were not retrievable. Not that they would have tried. They're not interested in useless pieces of paper.'

He spat out the words "useless pieces of paper"; everyone knew they were far from that.

'Can't you revise from text books? You know it anyway, Willy – you always do brilliantly in tests.'

Pauline was trying to find words of consolation, but these were not the right ones. The stress of the weekend exploded from Willy like a rocket.

'What a fucking stupid suggestion! How would you like to revise solely from a text book? I need my notes. I need to be reminded of exactly what we've covered, what we need to know, what we'll be examined on. I need it as it was taught and as I wrote it down. The text books are additional explanation, verification, supplementary back-up. I need my notes, written by me, in my handwriting. That's how I work.'

He was shouting, his round face like a red balloon, sweat dripping down the sides of his cheeks. His hands were shaking as he gripped the edge of the workbench and the tips of his fingers with their bitten nails were white with pressure.

'I know how I revise. You might think I'm a sponge, soaking it up. But I'm not. It doesn't come easily. My success reflects hours of hard work.'

He suddenly went quiet. He wiped his face on his shabby sleeve, ran his fingers through his wispy beard and pulled at his moustache, a habit they recognised.

'I might have said "Farewell" to my First.'

First Class Honours Degrees were rarely given in Pharmacy. Over the past decade, there'd never been more than one a year and at times no-one gained the ultimate accolade. There were rumours there never would be more than one and you had to be the best student of your year to be a contender. But nothing was stated openly, and those who quizzed the Head of Department on this learned nothing.

'Everyone gets the degree they deserve,' was all he would say.

They were all aware this year there were two contenders.

The discussions stopped when the next lecturer arrived. Kate listened and took notes in a distracted way. She realised the implications of this loss. The devil in her snapped his fingers and grinned at the opportunity. But she was a fair person at heart and kicked him out.

After the lecture, she went up to Willy. 'You can tell me to mind my own business, but would it help to borrow my notes?'

Willy was taken aback. 'Do you mean that?'

'I wouldn't offer if I didn't mean it. I know we're usually opponents, but I prefer an honest battle. Without boasting, mine are the best set you could borrow.'

'I thought about asking you but didn't imagine you'd go along with it.'

'You can have them next weekend. If you're going home to revise, you can make your own notes from them. I'm working on pharmaceutics next weekend so won't need them. But I will need them the following week. I haven't done any chemistry revision yet so will need them back promptly.'

She stressed the last few words and wagged a finger at him to make her point. They sorted out what he needed to borrow. Lectures would finish the following day in the run up to Finals. Kate said she'd bring the notes in for him.

She scribbled her phone number and address on a piece of

paper. 'I must have them back on Monday. No later. You do understand me?'

He nodded. Kate handed over a package the following day as promised.

'Take care of them, Willy. It's a big thing for me to part with my notes.'

'Of course, Kate. I appreciate this.'

When he didn't turn up on the Monday, Kate was furious. She couldn't believe he was abusing her favour.

The phone rang around nine o'clock in the evening. She grabbed it with relief. It was Willy.

'Kate, my dear. I know you were expecting me to drop off your notes. I've got a confession to make. I've been plucking up courage to call you. I've left your notes at home.'

'Willy, you idiot, you bloody idiot! What a way to repay me!'

'I'm so sorry, my dear. It was a total accident. I thought they were in my bag.'

'I can't believe an intelligent guy like you could be so stupid! When can you get them?'

'Well, I thought I'd ask my mother to post them on, although they'll be heavy. That might be quickest. I can't spare the time to go home again.'

'You can't spare the time?' Kate's voice rose to a shriek. 'Don't you have any thought for me? Well, get your mother to send them asap. You owe me big time, Willy, for this.'

Kate slammed the phone down and put her head in her hands. As her fury turned into tears she realised what a mistake she made in letting the notes go. She should not have trusted Willy. Maybe it was a genuine error, but maybe it was a tactic, delaying her revision schedule. The pressure of the recent weeks, the traumatic split with Jonathan, morning nausea she was trying to deny, the intense hours she put in with her books, weighed down on her. She allowed herself to sob.

Two days later, Willy phoned again. Pauline answered it and looked pale as she passed it to Kate.

'Kate.' He hesitated. 'I don't know how to tell you this. My mother can't find the notes. She cleaned and tidied my room after I left and says they weren't there.'

'I don't believe you. How can a fat bundle of notes have disappeared? You're doing this deliberately. What a way to repay my generosity!'

'That's unfair, Kate. I'm doing my best. I'm going home the weekend before the exams start. I can look then.'

'What's the use of that? It's too late. I need them now. Get her to look again. And search your room in case you've mixed them up with other papers. God, I hate you!'

Kate was obsessed with her missing notes. She had dreams about them. Sometimes they turned up unexpectedly and she'd wake up smiling only to realise she was fooling herself. Then Willy would feel too ill to revise and she'd relish the selfish satisfaction of revenge until she opened her eyes. Thoughts of the missing notes crowded her days when she tried to work on other subjects, ruining her concentration and putting her into a foul mood. They did, in truth, only cover one term's work. But she became convinced there'd be an exam question on those topics. She borrowed Pauline's notes and they were a help. Better than nothing, she said to herself, but not a patch on mine. And no way was she going to ask Willy for his notes – those he so recently made from hers.

Willy returned her notes two days before the first chemistry exam. His mother had found them. Tucked under the bed, hidden by the bedside table. She posted them as soon as she found them. Willy smiled, hardly a sign of contrition.

***

100

And now Willy was calling her "My Dear". He revelled in getting a First and stayed on in the department to do a PhD. Now he was Dr Gabriel Williamson. He went around muttering his future title from the moment the department made him the offer of a project. He even did it in Kate's presence, Kate who came so close. The best Upper Second. That was failure to her. She was convinced Willy determined not to return her notes in time for them to be of use. No, she was not his "Dear".

As she finished her makeup and brushed her hair, she shook her head, trying to remove the emotion these memories stirred up. Plotting revenge on Jonathan was bad enough, she thought. Payback for Willy was meant to be a light distraction, petty almost. But there was nothing light in the thoughts Willy provoked in her. And she wasn't sure in his case what she was going to do, whether she could do anything.

Chapter 9

Kate went down into the hotel lobby wearing a fitted emerald green dress that suited her perfectly. Worth every penny of the high price she paid. She chose an antique crystal necklace and matching dropper earrings that flashed as they caught the light. Her bulky silver bangles rattled as she moved. She approved of the reflection that walked alongside her as she glanced at the window. Turning a corner, she bumped into Becky looking flushed and untidy.

'What happened to you? Thought you'd be here earlier – at least for part of the reception. You abandoned me! I thought we were doing this together.'

Kate tried to prevent irritation showing through, although she was annoyed. Typical Becky!

'Yes, so did I. But there was something wrong with the burglar alarm at the shop. It's been playing up recently and in my rush I set it wrong so that it rang at the police station. I phoned to say it was only me being stupid but there was a new guy on duty who didn't recognise my voice. So I had to wait until he came out to check I wasn't a thief before I could lock up properly.'

She gabbled this out in a rush, hardly taking a breath. Becky's life was lived like that, dashing from place to place, cramming in twice as much as most people.

'Anyway, while I was waiting, I did my makeup so I only had to change when I got here.'

She gave Kate a peck on the cheek.

'You look elegant. Bit of a contrast to me. Haven't had time to make the best of myself.'

'Come here,' said Kate. 'Let me sort out your skirt. You've got the belt twisted and your blouse is half in and half out. I can see this was thrown on in a hurry.'

'Thanks. Par for the course! Anyway, glad you're here.'

She started to relax, tucked her hair behind one ear, put on a Becky smile and looked around.

'How was the reception? Who's here?'

'It was okay. And almost everyone has turned up. They're telling each other how great they look when in reality most of them are fatter, greyer and in the case of many of the guys, balder.'

'Except you, Kate. And I don't mean the bald bit!' Becky laughed at her own inability to string her words together in her excitement. 'I bet you got a few compliments.'

'Mmm. Well, yes, I did. From Jonathan in particular.'

'Wow! You're speaking to each other?'

'It would have been childish to ignore each other at an event like this and after so long.'

'So you've forgiven him?'

Kate felt the confused feelings within her, the emotion which was a mixture of loathing and longing, the wound which was still open. What if she'd given birth to his child? How would he have reacted to that piece of news?

'I'd hardly go that far but I'm not letting him know how I feel.'

She looked at Becky. Yes, she thought, I can trust her. A little, at least.

'Listen, Becky. I've decided to get something out of this weekend. I'm not one for platitudes and being pleasant to folk I'd rather not mix with, as you know. If you and Neil hadn't worked on me, I'd not be here. Since I am, I'm devising a few paybacks. If I need your help, will you go along with this?'

'Well, it depends. I'm here to enjoy myself. I've got nothing against Jonathan. I know he let you down, but it's not for me to get at him. I've always liked him.'

'I can handle him. I don't need any help there. There are a few others I'm targetting.'

Kate had a glint in her eye. She was on an adrenaline high with the anticipation of what she might do.

'Once I've dealt with Jonathan, my target is Colin. You remember how he pursued me in the first year. Made my life a misery with his constant requests. I always turned him down. I thought there might be mileage in being more positive towards him.'

'So how would that pay him back? You'd play into his hands. You're too devious for me, Kate.'

'Can't give my secrets away yet. If I need you to do anything, are you up for it? I might need a partner in crime.'

Becky's smile disappeared.

'I'm joking. Nothing illegal. A little revenge, that's all.'

'Okay. Sounds harmless enough to me. Count me in. Personally, I don't know why you didn't sleep with him. He's attractive and believe me, he knows what he's doing in bed!'

'Becky! I had no idea. When did that happen?'

'While he was pursuing you. He didn't concentrate on one girl at a time. I wasn't bothered about being a notch on his gun. I fancied a good time and I certainly got it.'

'Why didn't you say?'

'You didn't need to know, simple as that. It only lasted a few weeks. Colin's relationships were short. But we stayed friends of sorts. I didn't expect – or even want – to keep him for long.'

'But you don't object to my getting back at him?'

'No. He's always been a serial womaniser and has hurt a lot of girls. I'd like to see him get his come-uppance!'

They were moving towards the dining room where five round tables were laid for the group. Willy was taking charge again, ushering them in, telling them they could sit where they liked, saying it was casual, tomorrow would be the formal dinner.

His voice boomed over the gathering as he expressed his importance but no one took any notice. Everyone stayed in the bar area, eating peanuts and drinking, involved in their long catch-up on news, talking over each other in their keenness to join in, so he gave up trying to move them on and got himself another drink. It was whisky; Kate had correctly guessed he drank spirits.

She glanced at him and whispered to Becky, 'I need to talk to you about Willy, too. He's on my list.'

'I'm not surprised. You can't have forgiven him for his mean trick.'

'Too right. You know, he didn't just "lose" my notes, he destroyed my confidence. If I'd got the First, then I could have achieved anything. It had been my goal from about the beginning of the second year. I knew I could do it if I worked hard enough. Didn't say so to anyone, although I think in the end everyone knew the two of us might make it.'

'But you are a success, Kate. Your chain of shops. You can hardly say you've failed because of him. I know he was a sod but aren't you blaming him for too much?'

'I'm a success in spite of him. I had to pick myself up and change my direction. I had my heart on doing a PhD, as he did, and going into industrial research.'

'You could still have done it. You'd have found a placement, no trouble.'

'It was psychological. I felt I wasn't the best. I felt any research project offered to me would not have been the same as if I got a First.'

'But you don't know that.'

'No, I don't. I didn't even apply for a higher degree. If I couldn't do it on my terms, then I'd do something else. Pig-headed, I know – I can see you're about to accuse me of that!'

Becky nodded.

'I completed my pre-registration year and went into retail. The rest, as they say …'

'So you do have a grudge against him.'

'It's an underestimation of what I feel about him. It needn't have been like this. I thought we'd break departmental records and it would be the first time two Firsts were awarded. I didn't think it had to be me and only me. I wasn't selfish. I'd have shared the triumph. Clearly, he wasn't interested in that.'

'So where do I come into your schemes?'

Becky looked tentative as she asked, the force of Kate's acrimony surprising and shocking her. She'd come for a pleasant social evening, a chat with old friends and enjoyment. This was getting too dark.

'Not sure yet. I'm working on it. I might need a bit of distraction at some point. You were in DramSoc, too, and did more plays than I did. I bet you still have the old skills if you need them. Or perhaps I should say if I need them!'

'Haven't called on them for a while. But I don't like what Willy did to you so you can count me in.'

'I've been trying to think of an appropriate way of getting back at him. He lost my notes – or made out he had until the last minute – so it needs to be something to do with organisation. I need to make him feel disorganised, embarrassed, ill at ease... Let me know if you get an idea.'

'Oh, no. That's up to you. You want to do this so you sort it out. End of story.' Becky went to the bar. 'Refill?'

'I'll have a sparkling water with ice and lime. Need to keep a clear head.'

'Think I'll go and talk to Amanda. I hear it was a riding accident. What a shock seeing her in a wheelchair!'

She handed Kate her glass but before she could move off, Kate added, 'But that's not everyone.'

Becky stopped and turned, a look approaching fear on her face. 'What? Who else are you having a go at? I didn't realise you had so many enemies.'

'Not enemies. That wouldn't be the right term. I'm

exacting due retribution.'

'So who is it?'

'Can't you guess?'

Becky looked round the room and shook her head.

'Think money.'

'Kate, I can't keep up with you and I'm not sure I want to.'

Kate turned her gaze towards a well-dressed, tall man with a glass of beer in his hand and a commanding presence. He doesn't shop at a chain store any more, she thought.

'Simon? It must be Simon.'

'Correct. I thought you'd have homed in on him straight away. Didn't he get money out of you, too?'

'Yes, but not much as I hardly ever had any to spare.'

'Do you remember how he got us to feel sorry for him?'

'Yes – but why bother? Forget it. You have enough money now.'

'It's not the point.'

***

Simon would buy a cheap sandwich at the cafeteria when the others were tucking into fish and chips or pie and mash. Inevitably, someone would ask him why he ate so little.

'Had to buy text books this month so there's not much left over from my allowance for anything else.'

He had three brothers, two of whom were already at university.

'It's hard on Mum and Dad to fund us. They don't have well-paid jobs.' Occasionally, someone would treat him to lunch and he'd be excessively grateful. But he was such a sociable character people liked him; he was a "real nice guy".

Kate found him endearing. More and more they sat together at lunch and then in lectures. Towards the end of the second term, he asked her out.

'Kate, I know you probably think of us as mates, but I wondered, I wondered … could you fit in going to see a film next week?'

Kate took his hand. 'Thought you'd never ask!' She did wonder where the money for the tickets was coming from. They walked to the cinema rather than taking the bus.

'Sounds awful for a first date, but could you pay for yourself?'

This wasn't unusual. Kate shrugged her shoulders; she wasn't mercenary so didn't mind not having money spent on her. He rummaged in his pockets for whatever change he could find for his own ticket and while this was going on, Kate paid for both, even though she couldn't afford it.

'You're a star, Kate. One of the best.'

Afterwards they went back to his room and he made them coffee. It was the cheapest supermarket brand, instant variety, but just about drinkable. He put his arm around her and kissed her gently on the lips.

'You taste lovely. Come and lie on the bed.'

He held her face in both hands and continued his kissing, then ran his hands down her back and her arms. He was breathing heavily and Kate was expecting, hoping, his hands would move under her clothes. But they didn't. She was puzzled by this and so when he walked her back and asked if she'd go out with him again, she had to say "yes". He intrigued her.

On their second date, they went for a walk in the park. It was a mild March evening and the full moon threw huge shadows, great monsters preceding them round the lake. They waved their arms in the air and the monsters waved back. They held hands and ran silly races between the benches. He kissed her under the trees and she slid his arm under her coat. He held her close and nuzzled her neck.

'You are beautiful, Kate. I can't believe such a beautiful

girl is going out with me.'

They went back to Kate's room where the coffee was slightly better. His kissing was turning her on and she was wondering what she needed to do to get him to make a move.

'Have you had many girlfriends, Simon?'

'A few. I went to a mixed school and there was a lot of pairing off. Groping behind the bike sheds, that sort of thing.'

Kate wasn't sure she believed him; he spoke casually, as if he'd taken part, but his lack of conviction made her wonder.

'You know, I don't mind if you've not had much experience. I've not had a massive amount myself. My school was girls only.'

Simon turned crimson, got up and walked to the window standing with his back to her. He said nothing. Kate could feel embarrassment radiating from him.

'Everyone knows what to do these days. The guys would laugh themselves silly if they knew the truth.'

'But I won't, Simon. Come here.' She took off his T-shirt, then removed her own sweater. 'Come and touch me.'

Simon stroked her shoulders and slid his hand tentatively over her bra. Kate deftly undid it with one hand and threw it on the floor. Simon held her at arm's length and admired the view. He got braver and she encouraged him at each step. They were lying on the bed in a minimal amount of clothing, caressing each other, when he jumped up and ran to the bathroom.

'I'm so sorry, Kate, I'm so sorry. I couldn't help it. You're too desirable. I couldn't hold on.'

Kate was left wanting.

'It'll be better next time, Simon. And don't worry. I'm not in the habit of regaling my girlfriends with my activities.'

And it did get better. Kate enjoyed their sex together. She enjoyed introducing Simon to different pleasures, sharing what limited skills she had, and he was besotted with her. But after a while, the financial arrangement started to hurt. He moved from gratitude for the occasional hand-out to the expectation of regular funding.

'Doesn't Simon ever buy his lunch these days?'

She overheard a comment in the cafeteria.

And when everyone met up in the pub, Simon would arrive early and buy his half-pint before the others got there. No risk of being expected to buy a drink for anyone else, or worse still, a round.

'He can make half a pint of beer last longer than anyone I ever met!'

'He drinks a lot faster if he can see someone else paying.'

It became well-known Simon was a scrounger. Sympathy wore thin as he never contributed financially to anything. No longer was he a "real nice guy". His relationship with Kate showed the strain. As the first year was drawing to its end, she decided to end their partnership.

'I think we've run our course, Simon. I can't keep on funding you. I have no money. Can't remember the last time I bought anything new to wear. I can barely afford note pads and files! Time for us to split up.'

Simon was unhappy about it. He still doted on her, pleaded with her, told her he loved her. But he realised his time was over. They remained on amicable terms, but Kate stopped funding him. Or so she thought.

Towards the end of their second year, a trip was organised to one of the large pharmaceutical companies for those who were interested. Kate coordinated it.

'Simon, are you sure you want to come? We have to pay our own return rail fare. It's expensive. I'm struggling 'cos the department can't sub us.'

'That's okay. I asked Dad and he said he could fund it for me, just this once. He knows I'm keen on a career in industry.'

Kate collected the money from the group but Simon said his would be sent in the post in a couple of days.

'Are you sure, Simon? I'll pay for your ticket as long as I get it back. You do understand you have to pay me back. I can't afford to pay for you.'

Kate lost count of the number of excuses Simon presented but the mythical money never arrived. She couldn't believe he swindled her after all she'd done for him. Her lunches for the rest of term were meagre. She suffered more than anyone at Simon's impecunious hands.

***

Kate turned to Becky. 'Can you remember the business with the rail fare? I think I told everyone, I was so furious. And so poor!'

'You were too soft on him, Kate. But I still don't understand why you're bothering with him now.'

'I imagine you wouldn't object if we manage to get some money out of him this weekend?' Kate asked.

'As he positively reeks of affluence now, showy affluence at that, I wouldn't mind a legal robbery!'

'Did you see him in the Times again this week?'

'No. What was he up to?'

'A successful defence of a dodgy Contract Research Organisation. He's found his niche, that guy.'

Simon had made a success of his career. After graduation, he forgot about his industrial intentions, went on to take a law degree and made a fortune out of pharmaceutical legal cases.

'I wonder if he's bought any drinks this evening?'

'I'd put money on him still being a skinflint!'

Willy tapped a spoon against a glass. 'We do need to move into the dining room. The Maitre d' has been to see me. We're running half an hour late and he's not happy.'

'We'll have to continue our chat later or maybe tomorrow.'

'Haven't we finished?'

'Nearly.'

'It's getting over the top, Kate. I don't want to hear any more. Most of us have a few grudges but we put them behind us and get on with life. Live for now, enjoy yourself!' She started to move away but Kate reached out and touched her arm.

'There's one more. Just one. This will be a surprise to you, something you know nothing about.'

'Who now?' Becky looked wearily and impatiently at Kate. She wasn't interested; Kate hoped to trigger her curiosity.

'Someone who's not here yet. I imagine she's coming tomorrow. She wasn't on Willy's "non-attendee" list.'

'Hell, you do know how to drag things out.'

'Ah, but there's a story. Not one I can tell you in a hurry. So I'll leave it.'

She left Becky looking perplexed. Maybe she'd gone too far, perhaps should have stopped at Simon. But she might need further help.

Chapter 10

Kate and Becky moved off in different directions, Becky heading for Amanda and the conversation she wanted to have and Kate walking slowly, gauging which table would suit her best. She made a point of heading away from Willy to the far side of the room. Tonight she needed to concentrate on Jonathan and hoped he decided to concentrate on her. As she was debating her next move, he came up behind her and put his hand on her shoulder. She trembled.

'I don't know whether or not to be pleased I produce a physical reaction with my presence. It's the second time today.'

'You took me by surprise. That's all.'

'Do you mind if we sit together?'

'Not at all.' Exactly her ploy.

Jonathan was in high spirits. The wine he consumed earlier was collaborating with the G and T in his hand. He could take a lot of drink, she knew. And he got happier and louder. Never ill, never maudlin, never depressed, never aggressive. The tipsy Jonathan was amusing company, humorous, sexy and, she remembered well, desirable.

'Have you noticed Janet over there,' he whispered seriously, putting his face close to her ear so that she inhaled his subtle after-shave. 'She has a new job. She tests seam strength for the trouser department in John Lewis.'

Kate, who had taken his comment at face value, laughed loudly and then put her hand over her mouth. It was hard not to be amused by him. Janet was almost bursting at the seams. Her robust posterior was pointing towards them as she bent down to pick up something. Kate remembered his ability to notice details and to extract the humour from them. The old Jonathan was still there. Keep on track, Kate, keep on track. Don't betray yourself. Remember the baby you might have had. Remember the hurt.

They sat down and Jonathan continued to point out any unflattering details he could spot, the ladder in Eva's tights, the stain on Derek's tie. It was cruel wit but amusing.

'Why is Derek wearing a tie?' Kate said. 'No-one else is. It's meant to be casual.'

'I expect he wears it in bed. That's his idea of informal. He clearly gets plenty of use out of it as he hasn't had time to take it to the dry-cleaners.'

As he spoke and glanced around, he placed his hand on Kate's bare arm from time to time. She felt herself tense at each touch but controlled her reactions. On a physical level, she loved the feel of his warm fingers, the way he filled her glass, the way he caught her eye and raised one eyebrow as if they were conspiring together. It was so familiar, so reminiscent of their previous relationship, so real she felt twenty-one again. It was the warm, enveloping feel of a morning duvet. So it wasn't difficult to play the role she designed for herself and as she relaxed, she felt the tension between them pull him towards her like the filament of a web.

People were slow to sit down with so many years of stories fighting to be heard. Willy was sheep-dogging them from the bar area into the dining room.

'No speeches tonight, folks. You can enjoy your meal in peace. I'll torture you tomorrow!'

Sylvia, someone Kate hardly knew, sat the other side of Jonathan.

'Hello, you two.' She was jittery, biting the skin on the side of her thumb, looking at it and then gnawing on it again.

Most people had discarded their name badges with their afternoon clothes.

'Hi, it's Sylvia, isn't it?' Jonathan knew everyone. 'I remember you well. I remember you particularly from the time we had a flood in the lab.'

He went into the details of the overnight leak in the roof and how they started the day with mops and buckets. Sylvia organised them. He got Sylvia laughing in no time and her hands were freed from her mouth as she spoke; he was an antidote to skin-chewing.

'You know, I was worried about coming to this reunion. I thought everyone would be stuffy and would look down on me. I'm just a Mum at home, I don't work. Well, I do work, the kids make sure of that, but not outside the house. Not what you lot would consider a "proper" job. I gave up pharmacy during my first pregnancy and haven't returned.' She took a deep breath before continuing.

'At the reception, everyone was going on about their high-flying positions and their shops. Even if they weren't overtly boasting, if they were ordinary pharmacists, their lives are so different from mine. I had nothing to say to them, nothing in common with them. I'm out of date, don't know anything about the latest drugs or business practices. I felt beneath their consideration. I almost went home.' Her eyes were moist with dismay at what she wasn't and relief at what she now could be. 'It's such a joy to talk to you.'

'Don't run yourself down, Sylvia. Don't ever say you're "just a Mum". Looking after kids is an under-valued activity. And if you chose to do that, well done, you. It's hard work – I've looked after my two on my own and to be honest, going to work is easier!'

He worked his magic again. Always saying the right thing. Sylvia was devouring his words with motherly joy. Kate didn't join in the chatter but absorbed the information. She knew he could charm anyone, but there was no danger of him chatting up Sylvia; with or without a job, she didn't sparkle enough for him.

Kate spotted Becky at the adjacent table taking photographs. She called across.

'Can we talk sometime this evening? After the main course?'

Becky nodded. 'Okay. See you in the foyer.'

Then she saw Colin coming from the bar. He was aiming for the empty seat beside her. Damn, she thought, I don't want to cope with them both. This could spoil my evening. But he was there, throwing his arms around her like they were the best of friends.

'"Why, there's a wench! Come on and kiss me, Kate."'

'You are such a show-off. Half the room is looking at you. I know it's Petruchio from "The Taming of the Shrew", I acted in it, so you're not impressing me.'

'Oh, but I bet I am.'

He sat in the empty chair and grinned at her. This was not going her way. She wanted to work on Jonathan this evening and Colin was for tomorrow if all went as she wanted. Well, she'd have to make the best of it. Unless Becky could help.

'Well, Colin, since you've decided to honour me with your company, give me a potted history of your last thirty years.'

'If I must.' He made a play of trying to dredge up thoughts from the past. 'I went into hospital pharmacy for my pre-registration year, as many of us did. Then inertia took over and I stayed put.'

'What – in the same hospital the whole time?'

'No, I've condensed it a bit. I stayed a couple of years after registration. Well, they asked me to and I liked it there. Then I moved around to get promotions and am now a Chief Pharmacist.'

'Some promotion! You've done well for yourself.' Kate always thought Colin hadn't taken the course seriously.

'Yeah, I suppose so. I found my niche, my strength, found what I liked to do.'

'And family?'

'Got a daughter. Would you believe, she's starting a pharmacy degree next year? How old does that make me feel?'

'What does your wife do?'

'She doesn't. I'm divorced.'

'I'm sorry.'

'Don't be. We weren't the best match and we're both happier apart.'

He then wanted to know about Kate, and she went through her story. As quickly as she could. She needed more information about Colin.

'What do you do outside work, Colin?'

'Are you expecting me to say I relentlessly pursue unwilling females?'

Kate couldn't help but smile.

'I've given it up. In fact, it was hardly a career. You were the only one.'

'So the others were willing volunteers?'

'Something like that.'

The smoked salmon starter arrived and he poured out wine for them both.

'Actually, Kate, I was hoping you'd be here. I know it's belated, but I'd like to say I'm sorry.'

'So you should be. You made my life a misery in my first year. I couldn't understand you. You were hardly sex-starved. Why me?'

'Didn't plan it that way.' He wriggled in his seat. And the self-confident flirt looked embarrassed.

'As you know, I liked my women, and you were just another – until you refused me. Then you became special. You became a challenge.'

'It was a challenge for me to avoid you!'

'Feisty as ever. And you are a pretty special person anyway. Look what you've achieved. And, I must admit, you've lost none of your looks. If anything, maturity has improved them.'

'Colin Simpson – what can I say? Do I accept your apology graciously and thank you for your kind if somewhat OTT compliments? Or do I say you haven't changed but just got more subtle, or perhaps devious? Trying to charm me is more acceptable than saying you want a fuck.' She dropped her voice and mouthed the last word, not wanting to attract anyone's attention with her language.

Colin burst out laughing. 'How suspicious you are! I came here with no ulterior motives, believe me. It's my excellent fortune to be sitting next to a lively, attractive woman. Why wouldn't I make the most of it?'

'Okay. I partly believe you. But you didn't answer my question. What do you do for fun?'

Colin described his sporting activities and the drinking pleasures that followed. Kate began to wish she hadn't asked. Her interest was revived when he commented his daughter lived with him.

'Do you get on well together?'

'Yes, we do. Although I found it hard the first time her boyfriend came to stay and they slept together. My little girl.'

'You hypocrite! You never thought about me being my father's little girl!'

'Touché! Can't help your feelings, I guess.'

'So you'll be on your own when she goes.'

'Yep. Apart from the odd bit of female company.'

He said this deliberately. Kate sensed he wanted her to know. She was satisfied. He still had a roving eye; it was a useful piece of information. At that point, Jonathan spoke to her and she gratefully turned away from Colin.

'Tasty meal, isn't it?'

'It's okay.' Kate looked puzzled. This was strange small talk from Jonathan.

He leaned towards her and again she felt the warmth from

his body. 'Wondered if you needed rescuing. Didn't know how keen you'd be on resuming contacts with your stalker.'

'We've grown up since those days. It's no worse than resuming communication with him than with you.'

'What a barbed tongue you have!'

'Apologies, I needn't have said that. I'll try to be more civil.' She gave him a repentant smile, a betrayal to the child she lost.

Becky came up behind them and greeted Jonathan.

'Becky, I didn't realise you were here!'

They performed the two-kiss ritual.

'Late arrival. "Circumstances outside my control," you might say. Anyway, let's get a few photos.'

She clicked away, trying to make sure she included everyone. She leaned across to Kate just as Jonathan was about to say something.

'Sorry to interrupt, but I need to have a word with Kate.'

'I'm just going to the loo, Becky. Can we talk on the way?'

Jonathan gave them a questioning look but got no response. As they walked behind Colin, he tapped Becky's arm.

'Great to see you. Talk later, eh?'

The two women moved off, Jonathan and Colin exchanged a few meaningless sentences and both turned to their partners on the other side.

'Something important, Becky?'

'No! I thought as you said we needed to talk, I'd come and get you. A rescue mission! You hit the jackpot with the two of them, didn't you?'

'You might say that. Not exactly as I intended. I could do without Colin at the moment. In fact, I need your help to remove him.'

'Well, he said "talk later", didn't he?'

'Luckily, yes. Perhaps you'd come across after dessert.

119

Everyone will be moving into the lounge for coffee, I expect, so if you could be my diversionary tactic and keep him occupied, it would be perfect.'

'Sure, no problem. He's more amusing than most of the guys here. I've just had a blow-by-blow account of Brian's ten most difficult customers! It would have been funny if he told the story differently. Number one Mr Dull. Colin will be light relief.'

'And what are you going to do with Jonathan?'

'Need-to-know basis, Becky, need-to-know. You don't need that info, so best I don't tell you. I'm playing it by ear so I'm not sure myself.'

Becky shrugged; she wasn't bothered.

'You said earlier on you wanted to talk to me. What was it about?'

'I think we'll defer that. One thing at a time. Colin is the matter in hand.'

'Fine. I'm about to make the most of the meal. Glad I don't have such a complicated agenda as you do.' She flicked a strand of errant hair off her face and grinned.

Becky was in a buoyant mood, Kate was pleased to see. Her earlier irritability had disappeared. They walked back to the tables where waitresses were serving a predictable cheesecake. Kate ignored it.

'I think coffee's in the lounge,' Jonathan said. 'Shall we go in or are you tired of my company?'

'Are you tired of mine?' Hardly a risky question; more an invitation.

'What do you think?'

He ushered Kate away from the table, his hand resting on her waist, a light touch to guide her. She was acutely aware of the slightest contact, deliberate or accidental. Out of the corner of her eye, she could see Becky chatting energetically to Colin.

People had spread around. A group went out onto the terrace where the setting sun coloured their wine-rosy faces pink;

chatting women tested the evening air and hastily returned, wrapping their old-women's cardigans round their waistless bodies and grumbling against the cold, like their mothers had done. Others shunned the cooler air, preferring the liquid warmth of the bar. A couple of guys started up the departmental song but there was a lack of enthusiasm to join in; it was rubbish the first time around. An air of bonhomie pervaded the gathering. It was an atmosphere where everyone became an old friend.

Jonathan and Kate walked along the terrace, past the groups of empty tables and a solitary smoker leaning against the wall, cigarette cupped in his hand against the breeze. The only one, it seemed, to have retained the student habit.

'Are you okay out here?' Jonathan asked. 'Personally, I need a breath of air. The atmosphere was a bit thick inside!'

'Yes, as long as we stay on firm ground.'

Jonathan looked at her quizzically.

'I'm wearing high heels. They will be ruined on grass.'

Simple.

'Did you think of bringing your wife along this weekend, Jonathan?

'No. She wouldn't have known anyone and there are the children. Thirteen and eleven. Not old enough to be left alone for a weekend.'

'Must be hard for your new wife to take them on.'

'Yes and no. They get on okay with her. Love me, love my kids.'

'A real family man?'

'I've grown up since you knew me, Kate. The kids are everything. I adored Emily, their mother. Like I once adored you.'

Kate wasn't expecting such an admission and it disturbed her. He loves his children. She hoped the colour hadn't risen in her cheeks. She turned away and partly covered her face with her hand.

'The intervening years changed me and I wanted the

permanence of commitment. Her illness and death nearly killed me. It was only the kids that kept me going.'

'Then you married again.'

'I was lonely and life was hard. No family around to help, I was dependent on child-minders because of my travel. I met Liz while working and she was fun. I needed female company. It was a wild affair and for the first time in years I was happy. We married six months after we met.'

Jonathan, talking about what he called a happy time, was getting morose. This isn't like you, Kate thought. I need to break this mood. Apart from anything else, I'm starting to feel sorry for you. I must never feel sorry for you.

'Why so miserable if you were happy?'

'It was a mistake. She didn't like the girls. Or, more accurately, she didn't like the constraints they put on our lives. We started to argue.'

'How long did it last?'

'Little more than a year. She walked out. A total failure. A messy divorce. I swore I'd never marry again.'

'There is an obvious next question.'

Jonathan didn't reply. He was a man who needed a woman; Kate knew that. They reached the terrace again, having circled the hotel. Jonathan suggested they go in out of the cold. The warmth of the lounge hit them like sunshine and they rubbed their hands as they moved to the table where coffee cups were lined up.

'We're getting enquiring looks,' Jonathan said.

'Understandable. We haven't been seen together for a long time. I would prefer to be somewhere less conspicuous. There's no need to start rumours flying. Let's move across to the lounge on the other side of reception.'

'Good idea. That is, unless you're tired? I see the crowd has thinned out.'

'I've always been a night-bird. You know that. Too early

for me to go to bed.'

'How about a brandy?'

Kate said she'd love one and Jonathan headed for the bar.

She chose an armchair in a corner of the lounge where there was flattering illumination, away from the other occupants of the room. There was an elderly couple in another corner, involved in their own conversation, and a lone man with a newspaper and a drink. No pharmacists had migrated this way. She sat down and waited, straightening her skirt, fiddling with her necklace and re-clipping her hair. Jonathan came in with the drinks, large ones, a brandy for her, a single malt whisky for himself. These were not regular student drinks but he had introduced her to brandy after a lucrative job and remembered her penchant for Rémy Martin.

'It's the right brand. I hadn't forgotten, even if I couldn't often buy one for you.'

Kate raised it towards him in a toast. A pre-planned toast. 'To us, Jonathan. Together and apart.'

He beamed, his temporary dip in spirits forgotten. 'To us, Kate. I'm glad you came this weekend. I had a feeling you wouldn't. I didn't know if I wanted to see you here. I didn't know if you wanted to see me. I felt it wasn't your scene.'

'You're right. It isn't.' Her voice had a bitter tinge. 'I have bad memories of my university years.'

'I know I have a part in that. You're expecting me to ask a particular question. I can feel it hanging in the air.' Jonathan hesitated. He rubbed his hand across his mouth as if to prevent unwanted, rash words from escaping.

A waitress walked by, collecting glasses, and they both went silent. It seemed the silence lasted forever.

'I don't know if I am. If you do ask, I don't think I want to answer.'

Only Kate and Jonathan knew about the pregnancy. She told no-one else. Secrecy made it tolerable.

Only Kate knew the outcome.

123

'But if…'

He put his finger against her lips to stop her saying more. She remembered the first time he had done that. Its slight roughness tempted her to lick it.

'My bad memories were not only because of you. There wasn't a great incentive to come this weekend. But Becky was full of enthusiasm as only she can be and she persuaded me. I am glad I'm here.'

She rested her hand lightly on his arm and he placed his hand over hers.

'I'm glad you're here, too,' he said.

Kate was wondering where to go next. Successful so far, several difficult moments carefully navigated. It was an effort to control her emotions. Her senses were alert and vulnerable, as if on the edge of a momentous happening. Take your time, slow down; she tried to obey the composed, disciplined voice in her head.

'I shouldn't say this, Kate, but you are affecting me far more than I anticipated. You have powerful allure. You always did, but the self-confidence you now have makes you immensely attractive.'

'Are you making a pass at me?'

'That's something students do. I'm being honest, telling you how I feel.'

'So how am I meant to respond?'

'You could be honest as well.'

That would be a mistake, she thought. 'You left me, Jonathan, I didn't leave you. You left me at the worst possible time and I had to cope. I never lost my feelings for you. I had to channel them elsewhere.' To resentment and hatred, to feelings too complex to describe. 'You are still the attractive man you were. You still draw me; there is still a powerful tension between us. I can feel it now. It's why I reacted to your touch.'

Jonathan leaned back in the sofa and crossed his legs in

the way Kate remembered with the ankle of his right foot on his left knee. He looked at Kate for a while before speaking, his words chosen with care and spoken deliberately as if they were specimens rarely on display. It was hard for Kate to remain dispassionate.

'Are we going to do anything about this?' He sipped his whisky, his eyes intense.

'We are both married, Jonathan. Does that mean anything?'

'I suspect you've had the odd adventure during your marriage to your safe and loving husband. You've told me you need excitement.'

'And what about your new wife? It's a bit premature to be wandering, isn't it?'

'Absolutely. I have been faithful in all my marriages, believe it or not. But you have presented me with an unexpected situation. It's as if this is an unreal world. What happens here doesn't have any relevance outside. We are in a bubble. I can be faithful again tomorrow.'

His hand was now on her thigh and she didn't push him away. His warmth passed easily through her dress, up her leg and beyond. Only the guy with his newspaper was left in the room and he was uninterested in them.

'Are you coming?'

Kate said nothing. Jonathan got up and turned towards the door. 'Room 406.'

Kate let him go and smiled to herself. Jonathan had drunk a lot. Would he see this through? Five minutes later, she got up to follow him and then sat down again. Too soon. Let him wait. She picked up a magazine and flicked through the pages, reading nothing, barely registering the pictures. After a few more minutes she rose and wandered round the room, stopped in front of an old photograph on the wall as if it caught her attention, then left the lounge. As she passed reception, she saw Becky and Colin ahead of her. He had his arm around her waist and they were heading for the lift, giggling together.

She was shocked. I asked her to distract him not to get off with him, she thought. Bugger! This could be a complication if she's got him in tow. Kate was diverted from her own purpose by this unwanted development but then she stood still, told herself to handle one matter at a time. Colin was for tomorrow; she'd deal with him then.

After a brief visit to her own room to apply more perfume, she walked along the quiet corridor and bumped into Becky coming out of her door.

'Hello there!'

Becky jumped. 'You startled me. I thought everyone had gone to bed.'

'Heading somewhere interesting?'

'Making the most of an opportunity, you might say.'

'Well, don't get Colin too keen. I need him to be available tomorrow.'

'Are you psychic or what?'

'Saw you downstairs. Seriously, don't get in my way.'

'Kate, Kate – listen here. You have these hidden agendas and as I don't know the details, I can neither help nor hinder you. You make everything too complicated. I'm enjoying this evening. I take life as it comes. I'll do what I want whatever you say. You should know me by now. What happens tonight will be forgotten tomorrow.'

Kate was surprised Becky was still single. With her friendly, outgoing personality, she was always the spark that ignited an evening, the centre of a crowd. Perhaps it was the problem, Kate thought – too many men and no special one. As a student, she was constantly in and out of love. When things were going well, her blond hair curled frivolously on her shoulders and she wore red lipstick; when things turned sour, she tied every strand back severely and wore no makeup at all. Kate suspected her love-life was calmer now. Her hair remained in one style, well-cut, although a tendency to wildness remained. She hadn't seen her with a man for months.

'Okay. But he needs to be brought down a peg or two. Bear that in mind.'

Becky turned to go, then looked back. 'And you're heading where?'

'You can probably guess.'

Chapter 11

Becky was more than willing to go to his room with him. Colin remembered their relationship as students, a wild few weeks when they were rarely out of bed. Intense and passionate until it burned itself out. She was a fun, uncomplicated girl. It didn't take long to discover what attracted him thirty-odd years ago attracted him now.

'You haven't changed, Becky. You still have a wicked sparkle in your eye.'

'And you still have your silver tongue.'

A magnet pulled them together over coffee. They joined an animated group crammed into one corner of the room. Becky's right leg was squashed against Colin and he managed to stroke her thigh.

'Your technique is rather obvious. But you were never that subtle,' she whispered.

'Subtlety is overrated. Too clever at it and your intentions may never be known.'

Becky ignored this, but it enticed him more. She turned to Simon. 'I hear you've deserted pharmacy and moved into law.'

'Not strictly true. I have moved into law but I use both my degrees. I'm a specialist in pharmaceutical cases. Not many of us around, we're rare beasts.'

'Rare, rich beasts, I imagine.'

'It has its compensations.'

'Well, it must be a major change from your poverty-stricken student days. I recall buying lunch for you on more than one occasion. There was never much spare cash around then.'

Simon gave her a disapproving stare. Clearly, he did not want to be reminded of this. 'Well, I think I'll get myself a nightcap.' He rose to go to the bar, making a point of terminating their conversation. But Becky was quick.

'Good idea, Simon. Could you get me a whisky? Glenmorangie if they have it.'

Becky could hardly keep her face straight. She didn't normally demand drinks without being asked but this was a special case. And she wouldn't usually drink single malt. She thanked Simon profusely when he returned with her request but was glad when he moved away. Giggles were rising like champagne bubbles within her and she couldn't continue talking to him for fear of saying the wrong thing or simply exploding. He'd become stuffy, she thought, not the pleasant company he used to be.

'Colin, how about a breath of fresh air?'

'Why not?' He was delighted to go outside with her. They both folded up with laughter as soon as they were out of earshot.

'Good for you, Becky! That was brilliant. A perfect absence of subtlety there!'

They talked about Simon and his mean student ways, while wandering across the terrace. Becky spotted Kate ahead and wondered what she and Jonathan were talking about. And whether Kate was putting her devices, whatever they were, into action. Colin slipped his arm around her.

'Can I have another lapse of subtlety?' He bent down and kissed her. Becky responded and within five minutes she agreed to go to his room.

'Don't let's make it too obvious. We can go back in and socialise for a while.'

They returned to the noisy group where a number of bottles, many already empty, testified to the evening's consumption. Colin went to the bar and came back with a bottle of red and two glasses. He poured wine for them both and Becky wondered if he was trying to get her tipsy. She liked tipsy. As they joined in the general conversation, Colin's eyes followed her with the unspoken question, "How long must we wait?"

She kept her word and they turned back the clock to their student days. An hour later as they lay on the bed together, he said, 'Well, Becky, am I as expert as I used to be – or am I better?'

He reached across for his glass and poured wine into it, splashing it on the bedside table. The bottle was nearly empty. Becky shook her head when he tried to top up hers.

'You obviously rate modesty lower than subtlety. You weren't bad, I'll give you that.'

'Not bad? Come on! You enjoyed it, you know you did. How many men have given you greater pleasure?'

'You expect me to say "none", I know.'

'Certainly I do. We all have our particular strengths and I know what mine is.' He was starting to slur his words and the amiable flirt was degenerating into a loud-mouthed bragger.

He reached across, grabbed Becky round the waist and clumsily tried to kiss her again. She turned away and sat up.

'Colin, I think I'm going to bed. My bed, not yours.'

And she got up, dressed and went out. Colin was left deflated, confused and frustrated. He got off the bed in an attempt to stop her but rocked from side to side and she was gone before he reached her. Everything suddenly deteriorated and his befuddled brain couldn't cope. And to make matters worse, the room was rotating.

***

Colin half woke up and looked at the clock. Twenty past nine. Shit, he thought as he dragged himself out of bed and headed for the shower. He was in and out in minutes, rubbing the towel roughly over his body and hair, throwing on his clothes, grabbing his room key then rushing downstairs.

They were meeting at ten o'clock at the new department

for a guided tour. A couple of present-day students offered to show them round. He could see Kate on the coach by the hotel door, well made-up and classy as ever, talking to Pauline. As he jumped on to it, he heard a voice calling Pauline to come and see photos so the seat beside Kate was left empty. He threw himself down beside her, panting heavily.

'Made it! I overslept. I've literally just got up, showered, dressed and run down here.' He ran his hands through his wet, dishevelled hair. 'I'm starving! Hope they have coffee and biscuits laid on for us.'

'You do look bleary-eyed.'

'A touch too much vino last night, I think. You don't have any paracetamol, do you, Kate? My head isn't the best.'

'Yes, I do. But you need a drink of water to take them.'

'Ever the sensible pharmacist.'

He stood up and called, 'Anyone got a bottle of water on them?' One appeared and he took a large swig with the two tablets Kate gave him. 'I should have drunk more water before I went to bed.'

'Good God, Colin, apart from the fact we had lectures on the effects of alcohol as students, you've done the practical enough times. And you're a Chief Pharmacist.'

'I know. I wasn't thinking.' Otherwise occupied but Kate wouldn't know.

'Can't see Becky. I wonder where she's got to.'

Colin looked rapidly at her. Did she know? No, he thought, simply an unfortunately-timed casual comment about her friend.

'She said she would be coming when I spoke to her last night. Maybe changed her mind – or overslept like me.' Colin rested his head on the back of the seat and closed his eyes. 'Waiting for the painkillers to take effect.'

He feigned sleep but his mind was active, going over the previous evening. He wasn't sure whether the alcohol had blurred his memory. Could he remember it correctly? Bloody drink. He could usually knock plenty back without much effect. Shit, he must have had a skinful last night. Not like Becky to walk out on him. He tried to remember the fun they had before she turned sour. Mmm, it had been exciting.

He squinted and noticed Kate watching him from time to time. Maybe she'd be more amenable to his advances now? Little chance! Kate wasn't the type to get desperate with age – she could still have her pick and it probably wasn't him. But he might try. Bloody drink. He still fancied her. Paracetamol works fairly fast. Within half an hour he should be feeling better.

They got off the coach and split into groups for their tour. A couple of young lecturers welcomed them, neither old enough to have taught them. So much for a reunion, thought Colin; none of our lecturers have turned up. Two pleasant third year students volunteered to be guides and they set off in the unfamiliar surroundings. Colin stayed close to Kate who kept a one-sided conversation going. They went firstly into the pharmacology lab, a super high-tech room with television monitors at strategic points so everyone could see demonstrations at the front bench. Nostalgia swathed them like a warm, old blanket as they told their guide what it used to be like.

'A far cry from our time. We gathered around the demonstrator who explained what he was doing. No TV, no microphones. We stood and watched.'

'Well, we were only twenty people. Half of us at any one time.'

'There are two hundred students in each year now.'

'Can't imagine how they'd have a reunion in thirty years' time,' Kate said.

'Would you even want a departmental reunion? You'd never know everyone like we did.'

'I didn't want this one,' muttered Kate and Colin raised his eyebrows.

They moved on to the mock pharmacies, looking exactly like the real thing, shelves of medications in alphabetical order, counter displays of non-prescription items. A white coat hanging in the corner.

'Could have got my paracetamol here,' Colin joked, 'I assume these are real drugs?'

'Yes, they are,' their guide said. 'In date, too. We run the pharmacy as any pharmacist would except it's not open to the public. Proper training for real life after registration. We act as each other's customers to practise our counselling skills.'

'Makes our course feel out of date. I wish there'd been an opportunity like this.'

'It was one of the best courses of its time. But it's great to see how training has moved on.'

'I don't see a pharmacognosy lab.'

'Pharmacognosy? It's not taught as a separate subject now. And we call it Materia Medica.'

'It was hardly the most popular one when we were students – hours spent examining and drawing botanical specimens of bits of bark, seeds, resins, roots, learning their names and active constituents.'

'Well, natural products are still a source of drugs so we learn about the important ones.'

Colin suddenly had a vision of the pharmacognosy lecturer standing guard over a large block of opium resin as they filed by to look at it. How he supposed anyone could steal it was hard to imagine, but students were ever prone to mischief.

'Kate, do you remember the opium block?'

'Oh, yes! They had it so long, it was probably inactive. But they watched it like hawks when it was out of its locked cupboard.'

Colin was reviving. He had more colour in his face, and was joining in the general comments and jokes. As they moved into the chemistry lab, Kate tripped on a step, bumping into him and grabbing his shoulder to steady herself. He caught her and softened her fall, finding her face close to his, her hair flicking his cheek.

'You okay?'

'Yes, I think so. Twisted my ankle but nothing serious.' She leaned on his arm as she bent down to rub her foot. 'Silly thing to do.'

But it drew them physically closer to each other and although it was an accident, Colin was pleased it had happened. He could tell Kate was aware of his presence, a force now rather than a consumer of paracetamol.

There were a few more labs and lecture theatres to see but Colin lost interest.

'Do you want to escape with me and we'll go and find a coffee?' He whispered in Kate's ear, putting his mouth close and resting his arm on her shoulder.

'Too rude. We're nearly done. I think we should stick it out. We're ending up in the coffee bar on the ground floor, anyway. I assume your head is better?'

'Yes. Feeling myself again. Maybe I'll learn my lesson.'

'If you haven't learned by now, I doubt you will.'

Colin was back. He was eyeing Kate with what could only be described as a polite leer. He was his old self again.

'You know, Colin, if you relaxed and didn't focus so much on sex, you'd be a decent guy.'

They were drinking coffee in an up-market version of the coffee bar of their student days, far cleaner, better lit and without the ever-present pall of cigarette smoke, but also more clinical and bland. And the floor wasn't sticky. He looked surprised and feigned shock.

'Can't think what you mean! I haven't made a single inappropriate suggestion.'

'Not out loud, you haven't. But you have an eloquent face. I can almost read your thoughts.'

'Clever Kate. Tell me about them.'

'I will on the coach back to the hotel. Unless you're staying for lunch here? Some people are.'

'Would I stay here when I have the chance of your company? We could pretend to be students and neck on the back seat!'

'Don't push your luck, Colin!'

The half empty coach moved off towards their hotel.

'Well?' He asked.

'You were thinking you fancied me. You were thinking I was still an unfulfilled challenge. But the challenge is irrelevant now. We've ended up, by chance, years after your stalking, in the same hotel, and you'd like to capitalise on it.'

'Stalking? Is that how you remember what happened?'

'It was stalking, Colin, although I was too naïve to realise it. If that sort of thing happened now, it would be reported to the police.'

Colin's face paled.

'Don't worry. I'm not thinking of a retrospective court case.' Kate laughed, breaking the tension that descended on them. 'You were thinking if you could persuade me to join you in your room, you might stand a better chance with me now than you ever had when we were students.'

Colin looked dumbstruck. 'Was I thinking that?'

'You are now!'

Colin sat and looked at Kate. This was a new twist to events. He'd not come to the reunion with any ideas. Then Kate was there, more attractive than he remembered. Yesterday there'd been a bit of banter at dinner and he apologised for his youthful behaviour. Not that he felt he did much harm. And now he learns she considered him a stalker – a stalker! Yet seconds later makes an oblique suggestion she might be persuaded into his hotel room. Don't think too hard about it, he told himself. No benefit ever came of thinking.

Kate was looking out of the window, leaving Colin to his musings. They walked into the hotel, Kate saying, 'See you later,' to Colin and disappearing upstairs.

She had been in her room ten minutes when the phone rang.

'How about lunch, Kate?'

She was expecting Colin to ring and was disappointed. 'Becky! What happened this morning? You missed the tour.'

'I know. I didn't want to face Colin and he said he wanted to go on it.'

'What happened last night?'

'Can I tell you over lunch?'

'Okay. See you in the dining room in ten minutes.'

They found a table in an alcove, away from the buffet and not in the line of sight of the door. Becky was her usual, somewhat dishevelled self, her innate efficiency never giving itself away in her appearance. Her makeup had a look of the previous evening about it and her hair was still damp.

'Let's grab a bite then we can chat. Do you want any wine?'

'No, I had enough last night.' Becky mimed a heavy head.

'So, tell me about it. Is Colin still the expert lover?'

'Well, to be honest, he is. It became clear early on what his expectations were and I thought, "What the hell!" A bit of fun is a bit of fun. So I agreed to go to his room and it was as satisfying as the old days. In fact, with my eyes closed, it could have been the old days. He is more padded now – doesn't look as lean and hungry – but otherwise not much different.'

'So why didn't you want to see him this morning?'

'Well, he got drunk and lost his appeal. He started lurching at me for a second round of sex and turned me off. In spite of what I had to drink, it sobered me up to see him like that. He also irritated me with his excessive boasting. A little can be amusing but it got beyond acceptable.'

'So you abandoned him?'

'I went back to my room. I don't think he had a clue why but I might have got a frosty reception this morning. It's not a matter I intend to discuss with him. You said he needed to be brought down a peg or two. Well, I did that. And anyway, you said you needed him this morning. How was he?'

'Hung-over, in need of medication. But he recovered as the inveterate drinker does.'

'Did you get back at him? What did you do?'

'Nothing. Just planted a few seeds. I'm not finished with him yet. I was worried he'd be hot in your pursuit today, anticipating another wild night of passion.'

'Never a possibility.'

'Well, I'm glad you've had your fill. I thought I might have trouble pulling him back.'

'You're not going to sleep with him are you?'

'As I said before, Becky, you don't need to know all my schemes. Then you can't be blamed for complicity. Thanks for keeping him out of my way last night. It was useful. Your role in this charade is complete.'

Becky's phone rang. There was a pause then she greeted Mary, her locum; a frown changed her expression.

'Sorry, Kate, a few issues. See you later.' She went away with a worried look on her face, listening to some unfortunate tale.

Kate collected a coffee from the buffet and moved into the lounge, this time finding a prominent position. Somewhere Colin will find me, she thought. Like a fish on a line, I'll pull him in. Within minutes, he appeared.

'Hi Kate. Just called your room. Thought you might be down here. Can I join you?'

'Sure. Go and grab a coffee. Have you eaten lunch?'

'Yes. Went in as soon as we got back. Needed food. Didn't see you in there.'

'I was in the far alcove. With Becky.'

The brief shadow that passed over his face would have been imperceptible had she not known last night's story. 'Where is she now?'

'Sorting out a problem with her locum. It was a large frown issue so don't know how long she'll be.'

'Maybe I don't need a coffee. Or perhaps we could have one in my room? I'm sure Becky will find other company, sociable girl that she is.'

'Okay, Colin. I accept your invitation. To coffee. Be with you soon.'

Kate went back to her room to collect her thoughts. She changed her clothes, renewed her lipstick, brushed her hair and mentally told herself to get on with it.

Colin had coffee ready when she arrived, proper filter coffee ordered from room service, not the rough instant powder from the sachets provided. He'd also changed into a fresh shirt and she could smell after-shave. Expectations, expectations. She could see a part-used bottle of gin on the table.

'Coffee, Kate? Or would you prefer a G and T? I've got tonic water and a lime in the fridge.'

'Coffee will be fine. I would hate to think you were trying to get me tipsy. It is two-thirty in the afternoon.'

'Kate, you are delicious sober. Why would I want you any other way?'

'And do you want me?'

Colin widened his eyes and licked his lips, like an animal contemplating a pounce.

'This has got nothing to do with your being a challenge, Kate. Nothing to do with your being unattainable when we were students. It has everything to do with your sexy body and my desire, here and now.'

But he'd think he'd won in the end, Kate thought. And it would not be acceptable.

He came over to Kate, took a sip from her coffee cup and

placed it on the table. He raised her chin with his finger and placed a gentle, almost chaste kiss on her lips. Then he did it again. He was breathing more deeply, the only sign of any excitement. He took her hand and moved towards the bed.

'Slowly, Colin, I'm not one to be rushed.'

'Rushed? Thirty years is hardly rushing.'

'I like to take my love-making slowly. We do this on my terms.'

'Any terms you like.'

'Then draw the curtains and put the lamps on.'

He did as requested, the dull afternoon becoming more seductive.

'Now sit down and watch.'

She got up and unclipped her hair which fell on to her shoulders, shaking her head so that it swished like a shampoo advertisement. She walked over to him, turned her back and asked him to undo her zip. Before he had time to touch her skin she moved away into a darker part of the room and slowly dropped the dress to the floor.

'Do you like my underwear?'

'Yes. Yes, I do. It's beautiful.' Then he smiled. 'Not an M & S girl then?'

'More Agent Provocateur.'

She walked around the room in her high heels so that Colin could see her from all angles. She knew the effect it would have, knew she looked sexy. It was an old trick; she liked to perform.

Colin was agitated.

'Kate you are turning me on big time. But watching isn't enough. I need to touch.'

He got to his feet and Kate raised her hand.

'You can touch only what you can see.'

Colin ran his hands down her arms, sliding them from her shoulder to her thighs, then traced his fingers between her breasts across her stomach. He put his arms around her and kissed her passionately. She could feel the insistent beat of his heart and his erection pressing against her.

'There is nothing like the feel of skin and yours is wonderful.'

He went to undo her bra and she pulled away.

'Anticipation, Colin, anticipation. Don't you value it? It's the spice that takes sex from an activity to an experience.'

'Kate, this is getting ridiculous. I want you now. And it will be an experience, one you will enjoy. I'm a skilful lover, you know.'

'Then take off your clothes.'

Colin needed no further prompting. But standing there, naked, not allowed to remove Kate's clothes put him on edge. He turned away from her.

'Don't you want to look?'

He shot round to see she had removed her bra.

'The rules haven't changed. You can touch what you can see.'

He did, closing his eyes and savouring the moment. He caressed her for a long time, until he could bear it no more.

'What do I have to do to get you to take your knickers off?'

'Well, that's the question. You have to make me a promise.'

'What promise?'

Kate walked slowly to the end of the bed and hooked her thumbs inside the sides of her knickers. One movement would have them down.

'You have to promise not to fuck me.'

'What did you say?' Colin's voice rose to a squeak.

'You heard. I didn't say I would go to bed with you. I said I'd come for coffee. And I've done that – I've done more than that. I think you had a fair deal – you got a lot more than company.'

140

'You are a bitch, Kate Shaw. You deliberately led me on until I was practically exploding. You made me believe this would lead to a fuck.'

'You enjoyed it. Don't complain. I let you touch; I might have only allowed you to look. Remember, you are not God's gift to women. It is possible to resist you. I think we're quits now.'

Kate looked down at her own nearly naked body and back at Colin. 'So are you promising?'

'Bloody hell, no! I'm not playing your absurd games!' he yelled.

'Then I'll keep my knickers on.' She got dressed and Colin disappeared into the bathroom.

'Your amorous escapades haven't gone too well this weekend, have they, Colin?' She called after him. 'See you at dinner.'

Chapter 12

Kate returned to her room with a self-satisfied grin on her face. The Colin episode had gone well; she was pleased with her performance. What time had she got left to herself? Barely an hour, not long. She felt invigorated – that's what success does for me, she thought. Even so, she needed to remove all traces of Colin. His fingers were still on her skin, she felt sticky with them, soiled. But it wasn't just his touch. She needed to wash off his eyes, his greedy, acquisitive gaze. She stripped off her clothes, letting them land where they would and wandered into the bathroom. The shower had plenty of power and she turned it on full. She stood under it, letting the jets of water bounce off her head and cascade down. I shall block the drain with the men I'm washing off me, she thought with amusement.

After several minutes she emerged, wrapped herself in a towel and lay on the bed. Colin has gone, she thought, I'm renewed. She shut her eyes and tiredness crept up, hovering nearby like a nervous friend, not sure if this was an appropriate time to visit. She drifted into a half sleep, a cosy, relaxed place, her body glowing from the hot water, the duvet soft beneath her. The distant clatter of traffic two floors below was background to a reverie, a confused mixture of old and recent memories. One minute Jonathan was caressing her, telling her he loved her, but it was spoiled by the taste of revenge. Then the horrendous dilemma – should she abort the baby? Then she was complaining at Colin, telling him she wasn't interested but found him kissing her. This was interrupted by Becky telling her to forget the past. A clock on the church across the road chimed four o'clock and brought her back to the present. She was glad; her thoughts were troubling. She needed to be awake. The room was a mess and Kate could not tolerate mess so she busied herself with sorting out her clothes. Order calmed her. A vigorous rub of her hair, a deep breath and she was business-like Kate again, getting ready for the next venture.

Jonathan was still nagging at her mind, a weight she found hard to lift. She couldn't rid herself of him as easily as she could Colin. But it was time to move on. She needed to concentrate on something, someone else. It was Willy's turn next; he was a problem. All she had was the germ of an idea.

I need to find him first, she thought, so she wandered down into the hotel lounge hoping he'd gone there in search of company, maybe someone to impress. There was nothing official laid on, no guided tours or activities that afternoon. Most folk had gone into town to see how it had changed. There was a hum of music playing and a few people chatting in groups. But no sign of him. Becky was there, talking again on her mobile. She finished the call and sighed loudly.

'Still problems with the locum?'

'Yes. She's had a drug addict in, being abusive. We're known to be suppliers of methadone to addicts trying to get off heroin. They're never a problem, but other addicts are. She's frightened and it's our late night tonight. I made the mistake of telling her about my issues with the alarm, so that's bothering her too. I do wonder if it's becoming too much for her. But she's reliable and a lovely lady and I'd hate to tell her I was getting someone else.'

'How old is she?'

'In her sixties, not old. And she has loads of experience. But more nervous these days. I'm debating if I'll need to go back.'

'Oh, Becky, what a shame! You were the one who was so keen to come. You arrived late and now you're talking of leaving early. Surely Mary can cope. It's what you're paying her for!

143

Don't go!'

'I don't want to. I'll go as a last resort. But I feel my responsibility. You understand that.'

'Well, let me know if you decide to leave. You've been such a help with my intrigues, I was thinking I might need you again.'

'I thought you enjoyed my company. Am I only here as an accomplice?'

'Sorry, Becky, I didn't mean it. Of course I value your company. I didn't express myself well.'

Becky sighed and her aggrieved air diminished although Kate was aware she needed to think before involving her much more.

'Well, you'll be glad to know I got my own bit of revenge on Simon last night. I forgot to tell you at lunch time.'

And she recounted the "whisky nightcap" story. Kate roared with laughter.

'That was magnificent! Didn't know you had it in you, Becky. You are such an easy- going person.'

'I just took the opportunity – he set the trap himself and I sprang it. He's changed and become superior. I think he looks down on us "ordinary" pharmacists who've never moved on. So I was chuffed with my performance.'

'He may act differently but he looks much the same, apart from the smart clothes, don't you think? Oh, that reminds me. Have you got any of your photos with you?'

'Yes, I have. I was amazed at how many there were. Most of the parties we went to and lots of snaps of individuals. There's one of Simon, I know. I was intending to bring them to the dinner this evening and pass them around. Probably won't get the chance now.'

'Could I borrow them? They could be useful in my "Willy-plot" and you might not be here.'

'Certainly you can. Although it's beyond me how they

will help you get back at Willy. There's nothing incriminating in them.'

'Don't worry about it. If you're at the dinner, you'll find out or I'll tell you later. Do you think I could have them now? I'll come up to your room.'

So Kate took possession of a large envelope containing several dozen photos. There was the first year Christmas party, a Hallowe'en party where she was a witch's cat, a summer picnic, the attempt at the record for the number of people in a phone box, photos of Rag Week, plus various groups drinking together. Many of those; beer drinking was a significant activity. There was even a photo of her and Jonathan sitting on the floor in Becky's flat, laughing about something. She looked at it for several seconds.

'Thanks, Becky. You're a star.'

She went to her room and phoned Willy on his mobile.

'Hello, Gabriel here.'

'Willy, it's Kate. I know you're giving a speech this evening and I expect it's prepared. But I've got an idea. Becky's given me a load of photos from our student days and I wondered if it would be possible to scan them into a laptop and show them. They really bring back memories. I've got my laptop with me; you can use that.'

'It's not a bad idea. To be honest, I did think of doing something like that but couldn't find my photos.'

Trust you to take ownership of the idea, Kate thought. Bet it never crossed your mind.

'Where are you now, Willy? Can we meet up somewhere?'

'I'm in my room.'

'Do you want to join me downstairs in the conservatory? We can go through them over a coffee. I'm sure the hotel will have a scanner in their Business Centre and a screen is standard equipment.'

Willy came down with a bulky folder and a busy air. He

nodded at the girl on the desk and said loudly if anyone wanted him, he'd be in the far corner of the conservatory. Giving Kate a rapid up and down appraisal, he indicated two armchairs by the window. They spent some time going over the photos. Willy went into ownership mode.

'Don't think we can use them all. There are too many. Pity because they tell the story of the three years. But if we take several events from each year and include groups and individuals, it should work. See if we can get most people in one or other picture. Glad I asked for the private dining room this evening.'

'I assumed you had. Giving a speech with an assortment of random folk in the room doesn't work, does it? We need to be able to hear your words of wisdom.'

Willy missed the irony.

Kate helped him to sort the photos into order so they followed the group through the three years. Becky had annotated each on the back with names and dates and Willy made notes to make sure he got the details right.

'What photos did you have, Willy?'

'A superb set. Better than these although similar. Annoying I've misplaced them.'

'Obviously you still have a problem with losing things.'

His blank look was replaced by realisation. 'Kate, you're not harping on about that accident, are you?'

'It may have been a minor, forgettable incident for you, but it wasn't for me. You caused me not to get a First. There was a question on tetracycline structure and those notes covered it exactly. I made a mess of it.'

'You've never made a mess of a question in your life, Kate. You are too clever by far.'

'A relative mess; I didn't answer it how I should have done.'

'And it's my fault? I don't think so.'

'Willy, nothing either of us can say will alter what

happened, so I'd like to know the truth. Was it really an accident you left the notes at home?'

'Yes, it was. A stupid accident, I'll admit.'

'And it took your mother all that time to find them?'

'Unfortunately, yes.'

But the tiniest hesitation before he replied told Kate he was lying. He saw the look of discovery flash across Kate's face, a "Eureka" moment, and knew he'd given himself away.

'So now I know, Willy. You did leave them behind by mistake but you could have got them back to me sooner. I don't know how you could do it.'

'You know as well as I do they were likely to award a single First. And suddenly, I was presented with this piece of luck. Not foreseen, just an opportunity that fell in my lap. The First had to be mine.'

'So zero thought for me. No gratitude for the help I was giving you. It was despicable. You treated me like shit.'

'I knew you would do well, whatever. You didn't need the First like I did. You had eloquence and persuasiveness to get you through, to say nothing of your looks. Your enthusiasm brought you to life when you talked about pharmacology in a way mine never did. I needed a top-rate, solid piece of paper to prove my worth.' He waved a photo in the air as if it were the paper he spoke of. 'My family expected it. You don't know the pressure I was under, an only child with everyone's expectations resting on me. Your initiative was always going to make you a winner. And you are. A chain of pharmacies bearing your name. You didn't need to tell me Kate – I knew you were the owner.'

Initiative, eh? Well, we'll see what initiative can do today.

'Let's talk about something else, Willy. This makes me angry, and I don't want to have any further arguments with you. I'll keep the peace for the sake of the reunion.'

She took a long drink of her coffee, swallowing the acrimony in her mouth.

'The photos – have we made the best of them?'

'I think so, Kate. I'll go along to the Business Centre and get them scanned in. I'll ask them to set up a screen as well.'

'I can do that. Give you time to think how the photos will tie in with your speech.'

'I was wondering how to integrate the slide show.' He opened his folder and took out a set of index cards on which he made notes. 'Always work from prompt cards. Dislike speakers who read the entire text like a newsreader. I do enough speaking at local Branch meetings. I'm used to standing up on my hind legs. And there are always presentations and the like at work.'

'I'm sure you are an experienced speaker.'

He nodded and spread out his cards. They were decidedly more than adequate prompts with a substantial number of words on each. Kate, a skilled speaker herself, spotted the nervous jottings of someone who wasn't as confident as he made out.

'Do you want to give me an outline?'

'If you like. There'll be the usual welcome, especially to those who've travelled a long way, mention of the staff members who are joining us. There'll be a couple of them, the ones we thought would show up this morning but didn't. Then something about the new department, comparing it with the one we had. I've got a few funny lines there, a few mild digs at the lecturers.' He laughed, a pig-like snort, in anticipation. 'A few stats, numbers of students, what graduates go on to do, reputation of the department. Then anecdotes from the past, escapades we got up to and so on.'

He proudly reviewed his memories, each one listed in tiny writing on the cards. 'Maybe I'll insert the slide show there. Or perhaps intersperse the anecdotes and the photos. I'll work on it. Then I'll finish by asking people to let me know what they thought of the weekend and whether we should repeat it in the future.'

He sighed and puffed out his cheeks. Kate guessed he could already hear the congratulatory remarks, the applause, the grateful thanks.

'What do you think?'

'Sounds fine to me. I'm sure you'll do it well.'

Kate was glancing casually through the index cards as Willy pondered his best approach when a voice called from across the room.

'Hi, you two! What are you plotting with your heads together?'

A strange creature appeared, pulling an older man by his hand. Both Willy and Kate stared as she tottered forward on unmanageably high heels. She was wearing something that looked like an outfit from a dressing-up box. Her short skirt was layered with net frills round the hem, the much decorated top overlapping it in a haphazard and ragged way. She wore lacy, fingerless gloves that reached to her elbows and a large bow of ribbon in her hair. Her wrists were weighed down with chunky bracelets. The whole outfit was in pink and black. It was, they both realised, Susanne.

Making a statement, thought Kate. Why ever is she dressed like that?

'This is my husband, Martin.'

She presented him like royalty, someone they'd been longing to meet. He shook their hands for slightly too long, giving each a formal nod and a glimpse of his even, white teeth. He was short, only a few inches bigger than Susanne, with curly hair and a neat, carefully trimmed beard.

'We got married exactly a year ago. Well, a year ago yesterday. It's why we weren't here for last night's meal. Martin took me to a two-starred Michelin restaurant.' She tipped her head to one side and gave him a newly-wed smile. She fluttered her dark blue eyelids. 'Martin's a retired dentist, so he'll fit in well with us. He'll understand any pharmacy jokes.'

She giggled and even Willy was silenced by her schoolgirl manner and the way she spoke for her husband as if he had no voice. She didn't look directly at Kate and for her part Kate wondered why she had come over to them. Their last encounter had been unpleasant. Well, it had been for Kate; Susanne may have remembered it differently.

So she's showing off a husband, Kate mused. Times have changed and so has she. Perhaps she wants me to know that.

'Well, delighted to meet you, Martin. You're a brave guy, joining a reunion of people you've never met.' Kate decided talking to him was preferable to listening to her.

'I don't mind that. Susanne wanted me to come so I couldn't say no.'

'A retired dentist? Have you been retired long?'

'Six months. Decided to go early and do other things. I had my own successful practice so I was able to sell it with no problem.'

Oh, God, another boaster, full of himself.

'Started off in hospital, like many of my contemporaries, then became an associate at an inner-city dentist's practice. Taught me a lot. In particular, it taught me I didn't want to stay there.' He straightened his shoulders to show he was above such places and made a noise in his throat that may have been an attempt at a chuckle.

'Managed to get a substantial loan to set myself up in Leamington Spa. Bought a small, well-run practice from a guy who was emigrating. It was onwards and upwards from then on. I specialised in orthodontics and you hardly see a child without a brace on their teeth these days. So work, private work in particular, was plentiful.'

Kate started to turn off. Life histories bored her and she didn't want to compete for accolades. Willy, on the other hand, was eager to counter these successes. His eyes were bright as marbles and his mouth was moving in anticipation of the words they were about to spout. He never tired of telling his story.

'Gratifying to hear about success. I've had my fair share of it, too.'

Kate heard him metaphorically saying "If you're sitting

comfortably, then I'll begin."

'Don't know if Susanne ever mentioned it, but getting a First here was difficult in our day. Usually only one a year was awarded.'

He kept his face turned away from Kate.

'Well, I was fortunate to get the First and it opened doors for me. I went on to get a PhD.'

'So you're a Doctor.'

'Yes, a proper one. Most medical doctors aren't doctors at all. I'm sure you're aware of that. It's a courtesy title. Not many have Doctorates in medicine. They mostly have a Batchelor's degree. MBChB: Batchelor of Medicine, Batchelor of Surgery. Had a few spats with a medic friend of mine about it!'

Willy laughed and Martin nodded several times until the spring in his neck ran down.

'Then I went into industry. Joseph Barker & Co. Ltd. Started off coordinating clinical trials in the UK, then managed a group with responsibility for European Studies. Later on, I moved to their manufacturing site, running the tablet manufacturing suite. Then I became Head of Production for a couple of years until I was promoted to the Site Lead Team. I was the youngest member of the Team.'

He beamed but got no response.

'Any time now I'm expecting to be moved to one of our European affiliates as the Managing Director of the site. A pretty rapid rise, eh?'

He finished his announcement but there was no applause. No-one needed so much information. No-one asked anything for fear of being told. To fill the gap, Willy turned to Susanne who was sitting as close to Martin as was physically possible, stroking his hand.

'So, Susanne, what do you do now?'

'Oh, I stopped practising pharmacy a long time ago. Retail bored me. I got no joy out of advising old women about their

151

arthritis and selling tights and baby food. I took a counselling course and work with a gay-rights organisation. Stayed on the register in case I ever felt the need to return.'

'Do you think you might?'

'No, never. Membership is a waste of money. I don't think I'll renew it again. And anyway, I'm working reduced hours since we got married. I might stop working altogether.'

She looked fondly at Martin, her rich reason for giving up work.

Kate stood up, gathered Willy's index cards together and slipped them in his folder for him.

'There you are, Willy, don't want these to go astray.'

She put the photographs carefully in the large envelope in the order they decided.

'All set for this evening. I'll pop along to the Business Centre and get them to scan these. Good luck with the speech, Willy. I'm looking forward to it.' Kate said goodbye, see you later, to the others and walked away.

'Pardon me, I thought Susanne said your name was Gabriel?' Martin, a stickler for correctness, noticed the discrepancy.

'It is. Kate is stubborn and insists on using an old nickname. If you want to know, ask Susanne.'

On the way to the Business Centre, Kate popped into the Ladies. She took the photographs out of the envelope and shuffled them like a pack of cards before straightening them up and placing them back in the envelope. It took no time.

'Can I help you?'

The young girl on the desk in the Business Centre looked up as Kate entered.

'Yes, you can. I need these photos scanned into the laptop. Keep them in the order they are arranged so we can run them as a slide show. They are for Gabriel Williamson. Charge it to him. He will need them at dinner.'

152

'Oh yes. The gentleman organising the reunion.'

'When can I collect the laptop?'

'In an hour's time. Unless you'd like it delivered to the dining room?'

'No, I'll come and collect it. And please can you put a screen up in the private dining room?'

'No problem.'

Kate thanked her and walked out, fingering the two index cards in her pocket. He'd have to manage without those. How careless of him to lose them!

Chapter 13

Kate called Becky to ask what her evening plans were.

'Unfortunately, I need to go back to finish the evening shift and lock up. Mary is flapping too much.'

'Oh, no! When are you leaving?'

'Soon. I'll wait until just before dinner so I get chance to say my farewells to everyone. I expect they'll meet in the bar. I don't want just to disappear. Doesn't seem right. Who knows when we'll meet again – if we'll ever meet again?'

'Well the proposal is to meet early, around six-thirty, with the formal dinner at seven-thirty.'

'That will work for me. I can say goodbye and be on the road by seven o'clock. It'll only take me half an hour and then Mary can go home.'

'I need your help before you go. Can we talk?'

'Oh, Kate, can't you manage without me? I've got enough on my plate at the moment.'

'Please – let me explain the situation to you. You might feel differently then.'

'You do put demands on a friendship.'

'Come for a walk in the garden. A breath of air will help us both.'

Becky sighed. 'A short walk. I'll see you by the front door.'

Five minutes later, they wandered off along the path around the hotel, away from unwanted ears. Becky looked at her watch, making the point she needed to get away within the hour.

'I'm not sure I want to take part in your games anymore.'

She was becoming involved in Kate's life and her face showed she didn't like it.

'I've distracted Colin so you could work your evil wiles on Jonathan, whatever they were. Then I brought him down a peg or two, although that was more for me than you. I've embarrassed Simon into buying me a drink. Who now?'

'Susanne. I'll let you off dealing with Willy – it's in hand! Pity you won't be at the dinner to see. I think you'd enjoy it.'

Although Kate laughed, Becky didn't join in.

'Susanne, eh? So what's your problem with her? I didn't think you knew her well. She didn't mix much with pharmacists. There was a rumour she was gay but I wouldn't hold that against her.'

'It wasn't a rumour. She claimed to be bisexual, but I didn't discover that until right at the end of the course. After our encounter together.'

Becky started to show marginal interest in the story. She watched Kate closely.

'I've not told this to anyone before, Becky, so it's in confidence. Actually, I'm finding it surprisingly difficult to tell you. I think a glass of wine would help.'

'Kate, I don't have the time and I can't drink. You know I'm driving. Either you tell me or you don't. It's up to you but it needs to be quick.'

'Okay, okay. After Jonathan dropped me, I was a mess. The whole thing came out of the blue and I was unprepared. We were in our final year, I was determined to get a good degree but this knocked me off my feet. I couldn't work but knew I had to. I couldn't concentrate but the fact I wasn't studying was making me panic. I didn't know where to turn.'

'You could have turned to me.'

'I could but I didn't. You were in the throes of an affair with a guy from geography and, as I recall, spent most of your time with him. You weren't around.'

155

'Well, there was Pauline, the ever-caring Pauline. Your flat mate, for God's sake! She was always a sympathetic shoulder to cry on.'

'True. But I wasn't logical. I wasn't thinking straight. I can look back, as you're doing, and think of the alternatives. Hindsight doesn't have emotion to contend with.'

'So what happened?'

'I was leaking distress from every pore. I thought I might be able to work better in the library where there were no associations with Jonathan. The department and my flat were filled with his presence, his smell, his voice, his laughter – his betrayal.'

'Hang on, Kate. Keep to the facts. Don't overdo it. I don't need a DramSoc performance.' Becky interrupted, tired of being a listening service.

'It's still so vivid. But you're right. I'll keep to the bare bones. I was making an attempt at working in the library when I saw Jonathan go past the window. He didn't see me but it tipped me over the edge again. I rushed into the Ladies and sat on the floor and cried. That's where Susanne found me.'

'Fortunate she did. You needed someone.'

'She suggested I go back to her flat to talk through my problems. I thought maybe someone I hardly knew might be better than a friend. More dispassionate, more divorced from the situation. So I went back with her. It was a Friday afternoon and we talked all evening. I poured out my heart; I told her my problems – well, many of them. She made us cheese omelettes, I remember. At around midnight, she suggested I stay. There were no lectures on Saturday, I didn't have a reason to go back. It was neutral territory. It was an easy option.'

'Did you stay?'

'Yes. I slept in her bed with her. In her double bed. She lent me a T-shirt to sleep in and a spare toothbrush. She put her arm around me and smoothed my hair. Before we went to sleep, she kissed me on the cheek.'

'So what about her being bisexual? This sounds pretty innocent.'

'I haven't finished yet. I had no idea what her sexual preferences were at that point. She consoled me when I needed it, and I felt better the following morning. I had a decent night's sleep, the first since Jonathan left me, and had unburdened myself. It was cathartic. We spent Saturday together, wandered around the shops, kept away from the campus, did no revision. She said it was therapeutic for me to do something different. One day wasn't going to alter the degree I got after three years' work. And I believed her. She was right, the break helped but I'd never have managed it on my own, would never have seen it as a solution.'

'This is a long story, Kate, and so far I can't see Susanne has done anything but show you kindness.'

'I'm not drawing it out unnecessarily. You need to understand the situation I was in.'

'Keep going.'

'We bought a bottle of wine for the evening and crisps. Then mince and onions to make spaghetti bolognaise. I had gone into shadow mode, following Susanne, doing as she suggested. She was pleasant company, chatting away about inconsequential things, light-hearted, amusing. I was relaxing, my head stopped aching and when we put a silly programme on TV in the early evening, I actually laughed. I was in a parallel world where I could forget my problems. I remember she painted my finger nails for me. She always had beautiful nails herself. Still has. I noticed them today. The only feature I envied.'

They had completed the circuit of the hotel and were back near the door.

'Please, Becky. I need a drink for the next part. You can have a fruit juice.'

'If you must. I shall start to think you have a reason to delay me from leaving if you don't get on with this story.'

Becky gave her a suspicious look but Kate was too wound

157

up to notice. They took their drinks into a quiet corner of the bar.

'The wine slipped down easily and we drank most of it before the meal was ready so it went to my head. When Susanne started telling me I was beautiful, I thought she was trying to make me feel better. She put her arms around me and pressed me to her. And I responded. I was stupid. I had no idea what her motives were. I thought she was another Pauline who hugged everyone.'

Kate swallowed a mouthful of wine, then another. She ran her fingers through her hair, closing her eyes and biting her lip. She looked around to make sure there was no-one within earshot. Becky looked at her watch.

'Then she kissed me. Not the peck on the cheek of the night before but a proper kiss. I can remember the texture of her lips and how she pushed her tongue into my mouth. I pulled away, it was a reflex action, but she had her hand round the back of my head and it was difficult to escape. She finished the kiss and smiled at me. I remember her words.'

'First time, isn't it, Kate?' she said.

I nodded.

'Don't worry. I'll treat you gently. I'll show you how wonderful another woman's body can be, how velvet skin against velvet skin has the most ecstatic feel. I'll introduce you to new pleasures. This is what you need, Kate. A woman's touch. It will heal you and wipe away the hurt. There are delights waiting for you, thrills beyond your imagination. I can lead you there. Let me. You don't need a man, you don't need Jonathan. You'll never need a man again.'

'Her words were hypnotic. It was like a chant, an incantation luring me on. I never had any contact with a woman, physical, sexual contact I mean, had no lesbian thoughts. I was a man's woman through and through. I was out of my depth. I kept saying no, but she ignored me. She stroked my face gently, running her fingers down my neck and across my shoulders. Then she went into the kitchen, leaving me to think. My head was full of confused thoughts. Part of me said I should leave, take my wounds elsewhere and deal with them differently. But inertia and wine were winning. So I sat there as if in a trance not knowing what would happen or even what I wanted to happen.

'Susanne joined me again, emptied the remaining wine into our glasses and gave me mine, telling me to drink. So I did, we both did. We watched television with her holding my hand. Then we ate. I was extremely hungry and ate everything she placed in front of me. It was like being a child again, clearing my plate as my mother told me to do.

'By this time I was feeling unaccountably sleepy. It was a pleasant sensation and I couldn't fight it. She led me into the bedroom and suggested I got into bed. She helped me undress and then we were both lying naked on the bed. She placed my hands on her breasts and I can still feel how round and soft they were. Jonathan's words ran through my head; he always loved the softness of my breasts. I was doing what he did and it was wrong. I remember the mix of uncontrolled excitement and repulsion. Then her hands slid down my body and her fingers crept between my legs. She started to touch me.'

Kate stopped suddenly, breathless. She licked her lips as if the words had dried them out. Perhaps she had said too much.

'I don't need to give you the details. You can imagine the rest.'

'Seems you were not exactly an unwilling participant. You can't lay all the blame on Susanne. And anyway, you're not the first to have experimented sexually. It's harmless, you know. I don't know why this is bothering you so much.'

'I have my reasons, believe me. What happened next is hazy; it's like looking back through a mist. I was almost comatose. I know Susanne made love to me. I know she kissed me, licked me, used her fingers and her tongue in places that excited and reviled me. And I didn't resist, or my resistance was ineffective. I gave in to her will. It was as if Jonathan was there and I was

159

experiencing the pleasure he gave me but it wasn't him when I opened my eyes. And all this because Susanne slipped something into my last glass of wine.'

'What? Do you believe that? It's a major accusation. Are you talking about a sedative?'

'A drug like Rohypnol.'

'Oh, God. The date-rape drug. Where did she get it? We didn't have access to drugs in the department. Not things like that anyway. Did you go for a urine test afterwards?'

'No. Didn't think about it. I suppose I could have. I'm guessing what it was. And how would I know where she got it? It could have been prescribed for her for sleeplessness. Or maybe for a member of her family and she helped herself. She might have bought it illegally. But it was weeks afterwards when I thought through everything and realised what had happened – what I now believe happened.'

'So what next?'

'The following morning, Susanne was up before me. I slept late, presumably sleeping off the effect of the drug. Then I told her she had misread me, I wasn't interested in that kind of relationship. She laughed and said I'd change my mind. To go away and think about it. She kept touching me, my arm, my hair. Nothing forceful. She was like an insect I couldn't brush away. But I never let her get near me again. She tried many times. I got notes after lectures, pleading with me to see her again. Telling me I was wrong to reject her. Saying I was afraid of the unknown, she'd go slowly with me and I would learn to love her. I never replied. I never acknowledged her presence. Eventually she gave up. At least she wasn't as persistent as Colin had been.'

Kate downed the rest of her wine.

'Well, there you are. Now you know why I need to get back at her. What she did was unforgiveable, criminal. I felt nauseous when I thought of that evening for months afterwards. But it shook me up and I got back to working afterwards.'

160

'So something positive came out of it.'

'Becky, how can you say that? Can't you understand what I suffered? It's why I've given you so much detail.'

Becky shrugged her shoulders.

'You can't prove what she did. You didn't find it pleasant but I think the best approach is to put it behind you and ignore her. You're not obliged to talk to her.'

'No. I need my revenge. I need to get this out of my system. She's obviously besotted with that stiff dentist of hers, so I thought maybe I could get back at her through him. But I'll need her out of the way. Could you distract her? Tell her about the new department?'

'I didn't go on the tour so I don't know much about it. Anyway, I need to get away. I don't have the time. And I don't approve of this. You're going too far this time, Kate.'

'Becky, just twenty minutes? It's all I need with him. It's enough for me to formulate a idea, see how susceptible he is. Please engage her in something, anything. I know – show her your photos. I've got them back from the Business Centre. They've been scanned into my laptop. Willy is using them this evening as part of his speech.'

Becky took the large envelope from Kate.

'Okay, I'll show her the photos, assuming she's interested. But that's it. No more. I'm leaving. And don't tell me what the outcome of it is. As you said, it's on a need-to-know basis, and I don't need to know.'

'Well, let's see if we can catch them in the lounge before they go to their room. I wonder if Susanne is already dressed for dinner in that weird outfit or if we'll see an even stranger one? Be prepared for a sight!'

161

Chapter 14

Willy was still talking to Martin and Susanne when they returned to the hotel lounge. It appeared to be a game of ping-pong. I'll hit a minor success to you and see if you can counter it. Then I might be able to smash a real triumph across that you have no hope of returning. Willy was enjoying himself, there being no subject closer to his heart than himself. Martin was determined to appear superior to Willy in Susanne's eyes so was promoting his own achievements with vigour.

Makes me sick, thought Kate, but it did have the advantage of boring Susanne. She had a vacant look on her face that made her look like a doll, a badly dressed one, a six-year-old's attempt at style.

'Still here?' Kate asked. 'Thought you might have disappeared to get ready for dinner. I hear we're meeting at six-thirty in the bar.'

Willy glanced at his watch.

'Still plenty of time. I don't need long to put my make-up on.' He laughed at his own wit. 'But you girls might.'

He looked across at the three female members of the company.

'Sorry, girls. It wasn't meant to imply you didn't look made-up already. I meant women usually need time to get ready. But then, you might already be ready.' He addressed his last comment at Susanne. 'I think I'll shut up.'

'You know what they say, Willy. When you get yourself into a hole, stop digging!'

'Diplomacy was never my thing. A man of straight

162

words.' He could turn most situations to his advantage.

Susanne bounced back out of her day-dream like a puppet whose master had just pulled the strings.

'I'd like to go to our room. Are you coming Martin?'

'In a minute. I want to finish this story I'm telling Wi ...Gabriel.'

'Shall I go on up?'

Kate looked across at Becky and the eye contact said, 'Now's your chance.'

'Susanne – you might like to have a look at the photos I've got from our student years. You're on one or two of them, I think. Unfortunately, I won't be able to stay for dinner. I'll be popping in to see everyone in the bar but my locum has problems so I have to go and relieve her. If you're going upstairs, you could come via my room.'

Susanne looked across at Martin and tipped her head at him. He shrugged his shoulders.

'No point in me coming with you. They'd not mean anything. But you go and have a look – you'll enjoy it. I'll see you in our room.'

Willy got up, pleased to have the thread of Martin's tale broken. He had marginally lost the last rally and was getting tired of the game.

'Think I'll check the dining room. Make sure they've set up the screen and projector in the right place.'

Kate encouraged him. 'Best to make sure, Willy. I've picked up the laptop. The photos have been scanned in.'

Kate was left facing Martin. 'Then there were two. Would you like a drink?'

'Shouldn't really, but a pint won't hurt.'

Kate bought the beer and had a sparkling water with ice and lime herself. It looked like a G & T.

'Well, Martin, I'm glad to hear Susanne is married. You both look happy.'

'Oh, she's such a loving girl. I can't believe how lucky I am. Didn't think I would marry. She's the most wonderful thing that ever happened to me.'

'So may I ask - why did you not expect to marry?'

'Never met the right person as a student. Nor in my younger adult years. Dentistry can be lonely. Always with people but not socially. They are patients. And that relationship is formal and protected. Not done to fall for a patient, you know!'

Kate smiled sympathetically.

'And then my mother was ill, so I moved back home to nurse her. I know that sounds strange, a son looking after his mother. But we were close. And when my father died, his last request was that I take care of her. And I did financially. It was no problem. I never thought I'd end up as her carer, though.'

'When did she die?'

'Six years ago. I became lonely and put my efforts into work. And it had its compensations. I opened a second surgery and made a name for myself. But I felt I was missing out on life, the world had more than dentistry to offer. Then I met Susanne.'

'How did you meet?'

'In the strangest of ways. She slipped on the icy pavement one winter's day outside the surgery and banged her head against the wall. My receptionist saw it happen and went out. She suspected concussion, so they brought her in. Anyway, after a while she seemed alright but I took her phone number and called her later that evening to check. She invited me out for a drink to thank me. And it moved on from there.'

Kate reached out and patted his hand, a friendly gesture but she wanted to see how he reacted to the familiarity of an attractive woman. He smiled like a kindly uncle. Her touch had done nothing. It was unnoticed and unfelt. Or regarded as innocent. Sexual allure looked like a dead-end here. He was still a newly-wed with no thoughts of wandering. Jonathan had cheated on his new wife; this one lived in a faithful world. Damn it, first failure. Getting back at Susanne wouldn't be through Martin. She would have to find a different approach.

'I didn't know Susanne well as a student. Not for most of the course, anyway. We did have more contact in the final year. Has she talked much about her time here?'

'Oh yes. We talk about everything. It's one of the wonderful aspects of our relationship. We are completely open with each other. I've heard folk say we look – how shall I describe it? An odd match, maybe. But you can't judge from the outside.'

Martin was at ease. A pint of beer and talking about Susanne turned him into a different person with no need for self-promotion.

'Did Susanne say she was a happy student here?'

'To be honest, it was mixed. Her enthusiasm for pharmacy waned early on in the course. There was too much pure science in it and she felt she'd only get a mediocre degree. She considered changing to sociology or psychology. I think she should have done. As you know, she left the profession a long time ago. She didn't mix much with her pharmacy colleagues. She told me she felt an outsider, she didn't fit in.'

'I don't recall seeing her at any of our parties. But then, I didn't go to many of them. I was a swot!'

They laughed together.

'Now this may sound strange,' Martin continued, not wanting to move on from his dearest subject. 'Her social life seemed to centre on the gay and lesbian community.'

So she's told him her background, Kate thought. This is what I need to know.

'She's such a caring person. She got to know – I forget how or where – a young guy struggling with his sexuality. He told her his problems and how he was afraid to admit openly he was gay. She supported him. She was unthreatening and a patient listener and eventually he came out. Through him, she got to know other gay individuals and mixed a lot with them.'

'And presumably it's why she went on to get a job in the Gay Rights area.'

'Exactly. She felt she had a rapport with most of the community, even though she's always been one hundred percent straight herself.'

Kate hoped he missed the surprised look on her face. Our little Susanne is more devious than he knows, she thought.

'In fact, she had a most unfortunate episode in her last year as a student.' He looked around the room as if to check for eavesdroppers. 'Maybe I shouldn't tell you this.' Another pause. 'Well, it's a long time ago. I'm sure Susanne won't mind. Just keep it to yourself.'

'I will.'

'One of the girls she befriended took advantage of her. This individual, a lesbian, had been badly let down by her partner. Kay I think she was called. Anyway, Kay's girlfriend abandoned her unexpectedly and left her in a total emotional mess. Susanne had recently split with her boyfriend of the time so they were partners in distress, you might say. Susanne invited Kay to her flat where they talked through their problems. Susanne said they both felt much better for it and built up a rapport. They were enjoying each other's company until Kay ruined everything.'

Martin looked around furtively and moved his chair closer to Kate. He seemed to be getting a vicarious pleasure from telling the story and lowered his voice to create the right atmosphere.

'Apparently, Kay made a pass at Susanne. Being naturally friendly, Susanne took it to be affection and didn't resist. However, when it became obvious what Kay's intentions were, she called a halt. But she left it too late. They'd been watching TV and drinking wine and Kay had slipped something into her drink. Susanne thinks it may have been Rohypnol.'

'My God!'

'Poor Susanne was subjected to a lesbian assault. I won't go into the details of what Kay did although Susanne has told me.

166

She has never forgotten the incident. It scarred her badly. I think of this when I take her in my arms. I hope my love will wipe away the memory, or at least make it fade.'

'Was it a shock this girl wanted a relationship with her? With all her gay friends, she must have had approaches before.'

Kate was treading carefully but probing as much as she could.

'Susanne wasn't naïve. Yes, she'd been propositioned and she knew what went on. But being forced to participate by being drugged was unexpected and shocking.'

'Would you have minded if she'd been a lesbian at the time herself?'

Dodgy question, am I pushing my luck?

Martin frowned, his thick eyebrows joining in the middle, a stern, black line across his eyes.

'Well, had she been a lesbian, I don't think she'd have married me, would she?'

'I suppose I should have said bisexual, not lesbian.'

'It's a theoretical question. Can't say I've given it much thought. I'm not homophobic but I would prefer to have a straight wife.'

He gave Kate a look that said he knew she was with him.

Kate had a whirlpool of thoughts rushing round her head. Should she disillusion him? She could tell him a few truths, drop a few heavy hints. But while it might give him doubts about his lovely Susanne, there was a chance he'd not believe her. It could be a bigger failure than her attempts at seduction. No, she had to be more elusive than that. And time was getting short. She had to find inspiration before the evening was out. Martin was still talking.

'You must think I'm an old fool to be so captivated with Susanne.'

'Of course not. I'm pleased for you. But if you don't mind a comment, I do agree you are an unexpected couple. I'm talking

167

about appearances now.'

Martin threw his head back as he hooted with laughter. He looked down at his neat brown trousers with their sharp creases, his tucked-in checked shirt, leather belt and polished brogues.

'You're right there! I'm middle of the road with my dress sense. Smart, I like to think, but nothing to attract undue attention. Now, Susanne – she's amazing!'

'She didn't dress like that as a student. She looked much like the rest of us – jeans and a sweater.'

'Well, when we met, she dressed normally. I mean, nicely, she always looked elegant and pretty, but she's changed since she's been with me. She says I'm a new phase of her life. That I make her feel different, that I make her feel special.'

Martin coughed and looked self-conscious, perhaps revealing too much.

'Anyway, she gradually started wearing more unusual dresses. I'm used to it now and think it suits her; it's feminine. But she does surprise people. Especially those who haven't seen her recently, like the folk here.'

'She surprised me, that's for sure.'

'I may be a new phase in her life but for me it's been a total change. I never realised how wonderful being in love could be. All those years with myself for company. What a waste! But better late than never, eh? Maybe you also know the feeling?'

Kate thought of Jonathan. 'Oh, yes, I understand completely.'

'So you're married?'

'Yes. A long time. Twenty years.'

'Is your husband here?'

'No. He wasn't interested in coming. Anyway, he's busy this weekend preparing for an exhibition he's putting on soon. He's a photographer.'

'How interesting! What's the exhibition?'

Kate was getting bored. She learned all she could. And she

didn't want any more clichés about love in later life. But as Martin had talked so much, she felt obliged to offer information in return. She didn't want her digging to be obvious.

'It's called "Love Hurts". It's a photographic representation of the suffering that can result from loving and caring. He photographs people. Not formal portraits or family groups – although he might earn more money doing that – but people in interesting circumstances. He has wonderful, heart-rending pictures for this exhibition. One in particular, of a child being dragged away from her mother as the mother is arrested. How he gets them, I don't know; he has an eye for catching the right moment. This exhibition is different in that there is a description under each picture giving it background and context. He doesn't normally add text. But it works well here, gives depth to the whole concept. He is talented; he's won awards for his work.'

'Well, I'll keep my eye open for this one.'

As Martin downed the last of his beer, Susanne walked in.

'Thought you were coming up. I went to our room but couldn't get in as you've got the key.'

'Sorry. Got chatting to Kate and didn't notice the time. How were the photos?'

'It was nostalgic to see them. I was only in two. One taken just after we started – a group of us outside the old department. I looked so young! Then another group one at Graduation. The intervening time seems to have disappeared.'

'Well you said your social life was elsewhere. We've been talking about it.'

Susanne glanced quickly at Kate whose face was blank.

'A bit of reminiscing. You have a delightful husband, Susanne. I've enjoyed getting to know him.'

Susanne nodded and turned her smile to Martin. 'Come on, we need to go to our room.'

'See you later, Kate'.

Martin patted her shoulder in a genial manner as he passed behind her chair. So much for my sexual attraction, she thought, as she made her way towards Becky's room.

'So, how did you get on with Martin?' Becky was rushing round her untidy room gathering odds and ends into her suitcase.

'I thought you said not to tell you, you didn't want to know?'

'I don't want the gory details. A brief resumé will do.'

'I got on fine. He's an easy guy to talk to. I got the impression he was trying to make up for many lonely years by talking as much as he could.'

'It doesn't answer my question. I've just wasted half an hour talking to Susanne so you could have time with him. Did you spill the beans about her nasty activities?'

'No. He's so much under her spell he'd never have believed me. And trying to flirt with him was a complete waste of time. So there's no way I can get back at Susanne through him. A total failure. But I did learn some useful information.'

'Well?'

'Sorry, Becky. A bit complex and you're in a hurry. Tell you later!'

'So do you have a Plan B?'

'At the moment I don't. And whatever it is, I'll have to manage it alone since you're deserting me.'

'You could let it go. Go and enjoy the dinner and forget about revenge. Be a normal person.'

'I could. But I won't. I know you don't approve. Don't give me that look.'

Becky rolled her eyes as she closed her suitcase. Kate bent down and fished a shoe from under the bed.

'Yours?'

'Oh, thanks. A bit disorganised this evening. I'm off now. Be sensible, Kate. See you sometime.'

Chapter 15

Becky was rushing from person to person in the bar saying her goodbyes, promising to keep in touch, hugging everyone, being Becky. She was on her way out when Jonathan wandered in with a large dressing on his ear.

'Goodness, Jonathan, whatever have you done?'

'I slipped down the stairs last night. Maybe had a nightcap too many! Fell against the corner of a metal table on the half-landing.' He indicated with his head the direction of the offending staircase. 'You won't believe this but I tore off a piece of earlobe!'

'Really?' A bad injury then?'

'No, not that bad. I'll survive! But it's a difficult place to put a dressing. I popped into A & E and they did it for me.'

Jonathan gathered a group round him listening to his story. Simon was attentive.

'You might have a case against the hotel for having a table in an unsafe place on the staircase.'

'Trust a lawyer to think on those lines!'

'I'm serious, Jonathan. People have won damages in cases like that.'

'It was my own fault. I should have watched where I was putting my feet. Or had less to drink. I'm not into suing unnecessarily. But thanks for your advice, Simon.' Jonathan smiled. 'Hope you don't expect me to pay for it! I'll buy you a drink though.'

Simon had his wallet in his hand, a fat object which he immediately pocketed at Jonathan's suggestion.

I walked in during this conversation and heard most of it. Jonathan handled it niftily, I thought. It was his first appearance since the previous evening and my stomach lurched as I saw him.

***

The previous evening with Jonathan. I took a large breath. Going back to his room was in my plan. There was still physical attraction; that was clear at the reception. The way he looked at me, his easy familiarity taking us back three decades. I needed that, needed to get him under my control. I'd worked out the sequence of events. Knew what I had to do. But once he began to kiss me and our bodies touched, reality took away my strength and resolve. I had no desire but to escape, was desperate to return to my room, the closeness of Jonathan being unbearable. My carefully laid snare was unworkable; I didn't have the guts or the concentration to go through with it. But as I threw my clothes on, Jonathan came across and pulled me back to the bed. He spoke quietly and intensely, calming me down, telling me we could turn back the clock once; we owed it to ourselves. I can't let this happen, I thought; I need to distract myself. And as he spoke, I hardened my will. There was one way to do it. I hadn't thought this through beforehand, but a ploy came to mind that could work. A way to keep myself strong and continue.

I let Jonathan undress me again, stroke me and continue his lovemaking. He was lying beside me, his old skills thrilling me, taking me back instantly to the past. But I had to occupy and divert my brain and knew a smart way to do it. An activity as far removed from love-making as could be. Calculations. Mental arithmetic. It was a skill of mine. I concentrated my thoughts. A straightforward sum to start with: 27 x 24. Two sevens are fourteen, two twos are four plus one is five. That's 540. Oh, God, I must keep focussed! Four sevens are twenty eight, four twos are eight, plus two is 108. The answer is 648. It didn't matter if it was right or wrong as long as it kept me occupied. It was succeeding.

Then Jonathan was lying on me, and slid easily inside me. I let him carry on, moved with him, cried out his name, groaned, dug my nails in his sides, told him to push harder, said I needed this, he was right, this was a special moment. 14 x 36. And inside my head, my mantra was repeating itself over and over, keep control, keep control. Three fours are twelve, three ones are three plus one is four. My actions had to appear spontaneous, but spontaneity was a risk. I knew I could so easily lose myself. That's 420 – or was it 440? No, 420. Jonathan did all I asked and we went through the love-making routine of our past. Six fours are twenty four, one six is six plus two is eight. That's 84. 420 plus 84 is 504. We changed positions and I sat astride him, leaning back so that my breasts looked their best.

'Is this still your favourite?' I asked.

'Oh, yes, but you can't do wrong, Kate. You can't do wrong.'

Exactly what I wanted to hear.

On and on, keep control, harder, faster, keep it going, raise the pressure, build the tension, keep control, keep control. 77 x 31. Three sevens are …Oh, I can't be bothered, I can't work out another one! Can I manage without the maths now? I think so. Jonathan was now absorbed with himself. He stopped caressing me in his tender, sensitive way and was lying on me, working towards his climax, anticipation driving him on. I knew he was close and started to bite his neck, moving my mouth towards his ear. He moaned. Keep control. Don't need the arithmetic any longer. But it worked. I knew precisely what I must do next.

As he called out and ejaculated, I bit his ear. I bit with all the force I could manage. As I planned, I bit completely through the lobe. I could taste the metallic bitterness of blood in my mouth and feel its stickiness; I forced myself not to heave. Jonathan shouted in pain and pushed me away. I spat out the piece of ear onto the bed, where it lay, a weird trophy, testament to my success. With tears running down my face and blood on my lips, I gathered up my clothes, dragged on my dress, stuffed underwear in my handbag and feet in my shoes. Jonathan was looking in the mirror, swearing vigorously and trying to mop up the pouring blood with pieces of toilet paper. There was a spotted, red trail across the cream bedroom carpet. I doubt he heard my final words as I opened the door to leave.

'You marked me for life; now I've done the same to you.'

I rushed back to my room, glad to see no-one on the way, and threw myself onto the bed. But nausea was more powerful than fatigue and drove me to the bathroom where I threw up violently in the toilet. I was exhausted, drained of feeling. I could not judge my own actions; I was confused by the plethora of emotions that tore through me. How close love and hatred are! After a while, my heartrate slowed and I started to think rationally. I could still taste his blood – impossible after repeatedly cleaning my teeth, I knew – but the sourness remained. I expected to be elated by success but elation, if it was there, was well buried.

And now it amused me that Simon was keen on suing the hotel for a bitten ear.

Chapter 16

Simon went up the staircase to look at the offending table. It was in a silly place. Not exactly blocking access but clearly dangerous if anyone slipped. Jonathan was stupid, Simon thought. Suing would earn him a decent compensation and make the hotel think, get their place in order. His lawyer's brain clicked into gear but he stopped himself. His business, he thought, not mine.

The bar was filling up. There was the chatter of discovery. 'Did you go into the new shopping centre?' 'Nothing like that when we were students!' 'We had lunch at a lovely deli. Mind you, wouldn't have been able to afford such prices thirty years ago.' 'Can't believe I haven't been back in all these years.' 'Should have had a ten year reunion or a twenty year one. A lot of courses do.' 'Isn't it funny how you pick up the threads of friendship where you left them?' 'People haven't changed much, inside I mean.' 'Well there are a few exceptions!' 'If you close your eyes, people sound the same as they used to.'

As Simon moved from the bar with a glass in his hand, Kate waylaid him. 'Hello, Simon. We've not had chance to talk yet.'

Simon looked her up and down, making no secret of his admiration.

'No, but I noticed you. You have an air of success about you.'

Kate looked shocked then said, 'Kate Shaw Pharmacies, Ltd?'

'What else? Gratifying to see you doing so well. I think success is attractive. It suits a woman.' Well, he hadn't intended to chat her up, but then you never know.

'And it suits a man.'

'Well, I can't complain. They say whatever the outcome of a case, the lawyer is the one who wins. I don't dispute it.'

He twiddled a thick gold ring on his little finger as he spoke, more a habit than a way of showing off. But it nevertheless drew Kate's attention to the large diamond embedded in the centre.

'So things have looked up since your student days?'

'Life is different now. I don't want to talk about those times. I hated being poor, really hated it. I enjoy my luxuries. It's one of the reasons I left pharmacy.'

'You can make an adequate living out of pharmacy. Don't run it down. You just need a bit of enterprise and the willingness to take a risk or two.'

'Yes, and capital to get you started. Or a guarantor. I had neither. So I sat down shortly after graduation and went through the options dispassionately. One thing was sure. I didn't want to be one of these.'

He cast his eyes around the roomful of pharmacists, trying not to show how little he thought of them.

'You're being harsh. And unfair. These are dedicated people who work hard. Where would our hospitals be without them? Who would staff our retail pharmacies?'

'I'm not knocking their jobs. If they've found what they want to do, I'm pleased for them. They have my admiration,' he lied, scorn polluting his words. 'It wasn't for me.' He took a swig of his beer.

'So why did you study pharmacy in the first place?'

'It's a mystery to me, too. I think I had a vision of owning a large chain. A competitor for Boots, something like that. Like you've done.'

'I'm hardly in Boots' league!'

'Perhaps not. But you're doing well. I've noticed an

increase in the number of premises carrying your name. Anyway, my teenage innocence hadn't looked into the finances required for a project like that. I then thought industry might offer rewards. The top bosses make a mint. You might remember we went on an industrial visit in our final year.'

'I do, indeed. There was the matter of the train fare, I recall.'

Simon shrugged his shoulders and raised his eyebrows to show he'd no idea what she meant. He remembered, undoubtedly, but wasn't going back there. The money was peanuts. He wondered why she'd become petty.

'But after a couple of interviews following graduation, I decided progression might be slow, so I abandoned the idea. I had a lawyer friend who also had a degree in physics. He had made a niche for himself dealing with highly technical cases involving nuclear power. It gave me the idea.'

'But did you think you'd enjoy law?'

'It was irrelevant. I had a goal. I swore to myself I would make money. Serious money. How I got there – providing it was legal – didn't matter. I thought I was bright enough to cope with the work so I simply went through with it.'

'I've seen your name associated with a few cases.'

'It's usually patent disputes. A generic company claims a drug's patent has expired and goes into production of a drug to sell it more cheaply than its current price. Then the drug's parent company points out there are several patents and not all have expired. Very complex, lots of picky details.'

'A lawyer's delight.'

'Yes. Well, yes and no.'

Kate gave him a surprised look – was there an adverse side to his job?

'Yes it's a delight financially. But you can get tired of the same type of dispute. I have a name in this area and am recognised for the success I've achieved. The major pharmaceutical companies hate me. But my niche is now extremely narrow. I can touch the walls on both sides!'

'So why don't you retire and spend your wealth?'

'I'm not ready for that.' He grinned mischievously. 'I'm in the throes of setting up a company to develop and market innovative over-the-counter products. Just about there, in fact.'

'So will this make you even more money?'

'It's the intention although not its main aim. We hope to find gaps in the market place where we can provide products that will work and be readily available. One of our first is a skin cream, a natural product to counter itching, better than the discredited anti-histamine creams.'

'And do you have a name for this company?'

'Clinavail. Keep your eyes open. With my legal background, I can easily deal with any licensing or regulatory issues, and over-the-counter products mean those are fewer anyway.'

'Hell, Simon, you won't know what to do with your money!'

'Don't worry about that. I'll work on it.'

'Well, rumour has it we're going to be asked to contribute to a "Needy Students' Fund" this evening. You will no doubt be a major donor.'

Simon turned his head sharply towards her. Being wealthy had its downside. 'Where did you hear about the fund?'

'I heard it mentioned. The new Head of the Department, Professor Cantwell, is joining us this evening. I believe he's going to make an appeal. In fact, he has just come in. He's over there with Willy. I think I'll introduce myself.'

Kate walked across the room to join a group of people who were talking to the new Head. Don't think I'm getting a second time around with Kate, Simon thought as his mind wandered back to earlier pleasures. I'd have enjoyed it. He watched her for a few moments then turned away. Disliking being one of a crowd, he decided to wait for a more opportune moment to present himself.

'Hello, I'm Kate Shaw. Good of you to join us this evening.'

'Hi, Kate, I'm Roger, Roger Cantwell. It's my great pleasure to be here. I've managed to attend every reunion since I joined the department eighteen months ago. It's important to keep in touch with our alumni. And these are usually interesting events.'

'How are you finding your new job?'

'Exciting, challenging, what I expected. My predecessor is a hard act to follow. But I'm doing my best. We get such excellent students here, always have.'

He looked around the room as if to prove his point.

'It's great the department maintains its reputation. Is the increase in student fees hitting you badly?'

'Well, we are charging the maximum. All the top universities are. So it could be a problem. Although students don't have to pay back their debts straight away. But psychologically, it may put the poorer students off. I wouldn't want any student to suffer that. If they're able enough to come, they should come.'

'There's a "Needy Students' Fund", isn't there? I remember it was being setup around the time we graduated.'

'Yes, but it never had much to give away. It seemed the word "needy" referred to the fund as much as to the students!'

'Well, I'd be happy to make a donation.'

'How generous of you, Kate! Perhaps you'd come and see me after the meal?'

'Certainly. And I'm sure there are others here who would do the same. You could mention it in your speech. Although please don't say the suggestion came from me!'

They laughed conspiratorially.

'Well, I was intending to talk about the "Small Change" fund, a new venture I've established. Maybe I should mention both. Don't want to alienate folk by being greedy.'

'Well, there are individuals who've made significant money. I'm sure they would like to give something back by way of thanks. And even the least well-paid of us owe part of our success to our time here.'

After a few more pleasantries, they parted, Roger circulating as Heads of Departments do. As Kate turned, Willy almost ran into her, shiny face excessively flushed and beads of sweat on his brow.

'Kate, where's the laptop?'

'Set up and ready to go. Nothing to worry about. You can go back to being sociable.'

He gave her a thumbs-up, sighed loudly to show his relief and returned to the bar. She moved on, wondering where the evening would lead. Hopefully not to Jonathan but they ended up unintentionally face to face. Kate expected him to ignore her or make a sarcastic, offensive comment. He was unlikely to make a scene but his feelings would be apparent.

'So here's the wild lady. I didn't expect such passion,' he said quietly. He had a strange look in his eye, not the disgust she was expecting.

'I'm not sure we have anything more to say,' she said.

'It will seem odd if we ignore each other after everyone saw us talking and laughing together last evening.'

Before she could answer, Colin butted in. 'Hope you get a better reception than I did.' He glared at Jonathan. 'What happened? Did she bite your ear off in a hot-blooded embrace?' He didn't wait for an answer, didn't expect one and walked away.

Jonathan looked hard at Kate. 'Surely you didn't tell anyone?'

'What do you take me for? Of course I didn't. It was simply a throw-away line from an aggrieved Colin. He happened to be fairly accurate.'

'So why was he aggrieved? Not stalking again, surely?'

'I don't want to discuss it. Nothing to do with you.' She wanted to get away from this unfathomable Jonathan. She could have dealt with his anger; he wasn't angry enough.

The clinking of a spoon against a glass alerted them.

'Ladies and Gentlemen. Will you please join me for dinner in the dining room?' Roger Cantwell was more successful in moving everyone away from the bar than Willy had been the previous evening. Kate needed to lose Jonathan but didn't want to be too obvious about it. She had to be near Simon.

'Kate! Over here!' Pauline called her.

With relief, she sat beside her, seeing Simon sitting opposite. Perfect. Martin and Susanne were seated at the same table; Jonathan was not. She could see him across the room; as she sat down, he moved one place to the left so that she was directly in his line of sight. Kate frowned at him and looked away. What was he playing at?

'Haven't had much time for a chat. We must catch up on the news.' Pauline caught Kate's attention.

'You never told me how you've managed to keep your figure and looks. What's the secret?'

'No secret. Going to the gym, spending more money than sensible at the beauty salon and hairdresser.'

Pauline moved closer to her so that she could speak quietly into her ear. 'What have you had done?'

'Done? You mean plastic surgery?'

Pauline nodded.

'Nothing, not even Botox.'

'Honestly? You can tell me, I'll keep quiet about it.'

'There's nothing to tell, Pauline.'

'Well, I had a boob job. Had to after three kids. It was inconvenient when they bounced against my knees! How come breast-feeding didn't make you sag?'

'I haven't got children, so the question doesn't apply.' A few months of pregnancy didn't count.

Pauline blushed and put her hand over her mouth. 'Trust me to put my foot in it. Sorry, Kate.'

'No need to be. You're assuming we wanted kids. I was never the maternal type, although we did try for a while. Turned out Neil has a low sperm count. So we decided we were happy enough as we were. End of story.'

'Well, the spin-off is you look great.' Pauline meant it; Kate didn't get many genuine compliments from women.

Roger Cantwell was on his feet and the murmur of voices stopped.

'Welcome everyone. Welcome back to the Pharmacy Department. I am delighted to join you this evening. As I've told several of you, it is a total pleasure to me to meet old students, to hear how you are getting on and to bask in your reflected success. It's gratifying to know your three years here set you up solidly for your future careers.'

Susanne looked at Martin and wrinkled her nose in disagreement.

'Much has changed here since your time. Changed in that we have a brand new building with vastly superior facilities, changed in that there are now two hundred or so students in each year as opposed to your forty. This means the whole dynamics of teaching has altered. We can't hope to know each student as well as your staff knew you although with our tutorial system, staff can build up strong relationships with small groups of students. I know some of you had a tour of the department this morning. I hope it impressed you.'

There was a murmur of assent and nods from all the tables.

'I would like to take this opportunity of publicly thanking our main benefactor, Charles Brookman, after whom the pharmacy building is named, for his huge generosity in providing much of the funding for the new premises. This was matched by the University and it's why we can offer facilities second to none in

Pharmacy education. Charles was a student here around thirty-five years ago but although he left pharmacy, he didn't forget it. He made his money on the stock exchange. It would be my pleasure to tell future students great wealth is there for the taking, but I'm afraid few of us end up in Charles' position.'

This raised a laugh and a few shouts of "Too true".

'Pharmacy is a worthwhile career, a rewarding career where most people's primary aim is to serve the community. However, we have to live and the financial rewards are not insignificant.'

He looked around the room. 'I hope I won't have a queue of hospital pharmacists coming to berate me for that statement afterwards!' He laughed at himself and someone pretended to boo. 'We have job security, few pharmacists are unable to find work...

'Long may it continue!'

'..and the scope and choice of jobs is wider than most professions can offer. In addition, I hear those of you who have left the profession have gone on to have great success elsewhere. Pharmacy is undoubtedly a preparation for life.'

This produced a round of applause and a cheer.

'However, although this is positive, we are always in need of additional cash. I would like to mention two present endeavours. The first is a project I started shortly after taking over the Headship of the department. I was aware it was difficult to give recognition in an on-going way to our students and wanted to be able to do this for specific endeavours. The problem was how to fund such awards.

'I came up with the idea of the "Small Change" award. You may have noticed a hessian sack tied up by the main door into the building with the words "Small Change" on it. We ask visitors – and we get many – to empty their change into the collecting box within the sack. It doesn't matter if it's a few pence or a few pounds. It adds up. When we collect fifty pounds, we make an award. What we make the award for is unspecified but we like to think it's for a "small change", a minor but significant contribution an individual has made, whether it is to the performance of the department or their own achievement record. All students can make nominations and a committee of staff members makes the decision. Usually there are several awards each term.

'So, tonight, I'm going to make the same request to you. Please take the weight from your trouser pockets or purses and make a contribution. It will be greatly appreciated.'

There was a general shuffle as everyone rummaged around to see what money they had with them.

'Please don't spoil your starter by delving in your pockets yet. I'll pass this bag round during the meal.' He waved a hessian bag with the appropriate wording on it in the air. 'I know you are probably hungry and I won't keep you much longer. I said there were two endeavours I wanted to mention. The other is one you may have heard of, the "Needy Students' Fund". This has been around for years, and as I told one of you earlier, the word "needy" usually applied to the fund itself as well as the students. It had little money to distribute. I'm trying to change this. So if you feel in your heart you could offer more than "small change", there are present struggling students who would be immensely grateful. I already have one offer of a contribution. Do let me know if you can help.'

He smiled to say enough, his begging was over.

'Well, I won't keep you any longer from your meal. I hope you're enjoying this weekend and will continue to keep in touch with each other and the department. There's always a welcome for you here.'

He sat down to a loud round of applause and the starter was served.

'I like the idea of the "Small Change" award. No-one misses their loose change.' Pauline was looking in her purse as she said this.

'Damn. I've only got twenty-three pence. Looks paltry

putting that in the bag. Wish he let us know beforehand. I suppose they can't object if I stick a fiver in, can they?'

'Silly question!'

'Well, I don't feel I can make out a significant cheque to the other fund, but I would like to give more than pence.'

'Easier for you guys who always have pockets of coins,' Susanne said. 'Personally, my handbag is so tiny I don't have a purse in it. But Martin will contribute for us both.'

He gave the smile of the bearer of cash and the payer of bills.

'You may not have a purse on you, but I never have loose change in my pocket if I can avoid it. It ruins the shape of my trousers.' Simon made his statement to the table.

'Savile Row, I expect,' Pauline muttered to Kate.

'So are your pockets empty now, Simon?' Kate asked.

'Entirely.'

'Well, I'm sure your wallet isn't. When we tip our purses out, you can do the same with your wallet!' She presented this as an amusing suggestion, but made sure he saw her hard look amid the mirth.

The hessian bag arrived at their table and Martin loaded it with a handful of change from his pocket. Kate tipped her purse upside down and a cascade of coins making up a few pounds tumbled into the bag. Others followed their example and the rattling bag reached Simon. All eyes were on him. Kate wasn't the only person to remember his scrounging as a student.

'Now then, Simon. A wealthy lawyer, like you. You won't miss a few notes.'

He extracted a ten pound note with flamboyance and put it in the bag.

'Come on,' piped up Jeremy who so far had been quiet. 'You can do better than that. I gave more in loose change and I'm a poor hospital pharmacist!'

The desire to extract as much as possible from Simon

bound the whole table together. Not just the memory of his student days, but his elegant clothes and his obvious wealth spurred them on. People turned to look from other tables. Simon twisted his neck as if his collar had suddenly become too tight. He screwed his eyes up as he looked round the table at the expectant, mildly antagonistic faces. Being the centre of attention was a familiar feeling but not in circumstances like this.

Grabbing a handful of notes, he pushed them rapidly into the bag and snapped his wallet shut. 'There. I'm wiped clean.'

A few people clapped and there was a cheer from Pauline. Well, that's the job half done, Kate decided. Simon turned and deliberately started a conversation with Caroline on his left; money talk was over.

Pauline tapped Kate's hand. 'You can tell me to mind my own business, but what's the relationship between you and Jonathan now?'

'There is no relationship.'

'You looked as if you were getting on well last night.'

'I decided it would be foolish to maintain a silence after all these years. So we are speaking.'

'Just speaking?'

'What are you suggesting?'

'Oh, I don't know. The way you were laughing together. Seemed a spark might have been re-ignited. You realise he can't keep his eyes off you?'

Kate looked up and met his gaze for a second, then looked away.

'Has he been staring?'

'Without a pause. I don't think he's noticed a thing he's eaten.'

'Well, more fool him.' Kate felt distinctly uncomfortable as she felt his eyes continue to watch her every move.

Chapter 17

A further tap of a spoon on a glass and Willy stood up, polishing his mouth with a napkin and rummaging in a folder. Everyone was now well into dessert, a contented glow of fellowship and alcohol enveloping the group. He savoured his moment, anticipating a successful speech and the warm admiration of the room.

'Well, I did warn you last night was your free night and I'd be torturing you today.'

He laughed loudly as he manipulated himself into position, pushing his chair back and placing his feet well apart. He swayed as he raised a glass of red wine to his lips.

'Oh, dear, I think Willy has been enjoying himself too much. Maybe the beginning of the meal would have made more sense. This could indeed be torture!' Pauline was keeping up a commentary in Kate's ear. She'd already applied her wit to various people round the room and Kate was grinning, trying hard not to burst into laughter.

'Looks like Willy's left sleeve escaped the attention of the iron!' Pauline noticed the wrinkles and creases wriggling their way down one sleeve of an otherwise ironed shirt.

'Pauline, you are the best company!'

'I'm sure you are dying to get into the bar – as am I – so this won't be long. I decided to wait until near the end of the meal as we have photos to show you. It fits in best here and it means your dinner didn't go cold.'

He beamed, casting his benign blessing on the assembled crowd. He enjoyed being the focus of all eyes, enjoyed the sound of his own voice. Then he looked down at the laptop which he had not turned on.

'Whoops! Better fire this thing up.' He fiddled with the machine, frowned and then abandoned it.

'Anyway, let's start at the beginning. Welcome everyone. It's great to see you at this thirty-year reunion. I think I've managed to talk to everyone and I have to say there was no problem in recognising everybody. The years have not made a huge difference to us. Maybe a little more weight.' He looked down at his own swelling belly. 'And a little less hair. But the same friendly folk inside.'

A murmur went round the room then everyone went silent as he got into his stride.

'There are some "Thank yous" I'd like to make.' He pulled out his first index card, made a strange barking noise in his throat and looked at the next one. 'That's odd. I had a list of names. Oh, well, I expect I can remember. Firstly, many thanks to Professor Roger Cantwell for welcoming us to the department and for joining us tonight. It's also great to see Dr Bob Passman and Dr Alan Cornish here. Two other people who haven't changed much.'

'Lies,' whispered Pauline.

Everyone turned towards the staff members and Kate caught Bob Passman's eye. He appeared to blush slightly before he turned away and mumbled to the odd-looking woman beside him.

'How stupid to bring his wife with him!' Pauline continued.

'Occasions like this take organisation and the departmental secretary has been invaluable. So Roger, please convey our thanks to ...' He looked down at his card which was no help. He scratched his cheek and coughed. 'To Marilyn.'

'Marianne,' Roger corrected him.

'To Marianne for sorting out the hotel bookings and liaising with the caterers. I couldn't have managed without her.

She's a star. And we should also give our thanks to the staff here for providing us with two excellent meals.'

There was a round of applause and the Maitre d' bowed, extending his arm to the hovering waitresses to include them.

'Then I must mention the guides who showed us round the department this morning.' In vain, he shuffled his cards to find where they were hiding. 'So sorry, I appear to have misplaced some of my notes. I can't recall their names.'

'John and Elizabeth.' A helpful prompt.

'Yes, John and Elizabeth. They did a great job. We were thrilled to see the new facilities. What opportunities today's students have! Having said that, I think we all share a nostalgia for the old, smelly building.'

He did a bit more card shuffling, trying to establish an order while a ripple of amusement followed his comment and the whiff of hydrogen sulphide briefly invaded everyone's nostrils. He would have preferred to go away, sort out his notes and start again but it wasn't an option. A fog of embarrassment was enveloping him and his normal, confident tone was turning to a hesitant stumble. He constantly sorted his cards but it served only to make him more frustrated. He wiped his hand across his sweaty forehead.

While they waited, Pauline whispered, 'You're still being watched.' Kate glanced across as Jonathan's eyes moved over her body. She wriggled anxiously.

'Without doubt, a major "Thank you" has to go to everyone here for making the effort to come. Big thanks especially to those who've travelled a long way.' He nodded at Trevor who lived in Northern Ireland. 'Reunions aren't always successful but I believe this one has been. We are fortunate in that the Register is an easy means of contacting everyone, but it's still no guarantee everyone will come. Only one person said they weren't interested which isn't a bad record. We were a group who got on well together and I think the atmosphere this evening testifies to the

189

fact relationships and friendships last. People don't forget.'

'How right you are,' Kate muttered to Pauline, who, in her innocence, smiled affectionately.

'I thought I would mention the incidents that have stuck in my memory and, I expect, yours.' He re-established his position, moving his shoulders up and down, pulling on his cuffs, and stroking his beard. A few glances were passed round the table.

'There was the dog. Do you remember when a stray got into the chemistry lab? A lot of chasing removed him but not before he knocked over various experiments. That was the best excuse I ever had for not handing in a report!'

It caused a wave of comments as everyone went through the "I remember that!" mode.

'Then there was the time Dr Passman brought the wrong lecture notes and we got an unexpected free period. A rare treat for pharmacists!' He looked at Bob Passman who smiled weakly.

'Sense of humour failure there,' Pauline said behind her hand. 'Not that Willy has noticed.'

Willy was mumbling to himself. 'I have a few more amusing anecdotes somewhere here. Well, never mind. Let's move on.' He looked at the laptop, pressed a few keys, swore under his breath and looked at Kate.

'Kate, could you get this thing started? It seems to dislike me.' Sweat was starting to run down his face. Kate went across and set it up.

'These are Kate's photos, a selection from our time here.'

'Actually, they are Becky's.'

'Oh, yes, Becky's. Thank you, Becky.' He looked around the room for her. 'Where's Becky?'

'She had to go unexpectedly.'

Willy started the slides, having found the card with the list he and Kate had put together.

'Right, now. This tells the story – well, the key moments – of our time here. I think everyone is in one or other photo, so look out for yourselves. The first is the group outside the department a couple of days after we started.'

He clicked on the slideshow and a photo of a large number of students in a phone box came up. A titter went round the room.

'That's odd, the first one should be the departmental group. I put them in date order.' He mumbled to himself and scratched his head. 'Never mind, maybe it's next.'

But the following slide was of graduation. Willy took a gulp of wine to hide his discomfort and the slide show continued.

'Ah, here it is. Don't we look young!'

The photos flashed up in random order. A party in the second year, a pub crawl in the first, a third year picnic after exams and individual photos taken at various times. Willy had worked out silly comments and witty remarks to go with most of the slides but couldn't find them; anyway, the haphazard nature of the slide show prevented him from knowing what was coming next. He tried to interject a few jokes here and there.

'Here's a young man struggling with a difficult piece of work!'

This was Colin with his arm around an unknown girl in a pub. Colin, his foul mood still hanging about him like a cloak, sniffed and turned away.

He tried again when a photo of the now bald Derek came on the screen. 'And here we have Derek with masses of hair – or were you wearing a toupée?'

Derek shrugged. Fortunately he'd overcome his sensitivity about hair loss. But a few worried glances passed his way.

'Bloody hell! Trust old Willy to put his clumsy foot in every hole he can find!' Pauline's commentary was continuous.

The photos captured everyone's interest and comments and quips were fired at them from all angles. It was a success. But it wasn't the sequence Willy anticipated nor the story he wanted to tell. It wasn't his success. He was annoyed he messed it up and his face was thunderous.

'Well, my apologies about the mix-up. I think I'll have to have serious words with the Business Centre about this. But I think it brought back memories for all of us.'

He was now beginning to slur his words – not badly but enough to appear comic and people were commenting to each other.

'I once heard a comedian say being sober on stage was the best advantage you had over a drinking audience. Seems Willy never heard about that!' Pauline was feeding comments again to Kate.

'He's made a real fool of himself. Not, I imagine, a situation he's familiar with.'

'Well, that's it, folks. I hope you're enjoying this weekend as much as I am.' His face belied his words and as he sat down with a thump, he knocked his glass over with his index cards.

Susanne had a fit of the giggles. Willy's antics delighted her and she was covering her mouth with her hand like a child.

'Shit, that's all I need.' The dregs of red wine splashed his pink shirt. He dabbed at it ineffectually with his napkin. 'If you will excuse me.'

He left the table to go and change, glad the unfortunate incident was getting him out of the room and away from what he suspected were mocking comments. As he moved away, Roger Cantwell stood up and interrupted his departure.

'Thanks, Gabriel. Perhaps you could delay your exit by a few minutes. I'm sure everyone enjoyed the photos – and it was fun for me to match current faces to your – slightly – more youthful selves!'

A surge of laughter went round the room, partly due to Roger's remark and partly the result of suppressed giggles bursting to get out, the result of Willy's fiasco.

'You've heard enough from me already, but before we leave the table, there's one more thing I'd like to say. When I joined the department, I decided we should try to recognise what our students achieve, not only while they are here with the "Small Change" project but after they have left. As many alumni have a thirty-year reunion, an award at that point would be appropriate. It's a time when most people are at the peak of their careers, have achieved many of their aims and made their mark in the world, at least in the world of pharmacy. And for most, it also heralds their first half-century!'

Kate felt an inner groan.

'So the award – a glass goblet with the winner's name engraved on it – goes to the student who has made the most of their career since graduating. It is independent of the classification of the person's degree, relating purely to post-graduation success. It's a way of recognising and thanking our students for taking what they learned here and putting it to use.

'However, I am not the person choosing the winner. I discussed this with the staff and we agreed it should be, wherever possible, a member of staff who taught and knew the students who are eligible. So in this case, Dr Bob Passman has chosen the winner. Over to you, Bob.'

Bob Passman stood up as people mentioned names to each other as possible winners.

'I bet Simon gets it. He's earned more than anyone else and has got the highest profile,' said Pauline behind her hand.

'I bet Willy thinks he's got it, though,' answered Kate. 'Look at his face. He thinks Roger stopped him leaving because he's the winner. But it might be Amanda – she's achieved a huge amount in the face of her problems. Depends exactly what they're looking for.'

As if to respond to her comment, Bob Passman told them about the criteria.

'Good evening, Ladies and Gentlemen. It is an honour for me to be asked to choose the winner and to make the award. Our previous winners were delighted and the assembled groups agreed they were worthy recipients. I hope the same will apply this evening. However, I have to say it was a difficult decision – you are a high achieving group. There were a number of close contenders. These were my criteria: firstly, I felt the achievements needed to be within the field of pharmacy.'

'Probably rules Simon out,' muttered Pauline, 'He's more a lawyer than a pharmacist now. I'm glad about that.'

'Secondly, I looked for consistent progress and impact on society rather than a one-off success.'

He paused, looked round the room and then bent down to pick up the trophy from a box by his feet. Kate could see Willy wriggling in his seat, straightening his cuffs and getting ready to stand, the red wine splashes temporarily forgotten.

'With great pleasure, for a major contribution to retail pharmacy, the award goes to Kate Shaw.'

There was a round of applause and several cheers. Willy clapped along with the others but could not disguise the displeasure on his face. Kate walked over to Bob Passman's table, accepted the trophy and shook his hand. He leaned across and kissed the air next to her cheek.

'Well done, Kate. The department is proud of you.'

Kate thanked him and said what an unexpected surprise and pleasure it was. Pauline hugged her when she returned to the table.

'I'm so glad it's you and not the insufferable Willy. He'll never speak to you again.'

'Well, that'll be an additional bonus! I wasn't expecting this. I can't believe I'm the most deserving person here. I feel embarrassed.'

'Don't be so modest. Enjoy it!' Life was always straightforward for Pauline.

As the dinner finished, people came by to see the trophy and congratulate her. Willy left the room, frustration sobering him up but spiking his grievances against the Business Centre. After changing into a clean shirt, he dropped in there, determined to give them a piece of his mind.

'Dr Williamson.' He nodded as he introduced himself. 'I am unhappy with the sequence of slides you scanned in for me.'

'Really? What's the problem?'

'They were jumbled. I had them in a specific order and that order was lost. Looked like someone shuffled them.'

'Well I apologise, Dr Williamson. Miss Shaw said to keep them in the order they were in and I passed the message on to the girl who did the scanning. I'll speak to her in the morning. She didn't mention she dropped any, but you never know.'

'Well, it's not good enough, not good enough at all.' Willy gave her a severe look, bumped into a chair, swore and stormed out of the office, his anger magnified by the recent disappointment.

He went up to Kate who was still chatting at the table. 'I've had words with the girl at the Business Centre. They made a pig's ear out of the scanning, totally lost the sequence. Did you notice how jumbled they were?'

'I did. Hard not to, seeing as they were in no particular order.'

'After the effort we put into sorting them out.' Willy was speaking too loudly, glad to ensure all knew the mistakes were someone else's responsibility. 'I shall go back in the morning and see if they've discovered what happened.'

'I wouldn't bother, Willy. Just accept things don't work out as you'd like them to all the time.'

'Unlike you to be so forgiving, Kate. Easy not to mind when it's me who has suffered.'

His clean shirt was already sticking to his chest as his body and his temper got hotter. In anyone's estimation, he was an unpleasant sight.

'Calm down, Willy. It might look different in the morning.' She gave him a knowing smile which was wasted. Willy was poor at detecting signals even when sober. 'Think I might also visit the Business Centre in the morning'. She'd make sure they didn't take the blame.

Willy wandered back to his seat and collected his redundant index cards. Kate followed to get her laptop. There was a general movement towards the comfort and coffee of the seating area with its sofas and armchairs. Susanne was still giggling and holding her head.

'This laughter is giving me a headache.'

'Sure it's not too much wine, my love?'

Martin was ushering her out more like an indulgent companion than her husband. She pushed his hand away. As Simon stood up, Kate tapped him on the arm.

'Have you met Roger Cantwell yet?'

'No, there were too many people round him earlier on. I'm not in the habit of queueing.'

'Well, I'm going to have a word with him. I said I'd speak to him after dinner. Why don't you come along?'

'Okay. He's got the contents of my wallet. He may as well meet me.'

Roger was leaning on the bar. 'Hello, Kate. Many congratulations! Bob didn't tell me who the winner was and I'm delighted. Would you like a drink? Must support my generous alumnus.'

'I'll have a sparkling water, thanks. Ice and lime.'

Roger turned to Simon. 'I don't think we've met yet, have we?'

'Simon Featherstone, pharmacist, lawyer and MD of Clinavail, a new pharmaceutical company about to be launched.'

'Now there must be a story there. But first, can I get you a drink?'

Not one to refuse, Simon asked for a whisky, saying nothing when Roger didn't order single malt although his face was eloquent.

'Right, Roger. I'll write you a cheque here and now.' Kate

got out her cheque book and wrote £100 in the amount box. 'Who do I make it payable to?'

'The "Needy Students' Fund". I'll get Marianne to take it into the admin office on Monday.' He glanced at the cheque. 'Thank you. It's most generous.'

Kate looked purposefully at Simon as she spoke to Roger. 'I'm sure Simon would be delighted to contribute, too. He must be one of our most successful students. I'm sure you'll be interested in what he has achieved. Maybe not in the league of Charles Brookman, but doing extremely well.'

Simon tried to turn his grimace into an amiable smile. He was cornered, trapped by his own vanity. Kate was a cunning woman and had duped him. As he removed his cheque book with a flourish – making the most of the display – he muttered, 'Touché.'

Making sure Kate could see, he entered £100 in the amount box. He wasn't going to be outdone.

'Oh, Simon, aren't you missing a zero?'

Both men looked at her with wide eyes. Roger's face gleamed like a beacon; Simon's had no expression. He added the zero, entered the words "One thousand pounds only", signed and dated it.

'Well, I'll leave you two together as Simon has already told me his amazing story. It's worth hearing. One you might like to repeat to show what students can aspire to.' She offered her hand. 'Lovely to meet you, Roger. Hope we meet again soon.'

She gave him her most winning smile and headed across the room. Seeing Pauline, she pulled her to one side. 'Come here, I must tell you this.'

Intrigued, Pauline followed her out into the reception area. Kate made a fist and thrust her arm into the air.

'Yes! Yes!'

'Whatever have you done?'

'Got Simon the Rich to write a cheque for £1000 for the

197

"Needy Students' Fund". I was sickly sweet about his achievements but it worked!'

'Never! You're brilliant, Kate. Can you get him to write one for me?'

'I wish.' She recounted quickly what happened then they went back to join the boisterous crowd arm in arm, almost bumping into Jonathan on his way out. He fingered the dressing on his ear.

'Did you have anything to do with Willy and the debacle in there?'

'Me? Why do you ask that?'

'I think it had Kate stamped all over it.'

Kate tried to remain expressionless but there was the glimmer of a sparkle in her eye. 'I couldn't possibly say.'

'Mmm. Well, I need to go and re-fix this dressing. Too much throwing of my head back with laughter has dislodged it. I don't suppose you'd care to help?'

'No, Jonathan. You are more than capable.' He shrugged and went up the stairs.

Pauline put her hands on Kate's shoulders and turned her so they faced each other. 'The way you two look at each other. Something's going on, I know.'

'No, you don't. And let's leave it that way.'

Chapter 18

Susanne was leading Martin to a welcoming sofa. Amanda was pushing her wheelchair the same way. A few guys were gathering chairs together for the group. Kate quickly took in who was there.

'Shall we join them?' Pauline asked.

'Why not? They're a friendly crowd.'

No Colin, no Willy, no Simon, no Jonathan. They had disappeared for their own reasons. The number was down to around twenty, one big, noisy group and a few smaller ones. Coffee cups clattered on the table and a waiter brought several large cafetières. Bob Passman was hovering near the door and came over towards her.

'I'd like to have a word, Kate, if you don't mind.' He indicated a stool by the bar and Kate sat beside him.

'Another drink?'

'No, I'm fine, thanks.'

He ordered a beer for himself and started to talk to Kate without looking at her. 'Glad I was able to give you that award. Felt it was a type of compensation.'

'Compensation for what?'

'For the fact you didn't get the First you deserved.'

'Sorry, but I don't understand. Much as I was thrilled to win, it has nothing to do with my degree. Roger said as much.'

Bob ran his finger round his collar and loosened his unnecessary tie. He looked around him and turned to face Kate.

'I should not be saying this. Please don't repeat it. You should have had a First. Your marks were high enough. Gabriel's were higher but not by much. Professor Everett was adamant only one First a year be awarded. It had always been the case but we never had two contenders as we had in your year. He felt it devalued the degree to award more than one. The staff had a heated discussion about it. I remember it clearly. Anyway, it's history now but I felt this evening's award at least placed you above Gabriel and showed your worth.'

Kate could barely control her trembling. She had trouble speaking and her voice was hoarse.

'I can't believe you think tonight's award can in any way compensate for being "cheated" out of my First. I feel betrayed. Why ever have you told me this? Wouldn't it have been better to leave the past in the past?'

Bob was taken aback. 'I was trying to be helpful. I thought you'd want to know.' He coughed and added quietly, 'And it was a thank-you for your discretion.'

Kate knew exactly what he was talking about now. It was at the beginning of their final year. He had asked for volunteers to help for a few days at a scientific meeting at the university after the end of term. It was mundane work but it offered a chance to attend lectures and to mix with scientists and researchers without having to pay a registration fee. It was a taste of the real world. Kate immediately signed up.

She loved it, loved the atmosphere, loved finding out what research was about. She got a flavour of what she hoped to do herself after graduation and was on a real high. Several of her pharmacology lecturers were there and Dr Passman gave a presentation. Afterwards, she wanted to tell him how much she enjoyed it but he was busy. It can wait, she thought. Then as she was leaving, she saw him pass the window and ran out. Rounding the corner, she nearly hit him. He was in the arms of one of his research students, a French girl called Francine. They sprang apart and Dr Passman muttered that Francine was congratulating him.

Well, maybe, but she had an unusually ardent way of conveying a compliment, Kate thought. She hastily made a few remarks about how interesting she found the presentation and left. When she saw him the following day, he said nothing but placed a finger on his lips. And Kate said nothing. She enquired casually the following term if he was married and found out from Amanda he was.

'His wife is pleasant but amazingly frumpy. No make-up, wild, frizzy hair and a cardigan my Grandma wouldn't be seen dead in. I think she works in admin at the university. Any reason for asking?'

'I saw him with a woman in town – from your description, it was his wife,' Kate lied. 'Thought there might have been a bit of scandal!'

The incident disappeared from Kate's mind until a couple of years after graduation when she bumped into Dr Passman at another meeting. There was no doubt this time it wasn't his wife he was with, nor indeed was it Francine. Colour rose up his face as he recognised Kate. This time, he simply introduced his partner and they exchanged a few words. Kate wondered how many partners there had been. She wasn't bothered. If he wanted to be a serial womaniser, it was his affair.

And now he was here with his wife, wondering if Kate was about to bring up the past, and trying to find ways to avert an awkward situation.

'Dr Passman – Bob – I don't approve of bribes. If either the award or the information was to make sure I kept my mouth shut, it was a clumsy gesture and unworthy of you. I'm not sure I believe your story about my degree, anyway. I always respected Professor Everett. When he said everyone got the degree they deserved, I believed him.'

She hesitated a moment. 'Why ever did you bring your wife here?'

'I had no choice. She's Roger's Personal Assistant now.'

Kate loved the irony of it. She almost forgave the silly man for his amateurish attempts to win her silence, a silence he had anyway. Her anger disappeared.

'Tell me – without the ulterior motives, was I a worthy winner of the trophy?'

'Absolutely, Kate. Absolutely.'

She believed him, patting him on the hand as she left. He said he must introduce her to his wife.

She still had unfinished business and no way forward. Well, the only option is to create an opportunity, she thought. She found a free chair and sat near to Martin, poured herself a black coffee and took a single chocolate from the plate in the centre of the table. A reward for success so far.

She half listened to the conversation around her. Martin was delighted to have discovered Jeremy's wife, Diane, was a dental nurse. He was deep in discussion about the complexity of crowns and the last piece of equipment he bought.

'You're being boring, Martin,' Susanne complained. 'You shouldn't talk shop. No-one else can join in.'

'But everyone's talking shop, it's just a different shop!'

He carried on his conversation and Susanne pulled a face. She wasn't used to being second best. Martin usually did as he was told. This was a man she didn't know. She turned to Amanda.

'What do you think happened to Willy? Gabriel, I mean.'

'Odd, wasn't it? I think he had too much to drink and confused himself. Muddled his notes up or forgot his script.'

'But his photos were in the wrong order!'

'I know. But it made it all the more amusing. He's a decent guy – he did, after all, go to the trouble of organising this reunion. Shame he made such a fool of himself. Everyone seems to think it's acceptable to laugh at him.'

'You always see the best in people, Amanda. I'm not that generous.'

'Well, I admit he's always been too full of himself. Perhaps it brought him down to earth. Welcome to the world where things go wrong!'

'Pity Becky missed it. With her sense of humour, she'd have been in stitches! I wasn't ever aware of her taking so many photos, but I'm glad she did. I never had a camera, don't have one now. Wouldn't have anywhere to put it.'

Susanne held up her minuscule handbag, big enough for a lipstick and a tissue.

'Martin carries my mobile phone for me.'

'Anyone for another drink?' Martin stood up and looked around. 'Tell you what, why don't we ask them to bring a couple of bottles of wine and some glasses?'

There was general agreement and he sorted it out. He leaned across to Susanne. 'Don't have too much, darling, will you? You look flushed.'

'I'll have what I want.'

She made a point of topping up her glass. She wasn't used to drinking more than a couple of glasses of wine. But tonight was different. One bottle shared was their frequent pattern, with his share being the larger. When they went out, it was the two of them, to smart restaurants or the theatre. Mixing in a big group inspired strange behaviour. She knew she was behaving contrarily tonight. But then, she thought, so was he.

He seemed to be enjoying the company of these people. He told her he liked their humour, their openness. They weren't as stiff and formal as dentists. And she guessed he'd not noticed how much he was drinking and had gone way past his usual limit; he looked pleasantly merry. He discarded his jacket and tie and lay back in a large armchair.

'I'm amazed your first group photo was so formal. All standing neatly by the department. Didn't you have any tricks played on you?' Martin had the attention of the group now.

'What sort of tricks?'

'Well, I have a similar photo outside the dental school. However, unknown to us, the second years were behind the first floor windows, and when the photographer said he wanted a second photo, they poured buckets of water down on us! It's a brilliant photo!'

'Ah, we escaped! Our building was single storey!'

The volume of noise got greater and few noticed Jonathan's quiet reappearance. He sat away from Kate, chatting to anyone who would listen. But his mind was not on his conversation. From time to time he touched the dressing on his ear and fixed his eyes on Kate. She changed seats to sit nearer to Susanne.

'Tell me about the work you do. You must have the most unusual job of anyone here.'

Susanne looked at her suspiciously. But it was a valid question and she had no intention of being overtly unfriendly.

'It's a counselling job. Mostly teenagers struggling with their sexuality. Afraid to disclose to their parents. Unable to talk to anyone. We give them an open atmosphere where they can say what they like in confidence and sort themselves out. It's satisfying. And I do it well. I never felt so happy with pharmacy.'

'Interesting. But you worked in retail before that?'

'Yes, for about five years. I got sick of it. I was never a sparkling student. Think I did the wrong course but didn't relish starting over again. The hope everything would click with me as the course progressed was a vain one. Nothing academic ever did.'

Susanne put her hand up to her face and rubbed her forehead. 'I'm getting a headache. I think I should have a drink of water.'

She looked across at Martin but he was laughing raucously at a remark Diane made and didn't respond. She frowned.

'I'll get you one from the bar.'

Kate fetched a large glass and handed it to Susanne who took a few sips then rested her head against the back of the sofa and closed her eyes. She looked pallid and beads of moisture appeared on her upper lip.

'God, this has come on suddenly. I wonder if the meal

upset me?'

Martin heard her comment and turned to her. 'I think you ought to lie down. I think you've overdone the alcohol.'

'No, I haven't. Stop telling me what I've done.'

Martin was taken aback by her ferocity but didn't argue.

'Maybe I will go to bed. You needn't come up yet, Martin. You're obviously enjoying yourself.' She couldn't keep the rancour out of her voice. 'I can manage. I think I need paracetamol.'

'Don't you have any? You are a pharmacist.'

She waved her tiny bag at him. 'Not one of my priorities with a bag this size.'

Martin looked round the assembled gathering. 'Does anyone have any paracetamol?'

'I have,' said Kate. 'They're in my room. Come on, Susanne, I'll take you up.' She looked across at Martin to see if he was coming too.

'Don't think I'm welcome at the moment. Said the wrong thing. Thanks, Kate. I appreciate this.'

He handed the room key to Susanne who tottered across the floor on her high wedges, using chair backs and the wall as a support. Kate grabbed her arm as she stumbled and led her to the lift. They reached Susanne's room and Kate took the key and opened the door. Susanne went straight to the bed and flopped down on it, moaning.

'Shit, I feel awful.'

'Stay there and I'll go back to my room for the paracetamol. I'll only be a minute. I'll take the key so I can let myself back in.'

She returned to find Susanne throwing up in the bathroom.

'At least I managed to make it in here,' she called. 'I feel slightly better now, apart from my head.'

She emerged from the bathroom, a white-faced clown in her strange outfit, the pink flower in her hair falling out, her elbow-length, fingerless gloves splashed and damp.

'Come here, let's sort you out.'

Kate removed her gloves and the flower and told her to take off her shoes. Susanne obeyed like a child, then lay on the bed. Kate got a warm, damp flannel from the bathroom and wiped her face.

'Do you want to get undressed?'

Susanne gave her a strange look. 'Is that a proposition?'

'Shit, Susanne. How can you go there? I thought you weren't feeling well. I was thinking your elaborate outfit might be better hanging in the wardrobe than crumpled up on the bed.'

'Bad joke, Kate, that's all.'

She started to take off her clothes, fumbling and getting stuck. Kate helped with a sigh, got a bathrobe and told her to put it on. She hung the dress, a limp collection of bits and pieces of rag once there was no body inside it, in the wardrobe.

'I'll get you a glass of water and the paracetamol.' Kate gave her the glass and two white tablets. 'Come on, knock these back.'

Susanne did as she was told and lay with her eyes closed.

'I was surprised to see you married. Surprised to see you here.'

'Ha! It was the surprise element I was after. It's why I came. I wanted Martin to come, too. To show him off, I suppose. And he didn't object. Now it looks like he's having a better time than I am.' She spoke with her eyes still shut, a low, emotionless monotone.

'I could never see you as a little wife.'

'No, nor could I in those days. But my life had no stability. There comes a time when it matters more than anything else.'

'And Martin provided it.'

'Yes. I didn't pursue him. He just appeared in my life in a bizarre way.'

'He told me you fell at his feet, as it were, outside his surgery.' Susanne opened her eyes.

'Oh, yes, you and he were chatting when I went to look at the photos. I needn't have bothered. We saw most of them in Willy's comedy turn.' She closed her eyes again.

'Anyway, he seemed to fall for me in a big way. He spoiled me with presents and outings. I'd never known anyone with money before. I got to like his extravagant lifestyle. Well, it was extravagant by my standards. Before I knew it, he asked me to marry him and I accepted.' She put her hand to her head again and groaned. 'I think I need to go to sleep.'

'Here, take a couple more tablets.' Kate offered them with a glass of water, propping Susanne up.

'Have a drink. Wash them down well. Don't want them getting stuck in your throat.'

'Okay, I'm desperately thirsty, anyway. Mouth feels like sandpaper. Bloody alcohol.'

Kate studied her lying on the bed and took her phone out. 'Just need to send a text. Try to sleep. I'll stay a bit longer.' But Kate didn't let her sleep. She kept up a stream of conversation.

'What happened after university? Did you continue with your lesbian activities?'

'Oh, yes. Well, bisexual actually. I wouldn't say "no" to a good-looking, well-shaped young man. But it was mostly women. Lots of them. None lasted although I was with one partner for over two years. When that broke up, I decided I'd have to find a straight man for anything permanent. Loads of gays I knew had rock-solid relationships but I didn't seem to have the staying power. You shouldn't have denied me, Kate. We could have had a future together.'

Kate ignored the comment.

'And Martin knows about your background?'

Susanne opened her eyes and sobered up momentarily. 'You are joking! He'd not have married me if I'd told him, I'm sure of that.' She saw the expression on Kate's face. 'Kate, don't even think of it! He would never believe you!' She sat up quickly.

'Why wouldn't he?'

'Why should he? Your word against mine.'

'I have a convincing story. I could tell him about how you drugged me. I'd enjoy involving him in that conversation. A sweet revenge.'

'Why do you say I drugged you? You have no evidence.' There was panic creeping into Susanne's voice.

'I have enough evidence to convince myself.'

'Hell, this is making my head hurt.' She put both hands over her head and screwed up her face. Her dark, smudged makeup was eerie against her pallor. She lay back again against her pillow, wisps of hair radiating out from her head, like scarecrow straws.

'Two more tablets won't hurt.' Kate was there with the medication. Susanne pulled away.

'How many have I taken? Is this alright?'

'It's fine. Never too hot on dosages, were you?'

'Anyway, I've told Martin about that episode with you. Except, I didn't give your full name. I called you "K". But I twisted it to make it look as if you were assaulting me. So he'd never believe your version. Clever Kate, for once I've out-foxed you.' She managed a weak laugh and muttered, 'Out-Kated you,' to herself.

'Interesting story. How's the head doing?'

'It's still bad.'

'Well, a couple more tablets should do the trick.'

'Haven't I had enough? Are you sure?' She went to swallow them then gasped, dropping them on the floor.

'Kate, what have you been giving me? They were paracetamol, weren't they? You haven't been trying to poison me?'

'What? And get caught? Don't be silly, Susanne. I'm no

murderer. Look, here's the packet.'

She removed a box from her handbag to prove her point. Then she opened it and took out two foils, their coverings torn and the tablets removed. They had contained sixteen tablets. She placed it on the bedside table while deftly scooping up the tablets dropped on the floor.

'It's paracetamol alright. An empty box. Do you know how many you've taken, Susanne? I've been slipping them in. You've had more than you think. Can you remember what the maximum daily dose is? More importantly, can you remember what a fatal dose is? Should have been more attentive in the pharmacology lectures.'

Susanne was wide awake now, stunned and shaking.

'Paracetamol is more dangerous than most people think. Its therapeutic window is narrow. Can you remember what a therapeutic window is, Susanne? I expect you can't. Well, I'll tell you. It's the difference between the effective dose and one which gives severe side effects, even death.'

'But you can't kill me. Everyone knows you're with me. You're not stupid – you'd be incriminating yourself.'

'They know I came up with you to give you paracetamol. But it's all they know. I could have left them with you and returned to my room. In your confused and drunken state, you could easily have overdosed. No more than eight tablets in twenty-four hours is the recommended dose. You have been a greedy girl! And I'll give you more information. Paracetamol exists in a soluble form as well as a tablet. I dissolved some in the copious quantities of water you drank. So, my little abuser, my little Rohypnol user, this is a taste of your own medicine.'

Susanne was now crying and pulling on Kate's arm.

'Oh, Kate, what should I do? What should I do? I don't want to die.'

'I don't intend you to. There are means of counteracting the effects of the drug. If you're treated soon, you'll probably avoid severe liver damage. You are very pale, though. It's one of the early signs of paracetamol intoxication.'

Susanne sat up and looked across at the mirror on the opposite wall. Her face was drained of colour.

'Do you have any abdominal pains?'

Susanne put her hands over her stomach. 'I think I do.'

'Mmm.' Kate nodded wisely. 'To make sure you've had enough, I think you need to finish this glass of water.'

'With paracetamol in it?

'Correct.'

'That's like poisoning myself.'

'You have a choice. Finish it or I tell Martin about your past and how you abused me. It could be the end of your marriage.'

'I've told you, he won't believe you.'

'Yes, he will.' She held up her mobile phone. 'I recorded you while you were lying with your eyes closed.'

'That's just a phone. You can't have recorded me.'

'You need to keep up with technology, Susanne. Let me play a bit back to you.' She started the recording:

'What happened after university? Did you continue with your lesbian activities?'

'Oh, yes. Well, bisexual actually. I wouldn't say "no" to a good-looking, well-shaped young man. But it was mostly women. Lots of them. None lasted...

'That's enough I think. Drink up.'

Susanne choked as she forced herself to drink the rest of the water. Then she rushed into the bathroom and vomited in the washbasin.

'Oh, dear. Nausea and vomiting is also an early symptom.' Kate stood up calmly and picked up her handbag.

'I'm going now. I leave it to you to decide what to tell Martin. But if I am in any way implicated, I shall play him the recording without a moment's hesitation. You deserved this

Susanne. What you did to me was unforgiveable. Despicable and indefensible. You took advantage of my vulnerable state and I've never forgotten it. Now we're quits.'

She walked to the door.

'By the way, twenty to thirty tablets can be fatal. You're small, at the lower end of the range. And the antidote is called acetylcysteine. You should know that but I'm sure you don't.'

Susanne could see a smile spread across Kate's face as she opened the door, a satisfied, evil smile. She turned her face to the pillow and cried.

Chapter 19

Becky's phone rang as she was getting into the car. She rummaged in her handbag for it. 'Hello, Mary. What can I do for you?'

'Hello, Becky. You asked me to tell you if Mr Booth's shortfall on his last prescription had arrived. Both items came in late this afternoon. So I phoned him and he'll pick them up on Monday. At least you don't have to start the week chasing those up.'

'Great. Many thanks. How have things been?'

'Fine, no problems. Busy, but that's normal.'

'I can always rely on you, Mary.'

'Well, see you sometime. Although we hardly ever do, do we?'

Becky laughed. 'It's the role of the locum! You are a rock. Don't know how I'd manage without you.'

Yes, it was valuable to have a solid, efficient character like Mary to help her out. She painted a less than ideal picture of her to Kate, but it was a matter of necessity. She was about to put the phone back in her bag, then decided to send a text: "On my way. 30 min xx." She headed home, each mile raising her heart rate a little.

Her front door opened as she reached it and he was standing there with his arms out towards her. She dumped her overnight bag and handbag on the floor, kicked the door shut and put her arms around his neck. He kissed her with the ease of familiarity and the ardour of expectation.

'What complications!' Becky said. 'I didn't think I'd ever get away.'

'Well, I'm glad you did. I'd have felt an idiot sitting here on my own eating the beautiful meal I've prepared for us. And anyway, it's ages since we had time together. I'm suffering from Becky-deprivation.'

'What do you mean? I saw you on Friday evening.'

'Yes, but only briefly. You could hardly call it a romantic evening of love-making. More like a medicinal mating! I need proper time with you.'

Becky squeezed his hand and gave him another quick kiss.

'What story did you give them? What was your reason for the urgent departure? And for getting there late on Friday?'

'For Friday, I gave them the burglar alarm fiasco. Exactly what happened a few weeks ago. So it had the ring of truth. I just moved the timing. Then for today I said Mary had problems with drug addicts coming in – it has happened to us but not for ages – and she was worried about the alarm. It tied things together. I made a few worried false phone calls to her.'

'Yes, when I phoned on Friday and you called me Mary, I guessed she was implicated!'

'You shouldn't have phoned. You could have dropped me in it big time.'

'You can think on your feet, I know that.'

They moved into the kitchen where the table was laid, candles lit and the aroma of Burgundy beef filled the room.

'It smells delicious. I recognise it. One of my favourites.'

'Am I one of your favourites, too?'

'What do you think? You are my absolute favourite.'

'Then why the worried look?'

'I'm stressed. Not like me, I know. Carefree, happy-go-lucky Becky.'

'The meal won't spoil. Let's go into the sitting room and you can tell me what the problem is.' He picked up the two glasses of red wine he had poured.

'I'm not sure exactly what it is myself,' Becky said as she

sat beside him. 'I think it's the accumulation of multiple deceptions getting me down. I've been having odd dreams. I dreamt I was pregnant with your baby.'

'That's unlikely to happen.'

'Yes, I know. It's not on my wish list! But it would be lovely to have an uncomplicated relationship where we could go out, mix with anyone we wanted and be ourselves. But life isn't like that.'

He looked at her sadly. 'No, it isn't.'

'Then this weekend added to the strain. I went there thinking it would be easy to escape but Kate needed me. She wasn't keen to go as you know and I felt an obligation to support her.'

'Is she enjoying it?'

'Yes and no. I think she's getting satisfaction from it. That might be a better description.'

She could hardly go into the details, not that she knew what Kate was up to. She had her suspicions but nothing she was willing to share. Kate would have her own story so she didn't want to confuse things with her version.

'I'll no doubt hear about it.'

Becky sipped her wine and felt herself relax. She looked across at Neil. He was a fun guy. She enjoyed being with him. Bloody nuisance he happened to be Kate's husband. When he went back into the kitchen, she reflected on how they first met. Must be ten years ago, she thought.

***

She was having a coffee in town, tired out with Saturday Christmas shopping, when Kate and Neil walked in.

'Hi, Becky! What a surprise! Haven't seen you for ages. How are you?'

'I'm fine. Started working in this area a few months ago.'

Kate gave Becky a brief hug, making minimal body contact. 'This is Neil. You know I'm married, don't you?'

'Yes, I heard. It was a while ago, wasn't it?'

'Quite a while - about ten years. How about you? Snapped up yet?'

'Still single. No-one will have me! I think I like my own way too much.'

'We're in town to sort out the details for Neil's exhibition. He's a photographer.' Kate looked proudly at him.

'Yes, it's my first proper show. Can't believe I'm doing it. It's called "Two-Faced". I'm using the "Reflections" gallery at the corner of Broad Street and Church Lane.'

'Well maybe I should go along and see it. What's it about?'

'I've taken pairs of photographs of individuals to show how people react in different ways to happy and sad situations. It explores the variety of expression a face can show.'

'Sounds interesting.'

'I'm opening on Friday evening, this coming Friday. There's an informal reception. You know, a glass of wine and nibbles. Why don't you come?'

Neil's enthusiasm made his face shine with excitement. He looked from one woman to the other. 'Please come. We'd both like to see you there.'

So Becky went along and admired his obvious talent. She didn't speak to him much as he had more important people than her to impress. But she was attracted to him. Trust me, she thought. I always go for the married ones.

She didn't see him again for a couple of years. She spoke to Kate occasionally and asked after him. But he was an acquaintance, nothing more. Then she saw a flyer in the library for another exhibition, called "Playthings". Well, I don't need a personal invitation, she thought. I might go along to the gallery.

'Hello, Becky.' Neil made her jump as he came up behind

her.

'Hi there, Neil. I'm surprised you remember me.'

'Of course I do. I remember interesting people.'

Better than saying he always remembers a pretty face, she thought. 'Tell me about the idea behind this exhibition.'

'I'm looking at play at all ages. So I have the intent look of a seven-year-old building a tower from Lego over there.'

Becky followed his eyes across the room.

'Then two teenagers rolling in the grass, treating each other as playthings.'

This was a photo further along the wall.

'Then there's an older guy in a sex shop, looking for a different kind of plaything.'

They discussed the way he looked at play from different viewpoints, how he hit on the idea in the first place.

'This is fascinating. Looking at ordinary situations through a photographer's eyes. It gives a whole new perspective.'

As they talked, she sensed an undercurrent in their conversation; she could feel a reciprocal lure. She liked the way he guided her around the gallery, placing his hand occasionally on her shoulder to move her on, explaining the concept behind the photographs. There was intensity in the way he looked at her. A photographer's appraisal, she thought; although maybe it was more than that.

'I enjoyed myself, Neil. Many thanks for the personal guided tour.'

They looked at each other for a few seconds and then common sense took over; they parted on a "See you around" basis.

Seeing each other around came soon. A couple of months later she saw him in town, rushing along a side street with a canvas shopping bag in one hand. He was wearing a scruffy, brown sweater and old jeans. He needed a shave and a decent haircut. When she greeted him, he put a hand to his face and then smoothed his hair. He straightened up and tried to throw his embarrassment away with a toss of his head.

'Oh, hello, Becky. Excuse my appearance. I've been working and popped out to buy a bite to eat. I wasn't expecting to see anyone.'

'You didn't coat yourself with invisible paint. I spotted you.'

He laughed and looked relieved.

'How's things? You look fraught,' she said.

He didn't answer immediately. Then he examined her intently. 'Are you busy? Could you spare time for a drink? I could do with a friendly ear.'

'It's my afternoon off. Coffee would be pleasant.'

They went into one of the many coffee shops that proliferated in the town and sat down in comfy leather armchairs. Neil bought himself a baguette to make up for his missed lunch. Becky sipped her cappuccino and waited.

There was a long silence.

'This is a cheek. I hardly know you and now I'm asking you to listen to my problems. You don't have to, you know. We can have our coffees and you can go.'

'That's silly. Often it's easier to talk to someone you don't know well than to a close friend.'

There was another silence while Neil ate.

'If you're worried I'll repeat anything you say to Kate, then don't be. I'm discreet.'

Neil took a deep breath. 'Okay. Here goes. I think Kate may be two-timing me.' He looked at Becky for her reaction which was minimal.

'Why do you think that?'

'She's been working evenings a lot lately, more than usual. She says it's because she's expanding the business and it needs so much attention. She's been away overnight once. Twice, a strange guy phoned to speak to her. She said it was her new manager.'

217

'This sounds feasible. Why do you doubt her?'

'She's been less responsive in bed. Our sex life is usually vibrant. She's been tired, even turned me down. That's never happened before.'

'Tiredness and overwork can have that effect.'

'I know, I know. But my gut reaction tells me it's not that.' He hesitated, looking as if he was trying to decide whether or not to continue. 'Oh, I may as well tell you. We'd been trying for a baby without success. It turns out I have a low sperm count. It's had an effect on both of us.' Relief at saying what was on his mind was obvious, washing over him like a cloudburst.

'So what are you intending to do?'

'Nothing. Neither of us minds if we don't have children, we decided. So we're not thinking of adoption or any other alternative. It's not that.'

'So what is it?'

'It's the end of a phase of our lives. We now have to move on. Being told you have a low sperm count is like hearing you're a second-rate man. I would rather not have known. It knocks your confidence.'

'You seem a first-rate man to me.' Well, she said it.

He smiled. 'I'm glad you think so. But you don't have to make complimentary noises. I wasn't fishing.'

'I don't say what I don't mean.'

Neil leaned back in the chair and stretched his legs. Scruffy suits him, Becky thought. I can see why Kate was attracted to him. He looks nothing like Jonathan yet there's a Jonathan-like appeal to him.

'So do you think Kate is having an affair as a reaction to what you've both been through?'

'Partly, yes. Partly because she's always looking for a new stimulus. It's served her well business-wise. It's not so beneficial for a relationship.'

'Are you going to confront her with it?'

218

'I don't know. I haven't decided. Although part of the early passion has gone, I do still love her. I don't want us to break up.'

'But surely you don't want to be second-best? In her eyes, I mean.'

'I don't think she wants a break-up either. I suspect this is a fling. Nothing serious. I may have to accept this will happen from time to time.'

Becky placed her hand on his. 'Don't you think that's defeatist?'

'I don't know what I think, Becky. But thanks for listening. It's helped hugely.'

Becky was debating whether this was her cue to say thanks for the coffee and go when Neil leaned forward and said, 'Your turn now.'

'My turn?'

'Yes. I've done nothing but talk about me. I want to hear about you.'

'Not much drama there. Disappointing, in fact. I'm currently unattached. I was in a relationship for around three years but it fizzled out. No acrimony, no fights, we just decided our time was up. He moved out about six months ago. We're still friends. That's the story of my life. Most of my affairs are like fireworks. They start with a bang and loads of passion, then peter out.'

'That's sad.'

'I've got used to it. I'm independent and don't know if I want a permanent relationship. I thought I did once but now I don't know. Maybe I'm not cut out for it.' Becky looked at her watch. 'I need to go, Neil. I have things to do. I hadn't realised how long we've been here.'

They both stood up. It felt natural to give each other a hug.

As they reached the door and Becky turned, Neil caught her shoulder. 'Is Tuesday usually your afternoon off?'

'At the moment it is.'

'Coffee same time, same place, next week?'

Becky hesitated and gave him a quizzical look. 'Same time, same place, next week.' Was she lighting the blue touch paper again?

***

Neil broke her reverie by calling from the kitchen.

'Dinner's ready. Would M'Lady care to make her way to the table? I'm afraid the sommelier's off tonight and the maid phoned in sick so you'll have to make do with your humble servant to wait on you.'

'Well, humble servant, you've done a great job here. I bet it tastes as good as it looks.'

They sat down to eat.

'You look pensive,' Neil said. 'What's on your mind?'

'I was thinking about us. How we first met at one of your exhibitions, how we used to meet on Tuesday afternoons in the coffee shop. How I began to wonder if all you were going to offer me was cappuccino and the occasional croissant.'

'Then the first time you invited me back here. We were like a pair of guilty teenagers.'

'I think we were both worried about Kate. It was like a ménage à trois. With an invisible third person.'

'I can remember the first time we made love. It was an explosion after the build-up, weeks of build-up! I felt dreadful going home to Kate. I'd never been unfaithful before.'

'That's untrue! It might have been the first time you'd been unfaithful physically, but what about all those weeks devouring me with your eyes? They were hardly chaste glances.'

Neil agreed. 'I was amazed Kate didn't notice anything. I felt I had "adulterer" written on my forehead.'

'Very biblical of you. She didn't notice because she didn't look. And has never looked since. I am right, aren't I? She doesn't have any idea about us, does she?'

'I'm sure she doesn't. I've cultivated my middle-aged, stuck-in-a-rut image well. She wouldn't think I had it in me to have an affair.'

'That's what I thought. I felt two-faced at the reunion when she regarded me as her only friend there. Well, not the only one, but the one she knew best. I'm not behaving much like a friend.'

'No, but then Kate started it. She didn't behave much like a wife.'

They finished the meal and Neil took Becky by the hand and led her upstairs. 'Man cannot live by Burgundy beef alone.'

'Your jokes don't get any better.'

He put the bedside lights on adjusting the brightness to a warm glow, sat on the bed and pulled Becky towards him. 'Come here, my little temptress. What have you got to offer me tonight?'

He removed Becky's clothes slowly, stroking each revealed piece of skin. Starting with her shoes and socks, he kissed her toes. Then he removed her sweater, resting his face against her stomach; her trousers, throwing them across the room and running his hands the length of her slender legs. He slid his fingers round her waist and under the soft fabric of her knickers, drawing her closer towards him. He unclipped her bra and let it fall to the floor, her breasts warm through his shirt. Sliding her knickers down, he felt her whole body against his, familiar but ever new. His own clothes discarded, the jig-saw of their bodies interlocked as they had done so many times before.

But Becky wasn't in the mood.

'What's wrong? I've got a rag doll here, not the usual bundle of sexual energy.'

'It's Kate. She's on my mind. I saw a lot of her this weekend. She's normally a shadow in the distance, not someone I had several conversations with today, someone who values me as a friend.'

'We need to get rid of her. I don't want a third person in the bed. Come on, I'll give you a massage. It will wash away thoughts of anyone but me. Lie on your front.'

Becky did as she was told and Neil took a bottle of massage oil out of the drawer by the bed. He tipped a pool into his hand to warm it up then smoothed it down Becky's back. She blew out a large breath as he started. She loved the even, firm pressure of his broad hands and the way he stroked her. And as he moved down over her buttocks to her legs and then back up again to her shoulders and arms, she reflected on her friend. Kate the unfaithful wife; Kate the avenger; Kate the schemer; Kate who probably slept with Jonathan the previous night. Kate who never mentioned Neil to her all weekend. Kate who always thought about herself first; Kate who could most definitely look after herself. Sod Kate, thought Becky, sod her, sod her, sod her!

She rolled onto her back and looked at Neil, a mischievous gleam in her eye. 'You've worked your magic. You've got the old Becky back. You have the most wonderful touch. Where did you learn to use your fingers like that?'

'From Kate, I suppose,' he said without thinking, then added hastily, 'With the addition of my own natural skill and imagination.'

Bloody, Kate. I didn't need to know that. My fault for asking, thought Becky. But then we do have our similarities, we do like the same things. We like to do our jobs well. We like Neil, we like his touch. I suspect if Kate hadn't been so uptight about him, we'd both have liked Colin. And there was the not insignificant matter of Jonathan. Should she ever need a weapon against Kate, she could mention the couple of weeks' fling she had with him after their break up. One of many women passing through his hands and his bed at the time, insignificant for both of them. How Kate would hate that!

Then she grinned. 'Now it's my turn to massage you.'

Chapter 20

Kate was shampooing her hair when the hotel phone rang on Sunday morning. She sighed and frowned.

'Hello, Kate. It's Martin. Hope it's not too early. There's a problem with Susanne. Can I talk to you?'

'Go ahead.'

'No, I mean I need to see you.'

'Alright. Does it have to be now or can it wait?'

'I'm afraid it can't. Would you mind if I came to your room? It needs to be private.'

'Okay. Give me five minutes to get dry and dressed.'

Exactly five minutes later, Martin knocked on the door. His fraught face had fear written in every crease and there was a wild, needy look in his eyes. His uncombed hair was a tangle of matted curls and his beard looked smudged around the edges where he hadn't shaved.

'It's Susanne. I've told her I'll only be a few minutes so this has to be quick. She says she's taken an overdose of paracetamol.'

'An overdose? How could she? I thought the paracetamol I gave her was all she had.'

'It's so complicated. Can you go over what happened last night?'

'Well, I took her to her room and she flopped down on the bed. She was extremely drunk, you know.'

'Yes, I realise that now. But I didn't last night. I was enjoying myself, enjoying the company. We don't often socialise, don't often mix with a group of friendly, similar people. And I

223

didn't notice how much she had to drink. I did warn her once but got a curt response, so I assumed she knew what she was doing. I feel neglectful now.'

'Don't. She's an adult. She should know how to look after herself, how much drink she can take. Anyway, I went to my room to collect the paracetamol and when I got back she was in the bathroom, throwing up. She said she felt better, apart from the headache.'

'So she took some paracetamol?'

'Yes, I gave her two tablets with a drink of water. I helped her to get undressed as she was struggling with her clothes and hung her outfit in the wardrobe. I left the packet of tablets with her in case she needed another dose later on or this morning. But there were only four tablets remaining as far as I can remember. So at the most, she's taken six tablets. The maximum daily dose is eight tablets, as no doubt you know.'

Keep as close to the truth as possible, said Kate to herself. Don't make any additional traps for yourself.

'Have you found the packet of tablets?'

'Yes. There are two empty foils in it from sixteen tablets. She says her head was so bad in her confusion she continued to take them. She was in a dreadful state when I went back to the room last night.'

Martin sat down suddenly on the bed and put his head in his hands. He was near to tears.

'She insisted she'd taken too many and was going on about liver damage and not wanting to die. She wanted me to take her straight to hospital. I couldn't, not after so much alcohol. There was no way I could drive. She wanted me to call an ambulance and even tried to phone for one herself.'

He wiped his hand across his eyes.

'I didn't believe her. I thought she was rambling, thought this was the alcohol talking. Eventually, she fell asleep. We both did. Then this morning, I expected her to have forgotten about it or at least to laugh it off. But if anything she's worse. She says she's taken more than the one packet but I couldn't find any other empty foils. I sense there's something she's not telling me. There's a story she doesn't want me to know. I wonder if it's imagination although her panic is real enough.'

'I don't like to say this, Martin, but do you think this might be attention-seeking?'

'Yes, I do. I should have spent more time with her last night. But now I can't ignore her pleas. She'd never forgive me. And I feel dreadfully guilty. What should I do, Kate, what should I do?'

Kate felt sorry for him. Not for Susanne, but this decent man was desperate.

'Well, it's up to you. But if you're asking for my advice, I suggest you do this. Take her to A & E now and say it's a case of suspected accidental paracetamol overdose while drunk. But try to get the nurse or doctor to one side and say you suspect she hasn't taken too many so it may not be serious. In this way, you satisfy Susanne and show you care without making the hospital believe it's a true emergency.'

'Kate, I knew you were the right person to ask. Thank you so much. You don't know how grateful I am.'

On an impulse, he hugged her and then looked self-conscious about it.

'I'd better get back. Thanks again.'

The phone rang as he reached the door.

'Hello, Susanne. Martin is about to leave. Do you want to talk to him?'

'No. What have you told him?'

'I've suggested he takes you to A & E where they can sort you out. I'm so sorry this has happened but you'll be fine. I expect I'll be gone by the time you get back so I'll say goodbye. Glad to see you again, Susanne.'

That was lucky, she thought. Everyone is on the same

page. What a gullible fool Susanne is! She had six paracetamol, that's all. Yet she thinks she had symptoms of poisoning. What an inspiration to say there was soluble paracetamol in the water I gave her! Luckily, I can think on my feet.

She looked at the time. Breakfast must be in full swing. Time to go and eat, say my adieus, tie up a few loose ends and assess the outcomes. She finished her makeup, dried her hair and went downstairs.

Pauline was sitting in front of a large Full English so she went to join her with a more modest plateful.

'How's your head this morning?'

'Nothing that a couple of pain-killers and a fry-up can't cure! I did have a lot to drink last night.'

'Yes, I noticed. You were entertaining.'

'I didn't do anything I shouldn't, did I?'

'Of course not. Apart from dancing on the table in your underwear.'

Pauline's jaw dropped in mid-mouthful.

'You idiot! I'm only joking. But from the look on your face, it seems it could have been a possibility.'

Pauline slapped her on the arm. 'So how's your head?'

'It's fine. Some of us know how to control our alcohol intake.'

'Show-off. Oh, talking of alcohol intake, do you know how Susanne is? She was well gone by the time you went upstairs with her. I haven't seen her at breakfast.'

'Martin is taking her to hospital, to A & E. Suspected paracetamol overdose.'

'I don't believe it! Why? Surely, not deliberate?'

'Apparently, it was accidental while drunk. Martin thinks it may have been attention-seeking. I spoke to him before they left. Seems unlikely it's a true overdose but she's in a panic.'

'Well I wasn't expecting drama like that this weekend, that's for sure.'

'What drama is that?' Willy was standing behind them, plate in hand. 'May I join you?'

'Certainly,' Pauline said. 'We were talking about Susanne. She's gone to hospital, suspected paracetamol overdose.'

'Yes, I know. Martin phoned me before they left to say they wouldn't be at breakfast and to say goodbye. She was always an odd girl, Susanne, when we were students.'

'I'd say different rather than odd,' said Kate, 'But since getting married, she seems to have adopted a new persona. I don't understand her.'

'What do you know about the paracetamol, Kate? I hear you took her to her room last night.'

'Yes, I did. I've told Martin everything. I left her with a few tablets, but not enough to overdose.'

Willy looked hard at her. 'You don't know anything more?

Kate scowled. 'Of course not. I don't know why you ask, Willy.'

Their conversation was interrupted by Jeremy getting to his feet. 'Could I have everyone's attention for a few minutes?'

The room went quiet as they listened.

'This is odd at breakfast, I know. I was going to do it last night but Willy, I mean Gabriel, disappeared after the slide show and the award. I wanted to thank him on behalf of all of us for organising this weekend. It's been great fun to meet up with each other and find out what everyone's been doing. To be honest, I came with trepidation, and I think others did from what I've heard. But it was unnecessary. It's been most enjoyable. Many thanks, Gabriel.'

There was loud clapping and Pauline cheered.

'Can hardly toast you in orange juice and coffee, but I hope you realise we appreciate the effort you put into this. I think the success of this weekend means we must meet again in ten years for a forty-year reunion.'

There were cries of 'Fantastic!' 'Go for it!' 'Yes, yes!'

Gabriel, but still Willy to the present group, got up. 'I'm glad you enjoyed it. I think it's gone well – you never know with events like these. I have heard of disasters!' He laughed too loudly. 'A forty year reunion would be great – or even a thirty-five year one. I'm more than happy to organise it – unless there are other volunteers.'

He made the offer as a formality; why would anyone else want to do it after his success? As he looked around, there were shaking heads and several fingers pointing towards him. He nodded and grinned, sniffing in pleasure.

'I think I would enjoy organising the next event.' Kate spoke quietly and remained in her seat. 'After all, it's a lot to expect Willy to do it again.'

'I'll gladly do it again – no problem there!'

Ignoring Willy's interruption, Kate continued. 'Does anyone mind if I take responsibility for the next reunion?'

Most people were happy for anyone who was willing to take on the task, so there were no objections.

'Fine. Wait to hear from me.'

Kate concluded the conversation, if it could be called that, by turning to Pauline and talking to her. Willy told everyone to take care and have a safe journey home but the group wasn't listening. He screwed up his eyes as he glared at Kate's back, willing her to confront him. She ignored him.

Pauline stood up. 'That's me fed and watered. I've got a long journey so I think I'll be off.' She gave Willy a peck on the cheek and hugged Kate.

'We must try to meet up and not wait five or ten years. I've enjoyed being with you. How did we manage to lose touch?'

'The distance between where we lived, I suppose,' said Kate. 'And life happening. I was an unhappy person after graduation and avoided any reminder of my time at university. Foolishly, it included you but it shouldn't have done.'

228

Kate gave Pauline a second hug.

'You're right, we mustn't let it happen again.' She lowered her voice. 'By the way, you surprised me by volunteering to run the next get-together. Didn't think you were keen, especially as Willy was eager to take it on.'

'I'm not. Just didn't want to give Willy any more accolades. I expect I'll pass it back to him after he's suffered a bit.'

Pauline gave her a dubious look but being Pauline, shrugged it off.

Kate was left with Willy who turned towards her and grunted. 'I went along to the Business Centre to complain about the mess they made of scanning those photos. They said they'd been particularly careful to keep them in the correct order. But as a gesture of apology, they didn't charge me. Said they had no idea what happened. I've been thinking. You couldn't know more about it than you're saying, could you Kate?'

'Possibly. I might have been careless on the way there and dropped a few, putting them back in the wrong place. But I thought it was insignificant. Hardly worth mentioning. A person who gained a First would have no problem in thinking on his feet and coping with that.'

'Don't you ever forgive and forget, Kate?'

'In your case, Willy, no.'

'You're a devious, scheming witch.'

'Your opinion, Willy. By the way, what were you implying when you asked if I knew more about Susanne than I was saying?'

'Nothing in particular. A shot in the dark. Wondered if you had a grudge against her. Had a vague recollection you and she fell out in the third year.'

'And I gave her an overdose? That's an accusation!'

'I didn't say that. I'm sure you'd never be so obvious.'

'You have an overcharged imagination. One you could

have used last night.' She opened her handbag and took out two index cards. 'Yours, I believe.'

Kate stood up, smiled broadly and spoke so that others could hear. 'Thanks for an interesting weekend, Willy. I won't forget it.'

She shook his hand and offered him her cheek. Unable to do anything else, he kissed her.

Right, thought Kate, I've finished with him. She looked around the room to see who else was at breakfast. No-one of interest so she moved into the lobby. Simon was at the desk, checking out. She had time to observe him, unnoticed. He was dressed expensively, from his black cashmere sweater to his leather shoes. Hand-made, she thought. She waited until he settled his bill.

'It was decent of you, Simon, to make such a generous donation. Generous donations, I should say – both of them.'

He chuckled, an unusual noise coming from him. 'Although I hate to admit it, you outwitted me there. I walked blindfold into your trap so I deserved all I got. Since I've had money, I've deliberately buried my poorer days. Pretended they never happened. It was the easiest way to dispose of behaviour I wasn't proud of. So it was a shock to be reminded. Perhaps I've made amends?'

'I think you have, Simon. I thought you might be mad at me.'

'I was. But then I thought about it. I can afford the money. And your tactics, in retrospect, were clever and amusing.'

'So we part on amicable terms?'

'We do.'

They shook hands and Simon kissed Kate on both cheeks. Well, not what I expected, thought Kate, but I don't have a problem with that outcome. Simon took his car keys out of his pocket and she noticed the Lexus key fob. A discreet but noticeable display of wealth.

Now she had a quandary. Always one to finish what she started, she debated with herself whether she should seek out Jonathan and Colin. Susanne was dealt with; that had evolved without further action from her. Willy and Simon were easy. She needed their reactions and in particular wanted to make sure Willy knew what had actually happened. But Jonathan was an enigma. She was troubled by how he looked at her. And she wasn't sure Colin would speak to her, anyway.

She caught sight of Jonathan on his mobile phone. He was talking animatedly and then looked at his watch. He fingered his ear in the way she'd seen him do before.

'Goodbye, Kate.'

She felt a hand on her shoulder and turned to face Colin.

'It's probably one-all now. But if you insist on not forgetting, then neither will I.'

'Is that a threat?'

'Merely a statement of fact. Maybe we'll bump into each other before the next reunion, maybe in a Kate Shaw pharmacy. I live close to one.' He lowered his voice. 'I liked what I saw. I would still like to fuck you. Unfinished business.'

'Maybe we will bump into each other. But don't stalk me.' She also lowered her voice. 'I don't go in for much sexual activity in my places of work.'

He gave her a lustful look. 'There are ways and means. Shake hands, Kate?'

They shook hands. As she watched him go, she was aware of Jonathan looking at her. He walked across to her.

'I need to talk to you. Will you spare me a few minutes?'

'Do we have anything to say?'

He gave her a look that left her in no doubt. She went with him to the end of the lobby, trying to ignore his earthy aura and the way his hips moved as he walked.

'I have an important question. Was it coldly-calculated or passion driven?'

231

Kate didn't answer immediately. There wasn't an easy answer. So many emotions flooded through her as she thought about what she had done.

'It isn't an "either-or" situation. It was both. I could not have done it had I not previously loved you so much.'

'It had an amazing and unexpected effect on me.'

Kate raised her eyebrows.

'I was in agony initially. Then I was furious. I seethed with anger. I couldn't imagine how I would ever calm down. I hated you. I stood and looked at that piece of my ear on the bed for ages. I wondered what I would tell my wife. The falling against a table story worked here with a dressing on my ear. But, actually, I have a piece bitten off and my ear looks like a bitten ear.'

'It was my intention. As I said, although I doubt you heard me at the time, I wanted to mark you permanently. I wanted you scarred for life as you scarred me.'

Kate was utterly serious as she spoke.

Jonathan took a deep breath and then exhaled forcibly. He rubbed his face with both hands as he thought about his next words. 'I still don't know what I'll tell my wife. But I do know your biting me was a powerful aphrodisiac. But that's not all. I can't get you out of my head, Kate. I can't believe I was the cause of such profound feeling. And I'm now in a dreadfully confused state.'

'I'm glad my efforts weren't wasted.'

'You're sitting there with a smug look on your face, enjoying this. But I don't think you've understood what I'm saying.'

Jonathan was leaning forward, ardent intensity making his voice rough. He put his fingers round Kate's wrist and held it tightly.

'I'm not saying I got a brief thrill out of the incident, that it was a temporary, passionate turn-on, if it's what you think. I'm saying it's stirred feelings I didn't know were there, feelings I thought belonged to the past.'

He cast an anxious look at Kate.

'And another matter. I know you won't like this. Won't want to talk about it. But I keep thinking about the baby. Our baby. Not knowing what happened is disturbing me, scaring me. I can't get it out of my mind. When we flirted on Friday evening, I said we were in a bubble. I thought this weekend's happenings would belong here, belong to the reunion, and I'd go back home with a warm glow, a naughty memory and a commitment to being faithful from then on. I truly believed that.'

Kate was transfixed by what she was hearing.

'But you've come back into my life like an explosion. And like an explosion, you've disrupted its foundations. I don't want you to walk out the door with a self-satisfied smirk and leave me here, the victim of your revenge. You did more than bite my ear, Kate.'

'Jonathan, I do understand what you're saying. I understand the words. But I don't know what you're implying, suggesting even. You have a new wife. I have a husband. We can't ignore them. We can't return to our student days.'

'That's why I said I'm confused. I don't know what I'm suggesting either. All I know is I can't go back to where I was when I arrived here. A basic element of my life has changed.' He sighed. 'Perhaps it's guilt.'

It had gone wrong. She wanted Jonathan to be furious, to hate her, to vow never to speak to her again, to spit in her face. She could have coped with that, enjoyed it in a peculiar, macabre, satisfying way. But she didn't know how to react to his passionate, wanting presence.

'I don't know how to deal with this, Jonathan, any more than you do. You can't walk back into my life and expect me to welcome you. In fact, I'm stunned you think you can. And I don't want it. I don't need you in my life now. I don't want further contact.'

She had no desire for discussion. In fact, she no longer had desire for him. Jonathan was about to speak but Kate put up her hand to stop him interrupting.

'Let me finish. I think we go away into our normal worlds. You need to think about what you've said and decide if it's real. I think you might change your mind in a few days of ordinary life. We've been in an artificial world here, never-never land, the bubble you spoke of. Everyday life will prick it.'

Jonathan's mobile phone rang and broke the tension between them.

'You should answer it.'

Kate turned away and left him, his gaze clinging to her like glue.

Chapter 21

Becky liked a lie-in on Sunday mornings. Having Neil there made no difference; he could get up if he wanted but she would stay in bed. She surfaced around nine o'clock and could hear him in the kitchen. A smell of bacon wafted upstairs. Caring man, she thought, a bacon bap would fit the bill perfectly. There was music playing but then she heard a phone ring. She stretched lazily and swung her legs out of bed, running her hands through her tousled hair. A long soak in the bath first and then breakfast – or the other way round? She decided hunger won, so put on her dressing gown and wandered downstairs, yawning.

Neil was walking around the kitchen talking rapidly on his mobile. His eyes shone with eagerness and he waved his hand at Becky to indicate he needed a pen. She found him one and he grabbed an envelope lying on the work surface.

'Right. I can meet you at eleven o'clock. Will it fit in with your travels?' He nodded his head a few times. 'Okay. Give me your phone number in case.' Neil scribbled a number on the envelope. 'No, it shouldn't take long. We can work on the text to go with it later, easiest by email.' He listened for a few more seconds. 'Fine. See you at eleven. Bye.'

Neil finished the call and looked at Becky in astonishment.

'Well, that was an unexpected, strange phone call. Come and have breakfast and I'll tell you about it.'

They sat at the end of the kitchen table, still littered with the remains of the previous night's dinner. Neil cleared a space, put a few plates in the dishwasher and brought the bacon, brown sauce and baps across.

'That was a photographer, a guy I've met a couple of times at exhibitions and trade shows, an acquaintance rather than a friend. He heard about my next exhibition, the "Love Hurts" one we talked about. He knows my style, knows I'm always on the look-out for the unusual, the quirky. He's offering me a photo opportunity. Now this is the weird bit. It seems he recently had a wild night of passion with an ex-girlfriend he met by chance and she bit off a piece of his ear!'

'What? Took a lump out of it?'

'So he says. He has a dressing on it but claims you can see a piece has been bitten out of the earlobe.'

'It's taking love-making a bit far. Don't get any ideas! I prefer my ears as they are!'

Neil reached across and pulled one of them. 'I like them as they are, too.'

'So what is the photo opportunity?'

'His bitten ear. He says it exactly fits the title of my exhibition. She bit it in enraged love and revenge for an injury he inflicted on her years ago. And, as he said, it bloody well hurt! I don't have the details. But I'll need them for the text to accompany the photo.'

'I heard you mention eleven o'clock. Are you meeting him this morning?'

'Yes. He's driving home from somewhere and passing near here. I'm meeting him in town. We can go to the studio and do the photo, assuming when I see his ear, I think it will work. He said the photo needs to be done asap while the ear is still swollen and obviously bitten. And as he's going to be nearby, I need to make the most of it.'

'You seem taken with the idea.'

'I am. It's wacky. I hope it works. If it looks like a scrape from a rugby match, I'll have to abandon the idea. But he is a photographer – a travel photographer, not my sort of work – so he should know the requirements for an effective shot.'

Neil was now pacing around as he talked, throwing ideas about angle and lighting at the bemused Becky.

'I can see I'm second best this morning. Your mind is elsewhere.'

'Sorry, my love. It's wrong of me. Come here.'

He slid his arms under her dressing gown and around her warm, naked body. He buried his face in her neck and kissed her gently.

'I don't often get offers like this. In fact, it's the first time it's happened. I normally have to work hard to get unusual shots. That's why I'm so excited.'

'Strange this guy phoned you. If a lover took a chunk out of my earlobe, I don't think I'd want it publicised.'

'Well, he doesn't either. He's asked me to position him so his face isn't seen or is in shadow. He has a wife to consider, it seems.'

'Naughty boy. Imagine cheating on his wife!'

'Can't believe anyone would do that!'

'But I think it's odd he'd want a photo taken.'

'He started to tell me about the impact of the bite, the way it stirred old emotions. It's affected him a bizarre way.'

'Well, no doubt you'll find out.'

'Yes. He'll have to give me the relevant info but I want to make sure the photo's okay before I get him to write it.'

Neil started to clear away the breakfast things.

'I can do that. You'd better get yourself ready to go. When will I see you again?'

'Don't know. We're running out of reunions. Meant to tell you, I gave Kate a convincing description of my Modern Languages reunion to the point of boring her! I don't think she has any idea I wasn't there.'

Neil went upstairs to sort out his things and came down ready to leave. He gave Becky a hug. 'Mustn't forget Jonathan's phone number. Where did I write it?' He looked around the kitchen. 'Here it is. Can I take this envelope?'

'Er... yes. It's junk mail.'

Neil put the envelope in his bag as Becky sat in shocked silence, trying to control her reaction. How many travel photographers are there called Jonathan?

'Where did you say this guy was coming from?'

'Some university, I think. I didn't take it in. He's on his way south.'

Neil kissed Becky on the forehead and rushed away.

Hell, thought Becky. This has got to be Jonathan Carson. What has Kate done? That's why he had a dressing on his ear. I can't believe she'd be so vicious. But then, perhaps I can. There was a madness about her this weekend. This episode is going to rebound on her. And on Neil. The piece of text is going to be interesting.

Chapter 22

Neil drove back home quickly. He didn't want Kate to arrive before him. He let himself in, unpacked his overnight bag and threw the duvet back, ruffling the bottom sheet and moving his pillows. He'd be in trouble for not making the bed. Excellent. He made a quick mug of tea, drank a couple of mouthfuls and tipped the rest away, leaving the dirty cup in the sink. His "cover routine" as he thought of it was automatic these days.

He was sorting out his camera when Kate arrived.

'How was your weekend?'

'It was much better than I expected. But then you know I didn't have great expectations. An interesting experience.'

'I said you'd enjoy it, like I did. Give me a few snippets but don't bore me to death.'

Kate told him the story of Simon and how she coerced him into making a large contribution to the pharmacy department. She mentioned his mean behaviour as a student and everyone's delight at seeing him part with his money. It amused Neil.

'What happened with Becky?'

'What do you mean?'

'Well I bumped into her briefly on Saturday night. She mentioned having to leave early in order to lock up the shop. Said you'd explain.'

'She had a mixed-up weekend. She arrived late on Friday which made me cross. I was relying on her for support. She was the main reason I agreed to go. A complicated problem with the shop burglar alarm. She got there in time for dinner and made up for lost time. She's a real live wire, you know. Has an eye for a sexy guy, too. I think she may have re-lit an old flame on Friday night.'

'Really? You surprise me.' Neil coughed and turned his face away from Kate to hide his reaction. It wasn't news he was expecting to hear.

'Well, she is single. No man in tow at the moment, so she might as well have fun. She was thoroughly enjoying herself when Mary, her locum, called. Drug addicts in the shop, apparently, and she wasn't coping. Becky ended up having to leave before dinner on Saturday to relieve her. Personally, I doubt it was necessary, she was being overprotective, but it was her decision.'

Kate glanced around the kitchen, a cursory inspection, automatically washed up the cup in the sink and made herself a coffee.

'What have you been up to this weekend?'

'Not much. Went to the pub last night and ate there. It was when I was leaving I saw Becky. Otherwise, I've been working on the exhibition.'

'Thought you would. How's it going?'

'Very well. In fact, I had an amazing phone call this morning. You'll find this hard to believe. A photographer I vaguely know phoned to offer me an opportunity. He heard about the next exhibition and had a potential photograph he felt would fit in with my theme. I'm seeing him at eleven o'clock. Apparently, a couple of nights ago he had a fling with an ex-girlfriend who bit his ear and took a chunk out of the lobe in wild passion. Can you imagine that?'

Kate looked horror-stuck.

'Exactly. Just how I reacted.'

Kate opened her mouth to speak and then paused. 'Why ever did she do it? Do you have any more info?'

'Passion, revenge, punishing him for ending their relationship. A complicated mix of emotions. I need to assess if the photo will work. It may not but if it does, it could be a sensation. That's why I'm meeting the guy this morning. He's in the area, driving home from wherever this bitten ear happened. Then if I think it's suitable, I'll ask him to provide me with the paragraph of text describing the incident.'

Neil was back in animated mode, Becky's unexpected weekend activities forgotten, as he anticipated his coup.

'But why does he want to be photographed?'

'It's odd, I know, but he wants the affair recorded. He said it made such an unanticipated impact on him it couldn't be dismissed. He won't be recognisable in the shot, of course. I'm grateful he thought to contact me.'

Neil put his camera in its case and collected the rest of his equipment.

'I'm meeting him in town and we'll go to the studio. Now what have I done with his phone number?'

He rummaged around and found an envelope. Kate looked across. She saw a mobile number and the word "Jonathan" beside it. But it wasn't all that caught her eye. The envelope was addressed to Miss Rebecca Whitehead. She frowned then looked intently at Neil but he was busy getting ready to leave.

'See you later. This won't take long.'

Neil closed the door and she heard him start the car and drive away. She stared into the hallway for several seconds then sat down on a kitchen chair to collect her thoughts. She repeated to herself that Neil had gone to meet Jonathan Carson. It could only be him – how many bitten ears were there around? Come on, Kate, you can deal with this. There has to be a means of limiting the damage. Jonathan didn't want to be identified so there was a chance he wouldn't name her. But he might mention a reunion. There could be enough detail for Neil to get suspicious. Maybe she should contact him. But how?

Right, her pick 'n' mix brain went into action. Willy had asked everyone to put their contact details on a sheet of paper. He got the Business Centre to make copies – at no cost after the previous evening's fiasco – and handed them out. Where had she put hers? Folded neatly in her handbag, as expected.

She was annoyed she found herself in a trap. No way could I have anticipated this, she thought. But I can get out of it. She went to the phone, trying to compose what she would say, her mouth dry with impending panic. She dialled Jonathan's number and waited.

'Hello?'

'Jonathan, it's Kate.'

'Well, I wasn't expecting you to start chasing me. This is a pleasant surprise.'

She could hear a taunt in his voice and could see how his mouth would be starting to smile. This was no time for banter.

'I know about the photo shoot.'

'What? How did you find out about that?'

'Never mind. I'm not happy about it.'

'It's my ear, Kate. If I want it to be an exhibition piece, it's up to me.'

'I don't want my name implicated.'

'Do you think I'm stupid? The photograph will not identify me and I won't mention your name. That sort of exposure won't help either of us.'

'Right. But I would rather not have the circumstances made too clear either.'

'Well, I've already explained a bit about how it happened. It's the whole point. The exhibition is called "Love Hurts". If a dog had bitten me, the whole scenario would be irrelevant.'

'Well, perhaps you can avoid saying where it happened, omit the fact it was at a pharmacy department reunion.'

Jonathan's voice changed and he spoke more softly. 'So you're asking a favour of me? Why would I grant you a favour?'

'I could make sure your wife heard about our adventure together.'

'But you wouldn't, Kate. It's not your style. I think I'm

the one who's calling the tune now.'

'If you let me down me on this, it will be our last communication. I mean it.'

'I thought you said this morning you didn't want further contact with me, anyway. Kate, you can't blackmail me. I'm the one with the power this time.'

She could hear the triumph in his voice. Bloody Jonathan, curse you.

'I'm not one to grovel, Jonathan. But I do need to know the narrative you write is sufficiently vague. I have a reason but not one I can go into now.'

'We'll see, Kate, we'll see. I'll write what I want to write. Think next time before you go biting off a piece of anyone's ear. Need to go. I can see my photographer across the square.'

He cut off and Kate shouted, 'I hate you, I hate you!' at the phone.

She thumped the kitchen table, cursing and muttering to herself. It had been simple, this revenge, but it wasn't any more.

Chapter 23

Neil hardly saw Kate as the date of the exhibition approached. He was like a casual visitor, one with access to the fridge, the coffee maker and the linen basket. He gave her a brief kiss now and then but there was no intimacy; during his few hours in bed, he slept. Mornings began with photographs, he devoured them with lunch and they were aperitif and digestif in the evenings. Kate tried to make conversation but he was distracted unless she asked about preparation for the big day when he would erupt into life, eyes shining, breath gasping. He would pace around the room, describing how the photographs would be lit, which ones were linked to others, which were stand-alones. Mentally he was in the gallery, waving his arms around, oblivious of furniture and ornaments. Kate had to slow him down as she rescued a vase of flowers.

'Be careful! You'll damage yourself and our home!'

So Neil would stop and communication would be on hold again.

'I am interested, you know, Neil, but "Love Hurts" can't be the only thing we talk about,' she said one morning as he stuffed toast into his mouth while frantically typing on his computer.

It was her third attempt at a conversation. The first, about a new pharmacist she employed, produced a grunt and an automatic, 'Oh, she sounds okay'. The second, a comment about one of their neighbours, got 'Mmm.'

'Neil – have you heard anything I've said?'

'What?' he said, looking up. 'Er… something about David

next door, was it? And you said we couldn't just talk about the exhibition – right?' He looked relieved he remembered any of it.

'Did you know you have a dentist's appointment in fifteen minutes?'

'What? Oh shit! I'll have to miss it.'

'I can rebook it for you. I'll tell them you're indisposed – a bad case of preoccupation.'

She walked over to Neil and put her hands on his shoulders, massaging the back of his neck with her thumbs. He could hardly ignore her.

'I'm sorry, Kate. Please bear with me. I know I'm not much company at the moment but this exhibition is the most important thing that has happened to me as a photographer. There is such interest, you wouldn't believe it. It's so much bigger than my other exhibitions. I've done the usual local advertising, flyers and posters, but the word seems to have spread far wider. I've had a couple of journalists phone me for interviews and I know at least one editor will turn up at the opening.'

He was talking faster and faster and the excitement made him look younger; he had the enthusiasm of his early photographic days. He got up and walked around, detailing how the photos would be presented, who was helping him in the gallery and how the text that accompanied each image would be aligned. His elation reached a peak when he mentioned the bitten ear photograph and the wonderful text that went with it.

'Just wait, Kate. You'll see it on Friday!'

'Okay, it's less than a week to go so I'll put up with talking to myself. Let me know if I can do anything.'

Neil knew he wouldn't ask for help except on the night when the handing out of glasses of wine and canapés would fall to Kate. He liked his independence, liked being able to show what he could achieve without her, even if financially he wasn't a match.

'Kate, have you seen my flyers? Just realised I promised some more to the library and I haven't been back. I need to be off in five minutes.'

Neil was rushing around in bare feet, gathering scattered pieces of paper and folders.

'Are they in a packet or what?'

'In a cellophane wrapper, I think.'

They both looked round the kitchen and Kate picked up a large brown envelope propped up by the toaster. She looked hard at it. It was addressed to Miss Rebecca Whitehead but had clearly been opened. Sticking out of the top was the corner of a flyer.

'Neil, is this what you're looking for?' She waved the envelope at him.

'Great. You've found it. I forgot they were in an envelope. I think you're a witch. You can always find the invisible!'

'Why has it got Becky's name on it?'

Neil frowned and took the envelope. Oh, damn, what had he picked up at Becky's house? Was he getting careless? A bit of quick thinking.

'Oh, I remember. I took the flyers into Becky's pharmacy and the packet split. She gave me an envelope to put the remaining ones in. She must have been re-cycling.'

Neil laughed and busied himself with paperwork as a distraction. Well, it was a reasonable explanation. It might even be true. Surely Kate would never suspect. Not him and Becky!

'Well, it's lucky I trust you, Neil, or turning up with another woman's name on an envelope might make me jealous!'

'You, Kate? Never. A broad-minded individual like you! If I had an affair, you'd congratulate me on my initiative. And, anyway, Becky's hardly my type!'

They both laughed too loudly; there was a disturbing undercurrent. It's this all-encompassing exhibition, Neil thought. It's making us both slightly crazy.

Friday evening arrived, as it usually did, on the heels of Wednesday and Thursday, unaware this was by no means a regular ending to the week. Neil had spent several days going through the most minute details. His life was a maze of notes, a calendar of lists, a directory of phone calls. He made a point of thoroughly researching his invited guests, the magazine editors and critics he needed to impress. He knew who would arrive early and who liked to arrive late. He knew how to deal with them, their quirks and dislikes, their humour and their prejudices. He could predict what clothes they would wear.

The layout of the gallery was exactly as he designed with the photographs above their respective texts, texts in a large, bold, easily readable font. He learned that lesson at a previous exhibition when a miserable but influential critic pointed out he disliked having to put glasses on to read the legends. And the explanations were key to the theme this time; this was what made the exhibition special.

The illumination, after many adjustments, met with his approval. As Kate pointed out, lighting was his business; he had no excuses for it being wrong. Then there were the more mundane matters. He was picking up the trays of canapés from Waitrose at five o'clock. The wine was already there, the white in the fridge in the kitchen at the back of the gallery. He would unpack the borrowed wine glasses when he arrived. Mundane, yes, but needed if the show was to be a success. These offerings were expected. He asked Kate to help with the hospitality. She was experienced at the "meet and greet" job and it left him free to talk about his work. He felt guilty when he realised she would also have to act as cloakroom attendant if people needed to remove their coats.

The lull before the first arrival dragged out like the long twilight outside. Two teenagers in school uniform stuck their heads around the door, attracted by the large "Love Hurts" poster on the window.

'You can come and have a look, if you like,' Neil said. 'It's not officially open and I can't give you a glass of wine, but you're welcome.'

They giggled, looked hastily around and then left in a

cloud of embarrassment, mouths full of canapés.

Neil took Kate round every photograph so she could answer questions if necessary. She'd seen many already but not with their texts.

'Obviously, I'll answer as many questions as possible myself but if you know their background, it will help.'

'We should have done this at home. It would have saved time.'

'Yes and no. You have to see them here to appreciate their impact and anticipate the comments.'

Kate often pointed out the difference between a photographer's and a pharmacist's viewpoint, so shrugging her shoulders, she listened carefully. He explained the sadness of the young wife as she watched her husband leaving for "Nine months, two weeks and three days", the title of the photograph. He was a scientist going to spend the time at a remote research station in Svalbard, an island to the far north of Norway. He captured the shine of the tear as it ran down her cheek and the reflection of the departing aeroplane caught in the curved window through which she looked. It was a chance encounter, a precious moment a photographer seeks. The text explained why the two had to part, the conflict they both felt between his important work and their new love.

'Wow, Neil. I think I understand why you've been so animated, so totally involved in your work. I'm impressed. This is your best exhibition yet. You get the feelings and the emotion of the situation across.'

In a similar vein, they moved through the photographs until they came to one she had not yet seen, one she feared seeing.

'This is the photo I'm most excited about. We talked about it, remember? This guy had a piece of his ear bitten off in a passionate encounter. I'm pleased with the lighting here. It keeps his anonymity but shows exactly what happened. What do you think of the title?'

248

'Well, it's appropriate, that's for sure.' Kate wondered at her own words. Was it a "Love Bite?" She looked closely at the photograph and read the text.

They loved each other in their youth but he abandoned her when she was pregnant with his child. Many years later their paths crossed and the old passion returned, more wild and uncontrolled than ever. She bit off a piece of his ear during the climax of their love-making. 'You marked me forever,' she said. 'Now I've done the same to you.'

Neil looked at her greedily, wanting a comment, her opinion.

'It's brilliant, Neil. It does illustrate your theme. But then, so do all your photographs.'

Neil beamed. Kate said what he wanted to hear. He was glad she was taking a real interest.

The guests started to appear around half past six. Neil welcomed the early ones, gave them glasses of wine and led them over to the first photograph. Then Kate was left to manage on her own. Neil was immersed in his objectives and explanations, describing why and how he obtained his shots and how they tied into his theme. He had a knot of interested faces around him, a cascade of questions interrupting his flow, everyone's comment fighting for its right to be heard. He glanced frequently towards the door to make sure he didn't miss a significant arrival. Kate was there for every newcomer.

'Oh, Becky, you're here. Glad you arrived early.'

Neil spotted her and smiled.

'You don't mind lending a hand, do you?' Kate said. 'If you could top up the wine glasses, it would make life easier for me. I think if exhibitions are going to be as full as this on a regular basis, Neil will need to hire a waitress next time.'

'Happy to do whatever's needed. My rates are reasonable! Lucky I decided to come although I can't stay long.'

'Thanks. It's now I need help. When most people have

arrived and I don't have to deal with coats, it won't be a problem.'

There was a low buzz of comment and discussion as the assembled groups moved round the room. Neil was in deep conversation with a short, middle-aged man in a crumpled cream jacket with sweat stains near the armpits. As Neil talked, his companion nodded and frequently pushed his glasses back up his nose, even if they hadn't moved. He dug his hands deeply into his pockets, distorting the shape of his jacket so it rose up his back like a concertina and sagged misshapenly at the sides. Then he took a pad from a folder he was carrying and made notes. After several more minutes, the two men shook hands and the scruffy visitor left, rapidly knocking back a glass of wine on the way out.

Kate managed to catch Neil's attention. 'Who was the odd individual taking all your attention?' she whispered.

'That was the one of the arts writers from the "Sunday Times". I think the exhibition will be reviewed in the culture supplement on Sunday. Kate, this is fantastic!'

Neil could hardly contain his pleasure although was doing his best to appear calm for the sake of the other guests, pretending such reviews were everyday for him. But inside he was jumping up and down like a child.

'He was particularly taken with the "Love Bite" photograph. I had a feeling that one was going to be a killer!'

After another hour, people started to leave. Kate flopped on an ottoman at the end of the gallery with her untouched glass of wine.

'You looked whacked,' Neil commented as he walked by with enough energy for both of them. 'Don't worry, I'll get these last few moving.'

'Thanks. Can't think why I'm so tired. Don't think your adrenaline rush has spread to me!'

Becky wandered across, took a long look at Jonathan's ear and then sat beside her.

'I intended leaving half an hour ago but got chatting. I

must go now.'

'Thanks for helping. It was the first half hour when I didn't have enough hands. Neil is ushering the stragglers out.'

'My pleasure. I'll go to the loo and get my coat.'

As Becky disappeared, the door of the gallery opened and a dripping raincoat backed in. There was a whoosh as an umbrella opened and closed outside. Kate sighed wearily and muttered 'bugger' under her breath. Neil looked across to her and shrugged his shoulders, indicating he'd deal with the late arrival. She got up to throw away her unwanted wine and then stopped dead. A tall, dark-haired man was greeting Neil. He made a comment about the bloody awful storm, laughed noisily and left a wet trail across the floor. Kate turned quickly and walked into the cloakroom. There was no mistaking who had arrived. His hair was longer but it was definitely Jonathan.

'Are you alright, Kate? You look dreadful. You haven't been drinking too much, have you?' Becky looked worried as the two women collided with each other.

'Don't be stupid. Not at an exhibition as important as this.'

'Well don't bite my head off. I was only asking.' She waited for Kate to explain but impatience won.

'Well, tell me what it is. You didn't look like this five minutes ago.'

'Jonathan's here.'

'Oh, my God. Did Neil invite him?'

'No idea. But I wasn't expecting to see him. He's a travel photographer, for shit's sake!'

'Well, you didn't seem to have much trouble dealing with him at the reunion, so I assume you'll cope with him now.'

'This is different. The situation has changed. I don't want to talk to him. If he'd arrived earlier, I'd have tried to slip away without him seeing me. I'd have told Neil I was feeling ill. But there aren't many people left here now, we're nearly finished. It

251

would look odd. And anyway, the only door to the gallery is at the front. I'll have to face Jonathan.'

Kate was talking to herself rather than Becky. She put her hand on Becky's arm as she moved towards the gallery.

'Becky, I don't know what you suspect, what you might have guessed. And I don't want you to tell me. But can I ask you to be discreet? Please don't say anything you don't need to and please don't voice any speculations. You'll have to greet Jonathan on the way out.'

'Kate, my life seems to be a series of favours for you. Too many of them. What would you do without me?'

Kate looked so troubled that Becky stopped joking. 'Okay. You can rely on me.'

Becky walked back into the gallery to find Neil and Jonathan quietly discussing the exhibition. Jonathan looked up as she approached.

'Becky! What a surprise? Didn't know you were into photography.'

'Hi Jonathan. Didn't expect to see you, either. I'm a friend of Neil's. Always like to support his work. I live near here.'

'Oh, yes, I'd forgotten.'

Neil was looking from one to the other with his mouth partly open. 'How do you two know each other?'

'We met at university. Small world and all that,' Becky said. Then turning to Neil said how much she enjoyed the evening but she had to dash. 'Sorry not to be able to stay and chat. I've already been here longer than I intended. Nice to see you, Jonathan. Enjoy the exhibition. Bye, guys!'

'What a surprise – you two knowing each other,' Neil said to Jonathan. 'Shame she had to go.'

Jonathan shrugged and pulled at his ear, fully healed and now just an odd shape.

'I thought you said you weren't going to come to the opening,' Neil said quietly.

'I wasn't but then curiosity got the better of me. I thought by arriving late, there'd be few people here and I would go unnoticed.' He lowered his voice. 'My ear has healed remarkably well.'

As they talked they walked up to the photograph of Jonathan. It was true, Neil thought. It would be a clever eye that could match the image and the man.

Kate was standing near the open cloakroom door, listening. When she heard the front door close, she came out.

Neil shouted across to her. 'Kate, come and meet an unexpected guest, a photographer friend of mine.'

'Jonathan, this is Kate, my wife.'

The shadow of disbelief that crossed Jonathan's face was as inconspicuous as the teeth marks on his ear. He and Kate stared at each other and played a secret game.

'Pleased to meet you, Kate. Have we met before? Your face looks familiar.'

'As does yours. Our paths probably crossed at university. I heard you talking to my friend, Becky. We both studied pharmacy.'

'That must be it. I knew Becky quite well in those days.'

'So what do you think of the exhibition?'

'I've not had chance to have a proper look although Neil has talked to me about the concept and idea behind it.'

'Well, look out for a review in the "Sunday Times" this week. Their critic was most taken with this photograph in particular.'

Kate pointed at the photograph they had been looking at. 'Can you imagine, Jonathan, the passion, even the fury, that led to such a photograph? I find it difficult to get my head around it.'

Neil looked anxiously at Jonathan, wondering how he would cope with such questioning. Curse him for coming! He wanted anonymity and he was now putting it at risk.

'And to have a photograph taken of the wound is even

stranger. Why would anyone want to do that?'

'Ah, great emotion has enormous power. Maybe the guy felt this was a memorial to a significant moment in his life. Something that changed his life, perhaps. To be able arouse such feeling in a lover, even an aggrieved lover, is a compliment.'

'A compliment? What an unusual observation. I don't think I can agree with it. If I wanted to compliment a lover, I don't think I'd do it by biting off a piece of his ear.'

'Maybe not but I think I could imagine it. I would like to think I might make an impact on a woman, once in my life, that would generate such an explosion of feeling. Although I'm not expecting anyone to bite my ear!'

As he laughed, he fingered his ear, the unbitten one, and looked towards Neil to draw him into the conversation. Neil smiled weakly and made a movement of his head that could have been a nod or a shake, a movement of indecision or simply of anguish at the way the comments were going.

'However did you get the photograph, Neil?' Jonathan asked. 'It wasn't a threesome, was it?' He laughed conspiratorially, as if sharing a joke.

Neil tried to control his expression, feeling sure he was now several shades paler. Whatever had got into Jonathan?

'My god, no. An acquaintance, who has to remain anonymous, called me saying his experience fitted the theme of my exhibition. It was such a lucky break. I took the photo and he provided the words.' He rushed out his clarification, looking from Jonathan to Kate, searching for a means of changing the conversation. He tried to divert them to an adjacent photograph but without success.

'As I've said to Neil before, I think I'm too much of a scientist. You artistic people can get inside a photograph in a way I never can.'

Kate laughed at her trivial comment and Jonathan joined in, finishing the large glass of wine Neil had given him. Anxiety was hanging around Neil like a shroud and he was running his hands through his hair in a distracted way.

He looked at his watch. 'Kate, I think our last guests need their coats. Would you mind looking after them?' It was more a demand than a request.

'No problem.'

She beamed at an elderly couple who seemed in no hurry to leave but now made noises indicating perhaps they should. It was getting late and they didn't want to miss the bus.

'Well, Jonathan, I'll leave Neil to walk you round the rest of the exhibition. Hope you enjoy it.' She walked towards the cloakroom and Neil scurried after her.

'And perhaps, Kate, you could start collecting the glasses.' He lowered his voice. 'I'll join you as soon as I can. I'll make sure Jonathan doesn't stay long. We are technically closed now.'

'Yes, of course. Annoying he arrived so late but great to have other photographers interested.'

Neil's face lightened as Kate moved away and he looked again like a master of the situation; he was back to his confident self. He rejoined Jonathan, started talking animatedly and headed him across the gallery. As the men walked passed her, Jonathan turned, fixed his eyes on hers and gave her a half smile.

A fresh surge of anger engulfed her. She resented him – she resented herself – for the games they had been playing. She might have married Jonathan; she could have given birth to his child. She experienced for the thousandth time the sadness and horror of the blood- stained sheet. Would she have miscarried the baby if he had not left her? An unanswerable question she had never ceased to ask. Only Jonathan was aware of her pregnancy. Only she knew the loss.

No game.

Chapter 24

Dear Neil

It was a great pleasure to visit the opening of your exhibition on Friday. What a superb collection of images! You certainly deserve the critical acclaim that is coming your way. I've read the review in the "Sunday Times" and it was spot on. My most sincere congratulations to you. I appreciate your keeping my anonymity and I have to say the way the photograph was lit, the angle of my head and the overall atmosphere you created were excellent. I am delighted my mishap, injury, call it what you will, has served such a useful purpose. I'm pleased my ear has promoted your career so significantly! As soon as I saw the photograph, I felt secure no-one would recognise me although I did notice you appeared ill at ease when a group of us discussed the photograph at close quarters. There was no need.

In particular, there was no need to prevent Kate from discovering the identity of the sitter; she knows already. You might like to ask her about it.

I don't know if our paths will cross again but I wish you all the best.

Jonathan

Kate read the draft message Jonathan sent her. She didn't know whether to be furious or laugh. After the text he added,

If you would prefer me to miss out the penultimate paragraph, I'm happy to do so, but there is a condition. I want to meet you again. And I want to meet you soon. Your decision. Let me know asap as I intend to send the message to Neil by the end of today.

Kate clicked on "Reply" and then stopped to think. She didn't believe Jonathan would send the incriminating message. What would be the point? Revealing to a man that you have bedded – no, it sounds too old-fashioned, almost mediaeval – fucked their wife is unlikely to endear them to you. And it was rude and Jonathan wasn't rude. At least, a rational Jonathan was never rude. But she knew what might happen after several glasses of Sancerre – or a far cheaper wine. On Friday evening she was worried when he started on the alcohol. Their repartee was acidly enjoyable but it was reckless; they were on dangerous ground and there was the risk one of them would slip. Jonathan obviously enjoyed the sport. She was relieved when he left.

Although ninety-nine per cent of her was confident she had the upper hand with him, one per cent warned caution. A headstrong, careless moment was all that was needed to make life difficult for her. She composed carefully:

Dear Jonathan

I cannot believe you are seriously considering sending this message to Neil – the entire message, that is. It's not your style and you have better manners than that. Do you want to destroy my marriage? If I mean anything to you, destroying my relationship with Neil will mean you and I never communicate again. If I don't mean anything, then why bother?

Kate

She avoided his question; he would have to wait a little longer for an answer to that. Kate had a policy of never sending any controversial or difficult message straight away. This was how she operated in business and it served her well. So she saved the text and went into the kitchen to have a coffee. There was plenty of time to mull it over. She would have a second look before sending it later.

Neil was sitting at the table talking on the phone. It hardly stopped ringing all morning. Those who hadn't seen the opening of the exhibition were calling to talk about the review. Neil was so excited he barely ate any lunch, picking at the cheese board Kate put on the table, eating a grape or two. He finished his conversation, put the phone down and grabbed Kate around the waist. He hugged her and danced his own version of the polka around the room, Kate tripping and stumbling as she tried to keep up with him.

'Come on, we'll open a bottle of champagne! This has to be the best weekend ever! It's only three o'clock but who cares!'

He ran into the dining room, grabbed one off the wine rack and rushed back into the kitchen.

'Get the glasses, Kate!'

'Whoa! That one won't be cold. One of us had the foresight to put a bottle in the fridge.'

'Clever you, clever you! What would I do without you?'

Neil was talking in exclamation marks. Nothing was a simple statement or question. He was intoxicated with compliments and praise before consuming a drop of alcohol. He popped the cork and managed to pour out two glasses without spilling much.

'Here's to your continued success!' Kate said as they clinked their glasses together.

'And here's to us!'

A dynamic and enthusiastic Neil was also a sexy, appealing Neil. She watched how he moved, the stretch of his muscles across his back, his flat stomach. Fine lines left their traces near his eyes when he smiled, a sign he was not immune to time. But he was wearing well. She'd like to have him back. He looked like the person she met and fell in love with when he was animated. My God, it seems so long ago, she thought. But it was little more than twenty years.

They met on a skiing holiday in the French Alps. It was a typical holiday romance, a blaze of uncommitted ardour fuelled by vin chaud, admiration of his superior expertise on the snow and evenings of silly dancing in ski boots. Exactly the sort of romance no-one expects to last. But they discovered they lived near each other in England and tentatively arranged to meet after their return. Neil called her a couple of weeks later. He had to explain who he was as she didn't recognise his voice or his name.

'Oh, sorry, Neil. I didn't think you'd call. I didn't mean to be rude. Good to hear from you.'

She was unsure whether she really was pleased to hear from him. Holiday romances were best left in the resort. But he was a decent guy and she was currently uncommitted. They arranged to have dinner together the following Friday. In the course of the conversation, Kate mentioned it was her birthday the following day.

'You should have said! We could have made it more of a celebration!'

'Don't be silly. I didn't want you to think it had to be special. This is as much a celebration as I need.'

He frowned as if he'd missed an opportunity and it endeared him to her.

The following day, a large bouquet arrived for her with a tag that said simply, "Happy Birthday. Love Neil xx".

So it continued and although it wasn't the explosion that falling in love with Jonathan had been, it had its own fireworks. She tried hard but unsuccessfully to avoid the inevitable comparisons. And Neil came out well. It was with shock she realised there were similarities between the two men, their sense of humour, their athleticism, their joy in springing surprises. Especially the latter – the particular attribute that first attracted her to Neil. A year later when he asked her to marry him, she agreed with no doubt in her mind. And here they were, still together.

After several mouthfuls, he put the glass down on the table and took Kate's glass from her. He turned off his phone, pulled Kate towards him and kissed her. It was an accomplished kiss; Neil could kiss well. She pushed Jonathan out of her mind and responded.

They finished the champagne in the bedroom. Sex hadn't been as fiery and passionate as this for a while. A combination of champagne and success is powerful, Kate thought, getting dressed. It certainly turned Neil on. She wondered if she had also turned him on or if any attractive woman, available at the right moment, would have been acceptable. Even Becky! What an uncharitable thought, she mused, but it passed nevertheless through her head. As the effects of the champagne abated, she thought of the waiting message. Neil was once more on the phone so she disappeared into the study. She read through her words carefully, added in a few, changed her mind and deleted them. Short and direct did the job. She clicked on "Send".

Within an hour there was a reply.

Dear Kate

Don't think I'm fooling around. There is no doubt I will send the message if you don't agree to see me. It is purely a means to an end. I have no feelings about your marriage. Neil would initially hate me. It's never a pleasant feeling to be betrayed. But I would point out if you had not bitten my ear, he would not be enjoying his current success. So he should feel gratitude. He would think it was ridiculous but ultimately would have to agree. If he wants any further information about our previous relationship, if any of that would make him feel better, I'll tell him. But he won't want to know any more; he won't ask.

So, Kate, make up your mind. I expect a decision by return.

Jonathan

Bloody man! Kate felt trapped. She could not allow Jonathan to send the message. This was not how it was meant to end. She would have to meet him again; she had to make sure she became the winner. Without her usual caution she typed a brief reply.

Jonathan

I will meet you again. I don't know why this is so

260

important to you but don't have any hopes that a wonderful, new relationship will develop. It won't.

I expect you to keep your word and delete the penultimate paragraph before you send the message to Neil.

Kate

She read it through twice and clicked on "Send". Done. She breathed a sigh and wondered exactly what she had done. Closing her eyes, she thought through the sequence of events that brought her to this point. She was interrupted by Neil calling to her from the kitchen where he had logged on to his laptop.

'I've got millions of emails to work through. Folk who came on Friday and loads of others. You won't believe how complimentary folk are.'

'I'm happy for you. That's great.'

No comment on any message from Jonathan. Had he sent it yet? Had he kept his word? The phone rang yet again and Neil picked it up. He wandered around, waving his arms as he pointed out invisible photographs to an admiring someone, saying 'So kind', 'Glad you liked it,' and disappeared out of the kitchen.

As she walked past the open laptop, Jonathan's name caught Kate's eye. So he had sent a message. Amongst a whole page in bold, unread. She stopped, fighting the urge to do something she had never done, an act totally against her principles. Ever since her teenage years when her mother had opened a personal letter, she'd been passionate about respecting privacy.

But she needed to know. Neil was now in the garden, still talking, so she clicked on the message, scanned it, closed it and then marked it as "unread". She inhaled deeply and blew out a long stream of air. The penultimate paragraph was no longer there. Then, as if prompted by an evil gremlin, a force outside her control made her look again at the screen. An unread message from Becky. There was no reason to go near it; it was wrong. She could see the back of Neil's head through the window. She clicked on the message. The usual congratulatory words, too effusive, then

261

the final sentence, "See you on Tuesday".

Kate felt sick. There was no innocent explanation for this. Becky's name on a couple of envelopes flashed before her, mocked her. She closed the message as she heard Neil's footsteps, quickly marked it as unread and walked back into the study. She sat at her laptop, composing messages to Jonathan and deleting them, her mind elsewhere. Nothing was working. Focus, focus. I'm losing control. I must not lose control. She tidied the already neat desk, lining up her note pad and other papers with finicky precision, putting her pens in a line. Then doing it again.

So what would happen when she met Jonathan? He presumably didn't want to discuss politics or the weather. The only thing they had in common now was physical attraction. They would end up in bed. Did Jonathan think there could be more than that?

Did she?

Would she abandon Neil for him? She leant back in her chair and contemplated such a life. Neil did annoy her at times but he was her comfort blanket. They were happy together. At least, until a few minutes ago, she thought they were.

On impulse, something alien to her, she picked up the phone and dialled Becky's number. The anticipated answerphone told her to leave a message after the tone.

'Becky, it's Kate. Can you meet me Tuesday evening? I need your advice. Can't explain on the phone.'

She had no idea what she intended to say to Becky or why she called her. She wandered into the kitchen wondering what she had done. I've shocked myself. This isn't me, she thought. Maybe I'll call her back and say "Ignore my last message. All sorted!" No. That would compound matters, raise questions. I can talk my way out of most situations. I need to get my head sorted.

She opened a drawer and lined up the cutlery. She folded up the newspaper, smoothing out the creases. She polished a splash mark off the granite work surface. Gradually, order crept back into her mind.

She needed to attend to Jonathan and went back to her laptop.

Jonathan

I always keep my word so I will meet you again. However, think carefully. How much do you value your other ear? One accident falling down the stairs might have been accepted by your wife – but I suspect you'll have to be extremely imaginative to find a second excuse.

Suggest a date, place and time.

Kate

Reply sent. The following day, Kate received a simple message. The expression on her face barely changed; she shook her head and moved it to her 'Private' electronic file.

Kate

You win. For now.

But we'll meet. I'll contact you soon.

Jonathan

Well, had she won? It was a matter she needed to think about.

Chapter 25

Some time later, the test told her she was pregnant. It was indeed a matter she needed to think about.

91480588R00162

Made in the USA
Columbia, SC
21 March 2018